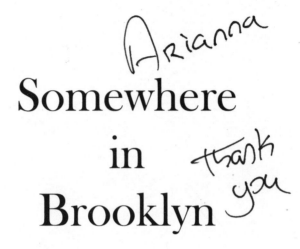

Somewhere
in
Brooklyn

HERU PTAH

 SUNRASON BOOKS

New York   Charlotte   Kingston

Published by
SUNRASON BOOKS

email: herumind@gmail.com
follow on instagram: @eyeofheru
facebook.com/heruptah
amazon: somewhere in brooklyn

Book ISBN: 978-0-9852881-9-8

Published 2019
Printed in the United States of America

Somewhere in Brooklyn is a work of fiction. It is fiction that takes place in very real places, and deals with very real issues—nevertheless it is fiction. It reads at times like investigative journalism, but it is wholly a product of my imagination. I have taken liberties with reality, and altered things to fit narrative purposes, but any resemblance to actual persons, living or dead, events, or locales is entirely coincidental. This book is For the Fallen—Never Forgotten.

Heru Ptah

Prologue

Desmond Bishop felt nothing and because he felt nothing, he felt fear. He felt his breath. He felt every pull and every push. It was a strain, like lifting a weight too heavy. There was a light, then seven sounds in sudden succession; glass shattering, his body jerking; the sound of a car alarm—loud, louder than he has ever heard it—screaming.

He felt wet. His shirt was wet as were his pants, even his socks. He felt it in his toes. It flowed through his fingers. A face came to the window. The glare of the streetlight shined behind him. He shouted words, something, something about hands. Desmond looked at his and told them move. Covered in glass they just sat in his lap and let the wet flow.

A hand came through the window and opened the door from the inside. The outside became overt. There were people gathering, onlooking, curious, anxious, angry. "They shot him. Yo, they shot him." A hand unbuckled his seat belt. He was pulled from the car and laid face down. His wet wet the pavement. The ground tremored. The train above him roared. His hands were shackled behind him. His body gasped in anguish, but his mind felt nothing, and because he felt nothing, he felt fear.

It was hard to keep his eyes open. Every blink was a memory. Nine years old, fourth grade, after school, he stole a candy bar. His friends dared him to do it. It tasted good but felt bad in his stomach. The next day he returned and repaid the seventy-five cents. The shop owner took his money but not his apology. His eyes opened to many feet, black leather, blue slacks, glass on the ground, McDonald's paper bag in the gutter, a rat pulling at the bag. The wet spread to his chin.

He blinked and recalled a memory he had no prior memory of. It was of his mother—but much younger—in a room of blinding light. Strands of hair lay flat and wet on her brow. He cried and she smiled the most beautiful smile. He opened his eyes and it was harder now. Everything was louder—noises, voices, sirens upon sirens. A force pulled on his eyelids like the sweetest sleep.

Ten years old, he rode his bike, with eight-year-old Cece on the handlebar, going downhill. They were going too fast to break. They zigzagged through traffic missing cars by milliseconds. *If we die, Daddy is gonna kill me because I killed Cece.* He opened his eyes, or at least he tried but like night cold gluing them shut it was hard to see. Everything was a blur.

He felt tired but feared sleep. He felt his father. The basketball went smoothly through the hoop. A crossover and a layup and it was over. At fourteen was the first time he beat his father. Dad was a mix of emotions. The competitor in him was upset he lost. The father in him was proud he had taught his son how to beat him. His pride won out and he hugged his son. Desmond wanted so desperately to hug his father now, because in his father's arms he always felt warm and safe and loved. He felt so cold, afraid and alone. His eyes closed.

* * *

There was a lot of traffic, much more than there should be at this time of night, even for Brooklyn. Brooklyn in the summer was always alive but this was more. On a Saturday after nine pm on Dumont avenue in Brownsville not too far from the L subway station, there were flashing lights everywhere. There were so many if it wasn't for the heat one might mistake late August for late December. These were police lights, however—nothing joyful about them. And was that a helicopter he heard above? Yes, it was. Something had happened, something bad.

John Bishop's right eye was twitching. Jumping was what his mother used to call it. It was blinking involuntarily. It came in fits every five or so minutes. Why it had come about he couldn't say. It began about twenty minutes ago. It was around the same time he started feeling an unprovoked sense of emptiness. Emptiness is a hard thing to articulate. You can't see it, but you can feel it but what you feel you can't describe.

He became anxious and was short of breath. It was a sudden sense of nervousness and . . . fear. He feared he was having a heart attack. He sweat, his pulse raced, his teeth chattered. It lasted nine minutes, and after it subsided it fell into the pit of his stomach like indigestion. His mother never liked when someone's eye jumped. It augured something ominous.

A man in his fifties got on the bus. Bishop had seen him before the times he had worked this shift. Beyond, "Good evening," Bishop had never really spoken to him. The tan Carharrt jacket he always wore told Bishop he worked with his hands.

"Can you believe this shit?" the man said as soon as he stepped in and dipped his metrocard.

"What?" Bishop asked. Having never spoken more than two words to this man, this was surprising.

"Damn police. They done killed somebody else's child and got that boy's body handcuffed and laid out in the street."

"Yeah?" All the police sirens, all the lights, the helicopter flying overhead, yes, now it all made sense.

"It never stops. They never change. We gotta do something about this. We can't just keep taking it like this." Bishop agreed with him but didn't say anything. It's not wise to engage passengers in political conversation. Things often turn bad. On the job he didn't just represent himself but also the Metropolitan Transit Authority. He might say the wrong thing and it might cost him everything. Bishop simply shook his head and the working man took his seat with an exhaustive sigh.

"They killed somebody else's child," Bishop repeated to himself. When you're a parent and you hear about someone else's child you automatically think about your own.

He called Cece. "Just checking in," he said. They shared I love you's and said goodbye. He called Desmond and he heard his voice. It was his voice mail. Bishop was disappointed he didn't reach him but not too concerned. Desmond would call back soon enough. He was on the other side of Brooklyn. He was safe.

Desmond Bishop woke up that morning like any other; his
lean athletic seventeen-year-old legs hanging off his full-size
bed, a bit of dried drool on his pillow and an erection between
his sheets. Involuntarily his hand slid down his abdomen. Realizing what he was getting himself into he got up and made sure
his room door was not just closed but locked. If it wasn't, Mom
had a habit of knocking then just walking in, as if knocking was
not asking for permission but merely a warning shot. Back in
bed his thoughts flashed forward to tonight.

Garfield was having a house party—nothing major just close
friends coming together at the end of summer. Sasha would be
there. He hoped she would wear a dress tonight. A dress is thin
and rides up the flesh easily. He imagined them grinding rhyth-
mically against the back wall. When you're young and you're in
love there's nothing better. They were a month in and still going
strong. He would be leaving for school tomorrow. He was going
away but Syracuse wasn't another planet. He would come back
every weekend or at least as many weekends as he could. Then
there would be the weekends when she would come up, if she
could somehow trick her parents.

He wanted to see her right now. He picked up his phone and
went to Instagram. However, before he could get to her page
something caught his eye. His feed was flooded with memes.
BLACK LIVES MATTER. REMEMBER THEIR NAMES.
This was how it starts. It happened again. Someone else had
been killed. There was his name. Cornelius Stewart. There was a
video. It was police dash camera footage synced with Facebook
live footage from inside the driver's car. A white Tallahassee
police officer approached a vehicle. He asked for the driver's
license and registration. The driver asked politely why he had

been pulled over. The officer wouldn't answer and repeated his command. They had a back and forth. The driver eventually relented and went for his paperwork. The officer shouted, "Let me see your hands," then fired off four shots as he frantically ran away, and the driver slumped over in his seat asking, "Why did you shoot me?"

Desmond stopped the video. He had seen enough. It was like all the others—different actors but same plot. It was sickening to the point where it began to lose its sting. Desmond had become, not indifferent but, inured to it. Police brutality was America's herpes. It flared up every three or four months; some unarmed black person was killed, sometimes two, sometimes three in a week. There was outrage, a call for justice, a call for calm, they led to protests, some were just marches, some were riots. Then it would simmer down again. People would go back to their regular social media, and in a few months someone else would get killed and the dance began anew.

Desmond was about to close out of Instagram, forgetting why he had opened it in the first place, when another video caught his attention. It was a documentary about a group of hippy looking black people with dreadlocks, and how in 1985 the Philadelphia Police Department dropped a bomb on their house. As he was watching he got a text. He opened his messenger app. It was from Garfield. REMEMBER TO GET THE THING TONIGHT. Desmond knew what the thing was. Desmond was of two minds about this. Part of him didn't want to bother with it. The other did want to get high with his friends. NP. I GOT YOU, he replied halfheartedly.

2

John Bishop slept like the dead. He slept as if he was in recovery rather than at rest. His body felt as if he had just gone back to the gym after skipping a few months. After five days of driving a thirty-ton bus for twelve-hours recovery was what he needed. His feet hurt, his back hurt, as well as his neck, as well as having a nagging headache, which he was unsure was born from a natural occurrence or an offspring of his hypertension.

He was six feet and a hair over two hundred pounds. He was built solid but would no longer be confused for an athlete with strong legs but a noticeable paunch. At forty he had already developed a working man's gut. He finished his shift at 2am. He got in at 2:25 and as tired as he was couldn't fall off until 4:00. He shouldn't have done it. He really did need the two days off. His wife was right. He was an overtime addict. He loved seeing the extra added to his check each week. He made well over 100,000 last year. However, he hated how much was taken out in taxes, which made him want to work to make up for what the taxes took out.

He felt her before he saw her. He inhaled her scent before he saw her face. It was a pleasant awakening. There were moments he thought Diane had never aged. There were moments when she smiled and the folds in her eyes seemed to be more the result of mirth than attrition. At forty as well, she was still that beautiful brown skinned girl he met at Georgetown University, with a button nose and a bright smile and an apple bottom.

He was on the basketball team and she was his English tutor. He got an A in that class. He didn't come by those easily; more to a lack of effort than ability. His efforts he put toward basketball. He had designs on playing in the NBA, or at least playing overseas and then working his way in. He tore the anterior cruciate ligament in his right knee during his senior year. He was devastated. At just six feet, his odds of getting in had always been a long shot. After his injury it became a miracle shot. Diane was his rock through it all—a bit too much. She became pregnant.

He had thoughts of working his way back and still giving his hoop dreams a go, but reality kept crashing in on him. A friend told him the MTA was hiring and that the job had great benefits. Working for Transit was the last thing he wanted to do. Then his son was born, and it was love at first sight. Bishop held him close and heard the treble of his tiny heartbeat next to his. He fell in love with being a father. He took the bus driver's exam the following week.

His wife could still get him hard, though that happened hardly. Diane worked days. He worked from the day into the night. When he came home—tired; she was still sleeping—tired. There was a tedium to it; days go by, weeks, sometimes months, without any intercourse; until it happens, and it was passionate, and it was good, and they both vowed never to make it go that long again, and then they go that long again.

He reached for her waist, slipped his hand to her backside and pulled her on top of him.

"What are you doing?" she asked with a girlish smile.

"Weh you think me a do?" he answered with the slightest of Jamaican accents. Bishop was born in the parish of Saint Catherine in Jamaica. However, he migrated with his family to America when he was seven years old. He assimilated into American culture quickly and his accent had a way of coming and going. His wife Diane was much the same, born in Montego Bay, Jamaica, but left when she was four years old.

"Don't start something you can't finish," she said.

"I plan on finishing," he said.

"We don't have the time."

"Then why you wake me up?"

"I woke you up because you're off today."

"No, I'm not."

"Yes, you are. It's on the board." A board magnetized to the side of the refrigerator, which showed the weekly schedule of everyone in the family.

"Yeah, I know. I didn't get to change it. Edwards had a . . . thing and I said I'd work his shift for him."

"John," she admonished. "C'mon, we planned this. We were both supposed to be off this weekend, so we can drive Desmond off to school."

"The plan doesn't change. We're not driving him until tomorrow."

"And what about today? What about shopping for all the things he'll need?"

"You can do that yourself."

Diane shook her head. "And what about Cece?"

"What happen to her?"

"John, how are you going to forget that she invited her friend over for us to meet."

"Which friend? Who? The white boy?"

"Yes, the white boy. We planned this and you agreed, and he's in the living room waiting."

"You mean right now?"

"Yes. Now get up, get yourself together and come say hello."

When did black girls and white boys become a thing? Being a bus driver brings you in contact with a large swath of humanity. Seeing so many human beings daily, you get to learn certain things. You see trends start and take hold right in front of you. The most prominent interracial coupling, to his eyes, had always been between black men and white women, and by and large it still was. However, black woman-white man had steadily grown from an odd occurrence to a notable one. He began seeing them on billboards and in magazines, and television commercials and subway ads. It made him wonder if it was advertising driving the movement or was the movement driving advertising. Either way black girl-white boy had become a thing, and that thing was waiting for him in his living room.

3

"My Dad is cool, you'll see," Cece said to Josh, **"he's real funny,"** as they sat on the sofa in the living room watching television. The television was on NY1 (New York 1). Beyond MSNBC it was her mother and father's favorite station. They could literally watch the news all day. Cece didn't understand how they did it.

Cece had the remote and could have changed the station but she wanted to make sure her parents were in a good mood, so she kept it on. Also watching the news would make her and Josh appear more civic minded and mature, and admittedly there was a story that had caught her attention.

"It's called AACT (pronounced act). That's A-A-C-T. It stands for African American Community Trust," the reporter explained while standing outside the Brownsville Community Center. "And it is the brainchild of Yalitza Noel," a professional looking cinnamon complexioned woman in her late thirties.

The news cut to a medium shot of Noel inside the Brownsville Community Center. "The trust is about cooperative economics. It's about pooling our resources together to create something greater for all the community. And all it takes is one dollar."

"One dollar?" the reporter repeated, both fascinated and incredulous.

"Yes. That's it. One dollar a week, four dollars a month. And as disenfranchised as this community maybe, everyone can afford a dollar, even the homeless. It's been a year since we started the trust and we've grown tremendously. So far, we have over 20,000 consistent recurring members. That's over 80,000 dollars the community generates every month."

"Wow, that is amazing. And what have you done with the funds?" the reporter asked.

"The first thing we did was open a daycare center. Quality affordable daycare was in desperate need here in Brownsville. And for being a trust member, you only pay one hundred dollars a week for daycare, when before they were forced to pay upwards of three hundred. We also opened another senior citizen center. And the senior center is adjacent to the daycare center. And we have a program where we have the seniors reading to and teaching the children. As we know reading to children is fundamental for their development and it helps keep our elders sharp and engaged."

"That all sounds so amazing. What's next for AACT?"

"We're currently working on an after-school center, which will provide free tutoring for our youth, grades one through twelve, and it will provide free ACT and SAT prep as well. And we've already leased a land from one of the many vacant NYCHA lots, and we're building a grocery store to provide quality affordable groceries for the community. And we're employing men and women in the community to do build it."

"And all this is achieved with just one dollar."

"Just one dollar."

"That is amazing. This is Nina Baksh here in Brownsville, Brooklyn for New York One news."

As the segment ended and switched to a forecast of the weather, Cece's mother and father entered the room. After taking twenty minutes to get himself together, Bishop met his daughter and her friend wearing shorts, his red, black and green flag t-shirt, and flip flops. The Bishops lived in a two-family middle income home in Canarsie, Brooklyn, a few blocks away from Canarsie Park, one of the larger parks in Brooklyn not named Prospect. They had bought the house just over ten years now and rented the bottom floor to help with the mortgage.

Josh had amber hair and sienna eyes. He was a good-looking kid and had a, seemingly, pleasant demeanor. Bishop could see why girls would find him attractive. There was only one thing Bishop truly cared about though, "Ya'll ain't fucking, right?"

"Dad," Cecilia, Cece, blurted, stunned and embarrassed.

"John," Diane called as well.

Yet despite the admonishments of the women Bishop looked at Josh and waited for him to reply.

"No sir."

"Well then as long as it stays that way and you never disrespect my daughter then we're good. Understood?"

"Yes sir."

"Josh, you look like a decent young man, and as much as I'd like to sit and talk, I worked two shifts yesterday and I have another to do tonight and so I'm going back to sleep and leave it to my wife to fill me in. It was a pleasure meeting you." With that Bishop extended his hand and gave Josh a firm but not too intimidating shake and left.

4

If Cece's cheeks could have shown red through her brown skin, they would have. The first boy she brings over and that's how her father greets him. She had no idea how Josh took it. He was always cool and would laugh off everything. Currently he and Desmond were laughing about something that happened in some basketball game. Cece wasn't in a laughing mood and excused herself and went into the kitchen. Her mother was there preparing refreshments to bring out. Cece stood by the refrigerator, arms folded and in a huff, looking like her mother just twenty-four years younger.

"Whatchu screw faced about?" Diane asked.

"You saw what Daddy just did," she said.

"Are you embarrassed?"

"Yeah-es."

"Embarrassment is more about your own insecurities than other people."

"He scared him."

"He didn't scare him."

"Yes, he did."

"Well then that's good. He should fear your father. Now if it scares him off then he was never worth anything and never meant you any good. If it doesn't, he will know to always respect you and treat you well because he knows there's a man in your life he will have to answer to. And that my love is more important than any minor sense of embarrassment you're feeling right now."

5

Desmond approached his father in his parents' bedroom as Bishop was getting ready to go back to sleep. "Daddy, you're crazy you know that, right?" Desmond laughed. "I'm dying. I can't even repeat what you said. Josh turned whiter than he normally is."

Bishop smiled uneasily, concerned he may have been too blunt. This was what they got for waking up a tired man. Cece was not happy with him right now. Still it was his job to protect her, and that meant not always being her friend. "What do you know about this kid?" he asked Desmond.

"Josh—he cool. I like him. Though I don't think Cece should be seeing anybody right now. She too young fi dat," Desmond finished with a twinge of patois. "Plus, these young dudes don't know how to act."

Bishop laughed, given Desmond was only a year and a half older. "And how about you, you know how to act?" Bishop asked his son.

"Hell yeah. Mi raise proper."

"And how about you and that girlfriend of yours?"

"Me and Sasha? We're good."

Bishop looked at him cautiously. "Make sure, you know. Wrap up. Wrap up," he advised his son. "Don't bring no babies around here. Not anytime soon. You got too much of a future ahead of you. Worst thing you can do as a man is get the wrong woman pregnant."

"Are you talking from experience?" Desmond asked.

"No," Bishop retorted recognizing how his son might misinterpret what he said. "I'm talking from getting lucky—but knowing how easy it was for me not to be."

"Cool . . . so . . . Daddy . . . I'm going to hang out with some friends at Garfield's tonight."

"Garfield? Where does he live, again?"

"Flatlands."

"Okay. You and your friends hanging out before you head off. Have fun." Bishop could always tell when his son wanted something. It was the way he idled and hesitated before spitting his words out. "Ask me what you wanna ask me."

"Can I borrow the car?" Bishop laughed. Desmond asked to borrow the car about once a week, and every week Bishop said, "Hell no." The kid was persistent. Bishop admired that at least. It was a war of attrition. Desmond imagined one day he'd finally wear his father down and Bishop would give in. "Well you know if you guys bought me a car, I wouldn't have to inconvenience you," Desmond said.

"Well, graduate college and we'll buy you a car."

"I just graduated high school; I don't get nothing for that?"

"What do you want, a cookie? You're supposed to graduate high school. You don't get props for just doing what you're supposed to do. Do you hear me asking for credit because you guys don't go hungry? You want a car, graduate college. Now that's a real accomplishment."

"What if I don't graduate college." Bishop looked at him crossly. "I mean, what if I ball out and I get drafted."

"Boy, you get drafted then you buy me a car." Bishop laughed, but then he looked at his son's disappointed face . . . and strangely found himself saying, "You know what . . . you can borrow it."

"Borrow what? The beemer?" Desmond asked, his voice in

falsetto, eyes wide open. Bishop didn't waver—externally. Internally, he couldn't believe what he said. "For real?" Desmond stressed for confirmation.

Bishop had already said it and it was never cool playing take-back with your kids. "I can trust you, right?"

"Yeah . . . yes—yes," Desmond repeated adamantly.

"Well you're just going to Flatlands," which was a ten-minute drive away, "and I'm carpooling with Owens." Owens was another bus driver. He also lived in Canarsie and when they worked the same shift, Bishop and he took turns picking the other up. Bishop hadn't seen his son look this happy since he was nine years old and got a bicycle for Christmas.

Bishop bought the brand-new BMW five series in baby-blue nine months ago. He had always wanted a BMW. He had worked hard the last two years, logging in hours of overtime. The BMW was his gift to himself. Bishop had allowed Desmond to drive the car before—but never by himself. Bishop had always been there to watch him. Desmond had driven Diane's car several times and there had never been an incident but, "You know, if you do anything to my baby, I'll kill you," Bishop said, putting his hand firmly on his son's shoulder.

"Oh, I know. Believe me I know. And Daddy, I just wanted to say—"

"Nah, nah. I hear the change in your voice, and I know where you're going. And we're going to have to go through it all again tomorrow when we drop you off. So, save it until then and let me sleep."

"Okay." Desmond said, and left the room before his dad could change his mind. He ran into his mother at the door. He hugged her tightly and gave her a big kiss on the cheek.

"What was that for?" Diane asked.

"Daddy's letting me borrow the car," Desmond said brimming with excitement.

"Daddy's letting you borrow his car? The beemer?"

"Yeah," Desmond said and walked off.

Diane looked at Bishop. "Are you sure?" she asked.

Bishop wasn't but what's done was done. "My father never let me borrow his car. I always hated that. And Desmond's a good kid, and he's just going to Flatlands and back."

"Okay," Diane said. "Your car your call."

6

Anti-crime units operated out of every precinct in the New York City Police Department. Anti-crime officers wore plain clothes and were meant to blend in with the general population. For the most part, to the untrained eye, they do. They dressed functional; loose fitting jeans and t-shirts, sneakers, timberland boots, and extra-large hoodies in the fall and winter.

Anti-crime Officers Brian McNally and Xavier Daniels approached the suspect outside of a laundromat on Atlantic avenue in Brownsville, Brooklyn. McNally was thirty-four, Irish American, with brown hair and brown eyes and had a slim to athletic build. Daniels was African American, twenty-nine and in impeccable shape. He used to run track in college, and he looked like he still could. The subject was dark-skinned and skinny. He was so skinny, he made skinny jeans look baggy. He wore them low. He wore a Louis Vuitton belt and some trickery of physics to hold them up. "Yo, why you harassing me, man? I'm tired of this shit. Ya'll always harassing me. This shit ain't right," Ramon protested.

"Ya'll? Who's ya'll?" McNally asked. "I never stopped you before. Have you stopped him before?" he asked Daniels.

"Nah, I never stopped him," Daniels answered.

"Ya'll. Alla ya'll. From the six-five, five-one, two-seven."

"Damn ma dude, you known all over. You ever think maybe the problem is you and not the police?" McNally asked.

"Hell no. I'm not doing nuthin'. I wasn't doing nuthin', just walking. Ya'll just roll up on me for no reason."

"And why you think that is?" Daniels asked.

He exhaled exaggeratedly, "'Cause I'm Dominican and you stay fucking with us. That's racial profiling. That shit ain't right."

"Nah, we ain't racial profiling. That is illegal," McNally said.

"But I hate to say it, but you do look suspicious," Daniels added.

"Fuck you, nigga."

"Hey—that's not nice," McNally said.

"What's that bulge in your pants?" Daniels asked.

"What bulge? I ain't got no bulge. That's ma dick."

"Really? And it goes all the way down there. You are one gifted dude," Daniels commented.

"Well, you know we blessed like that."

"So, if we search you, we're not gonna find anything?" McNally asked.

"You don't have any right to search me. I don't consent to a search."

Both Daniels and McNally laughed. "Dude, you been reading too many memes. We have every right. It's called probable cause, reasonable suspicion," Daniels said.

"Probable cause for what?"

"For one, you're about one hundred pounds, and twenty of it is in your dick," McNally said and both he and Daniels laughed again. "Now c'mon, up against the wall." McNally continued.

"No, nah. I don't consent to a search."

"Listen, we're being civil. Let's continue to be civil," Daniels said.

"No. No. Ya'll not searching me. Get off of me. Get off of—" Before Ramon could finish another plain clothes officer came between McNally and Daniels, grabbed Ramon by the arm and back of the neck, pulled him out, tripped him and threw him down to the ground in one fell swoop. Ramon skinned his knee, scraped his chin and almost bit off his tongue. The officer placed his knee in Ramon's back and proceeded to handcuff him.

"Damn Riley," McNally commented.

"Yeah, Sarge, we had it under control," Daniels said.

"What? Ya'll think I got nothing better to do than watch ya'll flirt with this asshole all day," Riley said.

"Yo, I think you broke ma rib," Ramon struggled to say.

"Really? Where?" Riley was white, thirty-six, two hundred and twenty pounds and just under six feet. He had a broad body and strong legs. With his knee in Ramon's back he moved it around until Ramon writhed in pain. "Yeah that's it."

"Yo that shit ain't right. That shit ain't right. And yo, I got you on camera."

Riley looked up and saw that they were being recorded by a teenager a few yards away. It wasn't the first time Riley was recorded doing the job. "That's nice, make sure you get my good side. Now get back."

"I have a constitutional right to tape you," the teen said.

"Great, just make sure you do it over there. You take even one foot in and I'm busting you for obstructing." The teenager continued to argue and record, but kept his distance. Riley turned Ramon over and proceeded to search him. Riley found the bulge in his pocket. It was a Ziploc bag with several baggies of heroin. "And what is this?" Riley said and shook the Ziploc bag in front of Ramon's face.

"Yo, that ain't mine. You put that there."

"You know your homie got this whole shit on tape, right?"

"Cuño," Ramon cursed under his breath.

"C'mon," Riley said, standing up, and all three officers held Ramon as they brought him to his feet. They walked him to an all-black Ford Explorer with tinted windows parked a few yards down. Another member of their unit, Officer Craig Roberts, thirty-five, African American, and broad built like Riley sat in the driver's seat. "You didn't think you should come out and help?" Riley asked Roberts.

"I was watching. You were good. Nice technique with the take down. You didn't need the big dog for that." McNally and Daniels began securing Ramon in the back.

"Yo ma man, you wash your ass today, ma man?" Roberts

called to Ramon. "I don't want you stinking up my ride."

"Fuck you, nigga," Ramon answered.

"Fuck me, huh? Well for your sake, let's hope your ass ain't as nasty as your mouth," Roberts said as they drove off.

7

Riley rode in the passenger seat. McNally and Daniels rode in the back with the perp sitting between them with his hands handcuffed behind him. As he drove Roberts looked at the heroin they had confiscated. "Ma nigga," Roberts called to Ramon in the back. "How you so dumb you walking with a bag of heroin in yo' dick?"

"Yo, don't call me nigga, man. I ain't no nigga," Ramon replied.

"Nigga what?" Roberts said.

"I said don't call me nigga, man."

"Well look at this. I woulda neva figured you for the type. What, you conscious my brother? What you in the Nation? Nah you ain't in the Nation. Maybe you a five-percenter. Or you know what, maybe you one of them hotepians. What your other name is, 'ankh-ra-fuck-mama' an' shit?" Roberts got high off his own joke when something occurred to him. "Wait a minute," when Ramon was led into the SUV, "you just called me nigga."

"Yeah, 'cause you black, you a nigga."

There were few times in his life when Roberts was ever flabbergasted, this was one of them. "Wait a minute. I'm black— I'm a nigga?" Ramon nodded yes. "And what the hell is you?"

Ramon looked at him as if it were not patently obvious. "I'm Dominican, man."

"What? So, you not black?"

"No."

"Nigga, you darker than me."

"That don't mean nothing. You got some Indian people, they darker than me, they darker than you. They're not black, they're Indian. I'm not black. But you, you a nigga. You black. Be proud."

Stunned, Roberts looked at Riley. With a sly smile Riley looked back and repeated, "Be proud."

"What the—yooooooo. This has got to be the dumbest shit I have ever heard in my life," Roberts railed. "You know what this reminds me of. You ever watch baseball? Don't answer that. Dumb question. You're Dominican of course you watch baseball. Well, I'm watching baseball and every now and again, they'll get on how the sport is dying, that there's not that much black people watching, cause not that much black guys are playing anymore. And that shit always confused the hell out of me. Because I'm watching it and all I'm seeing is a bunch of confused niggas. Like your dumb ass. Sammy Sosa bleaching ass mo'fucker." Ramon looked at him, steaming mad, biting his tongue. "Yeah, go ahead, say something else. Say something stupid. I'll put you in the back and rough ride your dumbass up and down Atlantic."

8

Niggers. No. Niggas. McNally listened to hip-hop. He knew the proper vernacular. Niggas was cheap. It was the cheapest word in Brooklyn, Queens, Manhattan, Bronx. Anywhere black people congregate you will hear it. It was almost as if there was some profit in it. If there was a penny given for every time a black person said the word, there would be a lot of rich . . . black people. They loved the word. They loved it like no other.

Here was the grand Negro conundrum as McNally saw it. They loved a word they hated anybody else saying. McNally didn't understand the conversation Roberts and the perp was having. He didn't understand how speaking another language or being born in another country changed who you are. He was Irish American, but he was white. It would be the same if he was Italian, Russian or German. When he looked at Ramon, he saw a black man—a bit more milk chocolate than dark, and darker than Roberts, but unmistakably black. Black people came in many shades. However, if this man demanded to be referred to as Dominican instead of black then McNally would oblige him.

McNally looked out the window as they drove back to the sixty-fifth precinct. The six-five covered Brownsville, Brooklyn. When people talk about the hood they are talking about Brownsville. It was a shit neighborhood as McNally saw it. Conversely, shit neighborhoods made for the best assignments. You did well in the hood, you rack up your arrests, you could write your ticket.

All of Brownsville was a housing project, nineteen housing projects to be exact, all jammed into a little over one square mile. It had the highest concentration of public housing in the country. For McNally it was dense and suffocating. It was over seventy-five percent black, nearly forty percent of which lived below the poverty line. People died ten years younger here than the rest of the city. The population dipped especially in the eighteen to twenty-four age group. What was the reason for the college age deficit? McNally had his ideas. Look at the children.

Black children always liked to put on a show. They made a spectacle out of everything. It seemed to him almost unnatural, not unlike watching reality TV. It's as if they know they are being watched and they are being their worst selves. And the people, the grown people, they said nothing. It recently occurred to McNally that they were afraid of them. They were afraid of their own children. All children talk. All children can be unruly. Black children were the worst. They have hair trigger tempers, and every perceived slight was a slander. They were always on the edge to explode. Most of the murders in the city were committed by teenage black males.

27

They turned off Atlantic and onto Rockaway avenue when Roberts made note of something that had been concerning him for the last three blocks. "You know, I think we're being tailed," he said, getting everyone's attention.

"Yeah?" Riley asked, looking at the passenger side-view mirror.

"Yeah. Tan sedan been on us since Atlantic," Roberts said.

Daniels turned around to look out the back window. McNally didn't attempt to. He had an ulcer. He had it for years now. It would come and go, and when it came it felt like hellfire in his stomach, and he would need prescription pills and bed rest to abate it. He started feeling it during their interaction with Ramon. It got progressively worse during the drive. He wanted to get a look at the car behind them, but he couldn't. He was doing all he could not to show how much pain he was in.

"Yeah, I see it," Riley said. "Well, we're at the house now," he said as they turned onto East New York avenue coming into the sixty-fifth precinct. "Let's see what they do?" Roberts parked at a diagonal at one of the free spaces outside.

The tan sedan parked across the street. Four people, all black, two men and two women, in their forties crossed the street and approached the officers as they were taking Ramon into the station house. They didn't look at all threatening, nevertheless, Riley kept his hand on his sidearm at the ready. "Hello Officers, my name is Ms. Forbes and we're with the Change Brownsville Neighborhood Patrol," one of the women greeted. "We understand that you arrested a member of the community."

"Okay," Riley said with overt suspicion.

"We're here to make sure that the community member was brought in safely and that his rights are being adhered to."

"Really?" Riley asked.

Ms. Forbes turned her attention to Ramon. "Brother, are you alright? How have you been treated?"

Having never seen anything like this before in all the times he had been brought in by the police, but happy for it, Ramon said, "Yo, they did me dirty, yo. They searched me. They had no right. Then that big white boy slammed me down. I think I broke a rib and busted up my chin."

The neighborhood patrol looked at the officers crossly. Riley looked at this entire display with amusement and was about to tell these people to get out of his way and let him do his job, when Daniels stepped forward and greeted them. "Hello, I'm Officer Daniels, this is Sergeant Riley and Officers McNally and Roberts. Mr. Reyes exaggerates, I assure you. In our search we found him with bags of heroin." Daniels showed them the contraband. "He resisted arrest. That's where his minor injuries came from. We're taking him in to be processed. You're welcome to come in and watch." This was not how Riley would have handled this situation and he believed Daniels was out of place for doing so, and he gave Daniels a sharp look for it.

Roberts had heard stories about this neighborhood patrol but this was his first time seeing them. "Never seen a patrol do anything like this—but whatever. But why ya'll here for him, though? He ain't black." He turned to Ramon. "Go ahead tell 'em." Ramon was silent. "Tell 'em." Ramon was still silent. "Oh, you ain't got mouth now. If this ain't a neeggaah."

9

The New York City police department was headquartered at One Police Plaza in Manhattan's Civic Center. It was a fifteen-story brutalist building made of concrete wrapped in red brick. It had been the home of the NYPD since 1973. On the eighth floor, once a week, CompStat meetings took place. CompStat was an amalgam of compare statistics. It was a system created in the 1990s designed to compile and compare exact stats of every crime committed in the city. It was used not only to record and categorize crime but also identify trends and how best to combat them. It was largely credited with decreasing crime in New York City from its historic highs in the 1980s and 90s.

Every week precinct commanders from all seventy-seven police precincts in all five boroughs gathered to look over the data. The room was filled with roughly two hundred members of the NYPD's upper echelon. Commanders were called at random to testify and explain the evolving trends in their jurisdiction. This week the commander of the 65th precinct was called. He stood behind a podium in front of all of NYPD hierarchy ranging from five stars to three: The Police commissioner, the Chief of Department, and his fellow commanders. Being called to present at CompStat can be a nerve-racking experience. Some commanders had been grilled to tears. Deputy Inspector Bertrand, however, was confident in his numbers. "Year to date, we have experienced decreases in five out of the seven major index crime categories, and no increases in the other two," he proudly said.

"Very good," The Chief of Department commented. "Very good, Deputy Inspector. Your precinct has historically been one of the highest crime areas in the city. What do you see as the overall reason for the downturn?" he asked.

"Just continuous solid police work, and community outreach with our NCO's (Neighborhood Coordination Officers) has taken root and is showing effects."

"That's good. But this isn't the time to pat yourself on the back. There is still a high concentration of gang activity in your area. A lot of guns out there and we need to get them off the streets."

"Yes sir," Bertrand said and then departed.

10

At the sixty-fifth precinct after Ramon had been processed and put in holding, the Neighborhood Patrol filed a civilian complaint against Riley—his eleventh—on Ramon's behalf, gave Ramon a card with the number for an attorney and left. Riley, Daniels, Roberts and McNally were at their desk having a laugh about the entire ordeal; McNally not so much.

Cashman, their Lieutenant, came over. "What's up Lieutenant?" McNally greeted with a bit of a grimace. Cashman, Cash as he was affectionately called, was a white man in his midforties. He had sandy blond hair and a stout build. He had been on the force over sixteen years. He had earned his white Lieutenant's shirt.

"What's wrong?" Cashman asked McNally. "You look like shit."

"I feel like shit. Feel like my stomach is eating me."

"Bleeding ulcer. I've had my share. Had my share of hemorrhoids too. The job will do that to you. Go home, call it a night, get better."

"Yeah?" McNally asked.

"Yeah. It ain't like you guys were doing much work out there anyway."

That was a dig. They all received it. Riley being the unit leader responded. "We just brought a perp in."

"Wow, one whole perp, with some baggies of heroin. Who gives a shit? Where the gun at, that's what I wanna know?"

"What gun?" Daniels asked.

"Exactly. What gun? You're the Gun Violence Suppression Division. You investigate gang violence. That's your job. You get guns off the street. Where the gun at? You haven't brought one gun in here in over two months."

"We've been going hard Lieutenant. We just haven't come across any," Roberts responded.

"Are you kidding me? This is Brownsville. You got nineteen projects in one square mile. Damn near each project has a gang and they all hate each other. If you're a gangbanger are you gonna walk around here without a gun?" No one said anything. "Exactly."

"Like Roberts said, we have been going at it hard lieu," Riley said.

"Well then go harder, or like McNally go home. Or maybe I should take your unit off this tour?" They all looked at him sourly. "Riley, I got you working evenings, primetime, because you're my top earner. Maybe I should have you working midnight." With that Cashman had made his point and walked off. All four of the men were visibly upset with being dressed down.

"You heard him. Let's get back out there and see what we can turn up," Riley said. Daniels and Roberts stood up to leave.

McNally gave a pound to both of them. "Alright you guys be safe out there. I'll see you all tomorrow."

"Feel better," Daniels said to McNally and he and Roberts walked off. McNally approached Riley.

"See you tomorrow, Sarge."

"Are you for real? You're really going home?"

"I feel like I'm dying here. And Cash said I should."

"He also said we haven't been doing dick lately," Riley said. They just looked at each other for a beat. "You know what, you feel that bad, if you feel like some Pepto won't hold you over, go home."

"Damn Riley, you're really riding me here," McNally said.

"I'm not. I'm trying to help you. Look, I'm already a sergeant. That's it for me. I got too much shit in my record. They ain't promoting my white ass any higher. I don't even want to go higher. You stop doing real police work and just deal with a lot of bullshit. Roberts, he's too dumb to make sergeant. Failed the exam three times already. Being in this unit is the best it's gonna be for him. Daniels is on his way up and out. They say he got third on the sergeant's exam. I don't buy it but that's what they said. And his rabbi is one of the big black chiefs. They been tight since Daniels was in high school. They love putting his ass on TV for community relations PR bullshit. His ticket is written. In seven years, he'll probably be running a precinct. In fifteen he might be Chief of Department the way things are going. You now, you wanna make Harbor. For that you need quality arrests, and we need guns."

"I hear you Sarge, I hear you," McNally said. "But I feel like shit. I can't tonight. I wouldn't be any good to you. Let me go home and get right. I promise I go hard tomorrow."

"Alright," Riley said his peace. "Take the unmarked I picked you up in today. Roberts will drop me home." He and McNally gave each other a pound and then McNally left.

11

It was 8:48 pm when Desmond pulled up behind a fifteen-year-old, champagne colored, Nissan sedan on Mother Gaston Boulevard. He felt uneasy being here. He shouldn't be in Brownsville—especially not in his Dad's car. If his Dad knew this was where he had taken the car, he would be in so much trouble. But Garfield had begged him to bring the weed for the party and Desmond begrudgingly obliged.

He was here to meet with his dealer. There were dealers around his way he could have bought from, but a good dealer was like a good barber, once you've found one you can trust you don't like messing around. You never know what people put in their drugs.

"This is ten-ten wins. You give us twenty-two minutes; we'll give you the world." The radio station was on the news. It was his Dad's station. Desmond didn't want to upset his father by messing with his settings, so he touched nothing. The news was reporting on the recent killing of unarmed motorist Cornelius Stewart in Tallahassee, Florida by local police and the resulting nationwide protests. A commentator said that Stewart had not followed police commands and that's why he had been shot. "I don't know how you are when you get pulled over by a cop. I know how I am all the times I did. When a cop pulls me over, I put my hands outside of the car, so he can see them clearly and I don't move them until he tells me otherwise."

The driver of the Nissan exited his car and entered the front seat of the BMW. Colin was white and in his late-twenties, lean built with blond hair pulled back into a ponytail. Desmond met him a year ago with one of his teammates on his high school basketball team. His teammate graduated and Desmond and Colin stayed in touch. Colin had been his weed man since then. "What's up, Des? Nice car," he said.

Desmond turned the radio down. "Thanks. It's my Dad's. Yo, why we had to meet in Brownsville?" Desmond asked.

"What's wrong with Brownsville?" Colin asked.

"It's just not ma hood. I never feel too comfortable around here. Dudes around here are just different."

"The hood is the hood, bro. They're all the same. Plus, my supply guy is around here. I had to re-up. And I gotta make this party in Harlem after this. This was the only time I had to meet you."

"Alright."

"So, what you need?" Colin asked.

"Gimme an eighth. That should do," Desmond said.

"Why don't you just do a quarter?"

"Nah an eighth is plenty. Plus, I don't have enough."

"You know what, just take the quarter. Same price as the eighth."

"Yeah?" Desmond said, surprised at his good fortune.

"Yeah." Colin pulled a baggie with a quarter of weed out of his backpack. My send-off gift to you."

"Alright. Thanks," Desmond said.

"And you know what, why don't you take an ounce?"

"How much you think we gonna smoke?" Desmond joked.

"Not to smoke, to sell."

"To who—my friends?"

"If you want. But I'm thinking more like at Syracuse when you get up to school," Colin explained.

"How would I do that?"

"Well you're gonna be on the basketball team, and you're gonna meet a lot of people. And nobody does more drugs than college kids. It's an easy way to put some money in your pocket. And believe me living on campus, you're gonna need it. And you just cash app me my cut and we take it from there." That all sounded a bit overwhelming and Desmond looked very unsure.

12

Colin returned to his car and pulled off. Desmond drove off as well and pulled up beside Colin at the stoplight. When the light changed, they nodded at each other, then Colin drove forward, and Desmond made a left onto Livonia avenue. It was time to circle back. He couldn't wait to get out of there. Hopefully his Dad wouldn't be anal enough to check the mileage on the car. Just then Desmond heard a siren and saw flashing lights in his rearview mirror. It wasn't a patrol car. It was a regular sedan. They must be undercover. *Shit.* But were they for him? He kept driving, hoping they were after someone else. The light flashed again. That settled it they were addressing him. *Shit.*

Desmond crossed the intersection and pulled over at the bottom of the block. The black sedan just made the changing light and drove past Desmond and pulled over a few meters ahead of him. Desmond had never been pulled over before. He had been with his father when he had been pulled over. Dad was usually cool and respectful, and things went smoothly. His Dad had told him, if he was ever pulled over to stay calm, be respectful and keep his hands in sight. However, Desmond was nervous. He shouldn't be here. If he got a ticket on the car out here Dad would know, and he would kill him. It also occurred to him he had an ounce of weed in his book bag sitting in the passenger seat. *Shit.* Should he hide it? Should he even move? Was an ounce of weed even illegal anymore? The laws were changing but he didn't know them and wasn't sure. He was literally a mess wondering what he should do. What if he got arrested for weed, in his Dad's car, in Brownsville? *Shit.* Dad would kill him two times. However, the police could not find the weed unless Desmond allowed them to search the car. So Desmond should not allow them to search the car.

All the things he had seen on the internet about how you should respond when pulled over by the police, and to know your rights, along with what his Dad had told him, kept running though his head and Desmond couldn't clearly remember any of them and this cop, just one, white, plain clothes, had just left his car and was walking towards him, and brought with him all the memories of all the police shootings he had seen. Desmond took a breath. He should just be calm, be respectful and cool and maybe the cop would let him go with a warning. He should show the cop his hands to show him all was good. That's what the white man on the radio just said. That was all he could re-member. His windows were already down. Desmond stuck both hands out to the side, fingers free, exhaled and saw a flash of light.

13

McNally approached the man—no not a man, a boy, he had the height of a man, but the face was definitely a boy, a boy's face, a scared face—gun drawn. He said, "Don't move," but the boy couldn't move. Bleeding from his right ear, all he could do was stare; eyes wide open; didn't blink once, not even from the glare of the streetlight. "Unhook your seatbelt and get out of the car." The unblinking boy couldn't do it. He couldn't do anything. All he could do was stare at him. McNally would have to do it for him. McNally put his hand through the window and opened the door from the inside. Shattered glass fell to the ground. He leaned in and undid the seatbelt and felt the warm rush of the boy's blood on his hands. He pulled him from the car and laid him face down on the pavement. Should he handcuff him? Should he not? He was bleeding badly. He was likely dying. Then again McNally was not a doctor. He looked bad but there was no telling how injured he was. He could still be a threat. McNally's safety came first. He handcuffed him, arms behind his back, the boy let out a restrained gasp, then McNally set about looking for the gun he saw in the boy-man's hand before he opened fire.

Where is it? Where is it? It wasn't on the ground. It wasn't under the car. It wasn't by the pedals, under the seats, the space between the gear shifts. "Where the gun at? Where the gun at?" Someone shouted. McNally took a glance around him and found himself hemmed in. Thirty or more people had suddenly appeared. "They shot him, they shot him," said another. This was too big for him. McNally needed help. He called for backup. He called Riley, he called for an ambulance in that order.

14

The police dispatcher received the call. "Officer involved shooting, Livonia avenue between Powell and Junius Street. All units in the area please respond." The call moved quickly through the chain of command, from Sergeant Riley to Lieutenant Cashman to Deputy Inspector Bertrand to the Chief of Department to the Commissioner to the Mayor. The Mayor was silent for a good twenty seconds. Police involved shootings were never good politically, especially during an election year. You lose one way or the other. "Has a gun been retrieved?" the Mayor asked.

"Not at this time Mr. Mayor," the Commissioner said.

"Okay. Contain this and keep me abreast."

"Yes, Mr. Mayor."

15

A patrol car and two uniform officers arrived two minutes after McNally made the call. McNally was glad to see them. Things were escalating quickly. Two other patrolmen arrived less than a minute later, and they kept streaming in; many he knew, many he didn't. Before McNally could blink, a helicopter and half of two precincts were on the scene. He was glad to see them all, especially his team, Riley, Roberts and Daniels. "What happened McNally?" Daniels asked.

"I saw him make a drug deal, I pulled him over. As I'm approaching, he puts his hands out the window and aims at me, and I fired," McNally said, trying not to bend over as his ulcer, which had abated somewhat in the last twenty minutes, kicked in again.

"You found the gun?" Riley asked.

"No gun," McNally answered soberly.

"You don't know that. You may not have found it yet."

"Maybe," McNally said, wanting to sound hopeful but certain they wouldn't find one. Riley and Roberts walked back to the car while Daniels stayed with McNally.

There was now roughly a hundred bystanders—and they were angry. They had watched a teenage boy lay bleeding handcuffed on the pavement for almost ten minutes before EMS arrived and took him away.

Riley always carried a black bb gun with him. To the untrained eye, and from a distance, it would appear to be a genuine gun. Riley had been carrying it for years. It was something he learned from a retired officer. This was in case he was ever caught with a dirty shooting he could finagle the scene. But he couldn't this time. There were too many eyes; ten of which were trained directly on him, almost as if they knew exactly what he had in mind. This was to say nothing of all the phones that were out shooting the scene from every angle, as if it was a Hollywood production. "No gun," he said to Roberts and he and Roberts walked back.

Mario Pacheco, McNally's union representative, had arrived and was by his side. Pacheco was in his forties, of Portuguese descent, and had over fifteen years on the job. The Firearms Discharge Review Board representative Arthur Chang was there as well. The review board took an account of every officer involved shooting. Chang was in his mid-thirties with roughly ten years on the job.

Chang had already taken McNally's service weapon into custody. "Now, why did you park ahead of the suspect instead of behind?" Chang asked.

"I would have had to park in the middle of the street. I didn't want to cause a traffic jam. It would have been chaos."

"Yeah, like exactly like what's going on now," His union

representative intervened. "This scene is madness. Why don't we get officer McNally outta here, before someone tries to take a shot at him."

"Um, okay," Chang said. "I'll meet you back at the sixty-fifth."

"Good," Pacheco said.

Officer Chang walked off.

In the presence of Riley and the other team members, Pacheco addressed McNally. "Now Brian, there's a cruiser over there, it will take you back to the precinct. I'll meet you there. And don't say anything to anyone else unless I'm present."

McNally nodded and began walking to the cruiser. As he was walking off he called to officer Chang, as Chang took notes of the scene, examining the shot up BMW and the blood stains on the ground. "What's his name?" he asked. Chang turned and faced McNally. "Did you find out his name?"

Chang looked at his notes in his memo pad. "Desmond Bishop," he replied.

16

Diane and Cece sat up in the sofa watching television. Though it was summer, the air conditioning gave the room a slight chill and they huddled under a light blanket. They enjoyed these mother-daughter nights when they could binge a show they had been meaning to get to.

There was a ring at the doorbell. Cece got up to see who it was. She looked through the peephole and saw two uniformed police officers. That was disconcerting. "Mommy, there are two policemen outside." It was never good to have police come to your home, at night, uncalled for. Hearing police, Diane perked up, paused the program, left the sofa and opened the door.

"Hello. May I help you," she greeted.

"Is this the home of Desmond Bishop?"

"Yeahhh-es," Diane answered cautiously. "He's my son." Why on earth were the police coming to her house regarding Desmond? What kind of trouble could he have gotten into? The police had never darkened her doorstep before. Desmond wasn't that kind of kid. He had never gotten into legal trouble. "What's going on?" Diane asked.

"We're sorry to say, but your son was involved in a shooting."

"A what?"

"Is he alright?" Immediately terrified, Cece asked.

"He's at Brookdale Medical Center. We just came to inform you."

They told her, her son had been shot and was in the hospital. They didn't say what his condition was, or who shot him or why? This was all left for her to discover at the hospital. Diane and Cece got themselves together and were out the door in less than ten minutes.

17

Bishop pulled the bus into the terminal and the last of his passengers departed. This was his final ride for his shift. His replacement was waiting outside to come in and take over. Bishop's eye had been twitching intermittently for over an hour and had gotten a bit red from him rubbing it with the back of his thumb. Beyond the twitching eye, an anxious feeling had crept over him and settled in his stomach like a bad meal. He couldn't articulate this feeling, besides to say he just felt off.

Bishop believed in God but wasn't quite sure he believed in spirits, omens or psychics. When his mother used to tell him, a jumping eye augured something ominous, he never took her too seriously. The woman used to soak stale bread in water before throwing it out and would warn against putting shoes on the table—as if anyone would ever put shoes on the table.

He felt his phone vibrating and pulled it from his back pocket and saw that it was Cece calling. That was unusual for Cece to do. However, he had called her earlier when he called both her and Desmond just to hear they were safe. When something is wrong you know it immediately. There was a delay before she said, "Daddy." There was an uneasiness in her voice; a bit frantic, confused and fearful. "Desmond was in a shooting. Desmond is in the hospital."

18

The family got to the hospital at the same time. They met each other in the parking lot. Diane and Cece came in Diane's Toyota Rav4, already packed with Desmond's things to take to school tomorrow. Bishop had taken an uber. They rushed into the hospital and Diane spoke to the emergency room receptionist. "Hello, we're the family of Desmond Bishop. We were told he was involved in a shooting and we should come here." The receptionist looked for his name in the registry, and when she found it, something she saw shook her for a half second before she looked up and responded. Cece saw it. *What was that look for? That look wasn't good.*

"Just take a seat right there and the doctor will be with you shortly," she said.

"But he's okay, right?" Cece asked.

"I really don't know, but the doctor will be right with you."

Within five minutes the doctor arrived, an Indian man in his mid-forties. He got to the point. "I'm sorry to say but your son sustained multiple gunshot wounds, and we tried our best, but we were unable to save him. I'm so sorry."

What? What kind of fuckery this man jus' say? Desmond

dead. How Desmond fi dead? Bishop's mind raged. Twelve hours ago, Bishop spoke to his son and now he was dead—just like that. He was going to college tomorrow. He was healthy, he had a life, he had a future, and just like that—dead. "No, no, no. You have the wrong Desmond Bishop. My baby is not dead," Diane said and held her stomach as if she could still feel him in her womb. "No . . . no . . . no," she said fighting back the tears and the truth.

"What do you mean dead? How 'im dead? Who kill him?" Bishop interrogated.

"All I know is that he was involved in a shooting with the police."

"With the police? Why? Desmond don't know nothing 'bout gun. Desmond not shooting anybody. Who shot him? Did the police shoot my son?" Bishop asked. The doctor didn't know the exact answer to give and so he could say no more than to offer them his sympathies.

19

You hear the words, but you don't truly believe it until you see it. Two hours later they were permitted to see Desmond's body on a cold slab in the hospital morgue. This was when Diane said her last prayers to God. She pleaded to the depths of her soul and even wagered with God to take her instead and let this not be Desmond and that he be alright. *Please God please. Please God please.*

They pulled back the sheet and revealed only the head. Dead bodies always looked different than the living. Bishop didn't recognize the face at first and was hopeful for a split second, but he needed only to look at Diane to be dissuaded. A mother always knows her child. When Bishop looked again, he could see it clearly. Yes, this was Desmond. The right ear was deformed but this was his son. There was no doubt. His son was gone. Diane bent over him, held her child, kissed his face repeatedly and wept, audibly, her voice cracking, her chest heaving as she repeatedly called Desmond's name.

Bishop always hated to see black women cry. Black women cried from the depths of their souls and it hurt your soul to look at it. Bishop closed his eyes and he heard it and it sounded worse in the dark. Bishop stood with one hand on Diane's shoulder and the other on the top of his dead son's head. He felt his son's coarse strong black hair glittered with shards of glass and caked with dried blood. Bishop cried like a man, behind clenched teeth.

They left the morgue and met Cece in the waiting area. Cece had been holding on to hope that it wasn't Desmond's body as well. Seeing her parents' faces shattered that hope. All three of them held each other tightly. Bishop tried to keep it in, trying to be strong for the women. He glanced at the television in the high corner of the room. It was on the news. He saw a report of a police shooting and killing of an unarmed black man in Brownsville, Brooklyn. The women looked in shock as Bishop fell to his bottom and let out a scream, like a howl stifled. They looked at him horrified and he pointed to the television, his voice cracking and gasping for air. "I was there . . . oh God I was there . . . the man tell me, him tell me, and mi neva know, mi neva know . . . Desmond did a dead, and mi neva know . . . I was there . . . oh God I was there."

20

There were five unions that represented the New York City Police Department, each corresponding to the rank of their respective officers: The Police Benevolent Association, the Detective's Endowment Association, the Sergeant's Benevolent Association, the Lieutenant's Benevolent Association and the Captain's Endowment Association. The PBA covering rank and file police officers, with its membership at roughly 24,000 was the largest in the NYPD. It was formed in 1888 with the rise of unions during the industrial revolution.

Before McNally met with the Firearms Discharge Review Board, he met with Pacheco his union representative, in his car in the parking lot of the sixty-fifth precinct, and they went over what he would say in his statement. "Look, they're not trying to fuck you, so don't give them reasons to. Don't lie. But say only exactly what you need to. And be succinct. But don't say anything that can be refuted later," Pacheco said.

"So, tell us what happened Brian?" Arthur Chang, the Firearms Discharge Review Board interviewer, asked as he and McNally sat in interview room 2 in the sixty-fifth precinct.

"It was a regular day like the rest," McNally began, still a bit frazzled from the shooting. "We had just brought in a perp, but then my ulcer started acting up. We were set to go out again. But I wasn't feeling well. So, I told everyone I was leaving early. This is around 8:30."

"Okay."

"I took an umarked car. Didn't drive to work. Riley had picked me up in it. Riley said I could take it home and Roberts would drop him off at the end of their shift. So, I pull out of the precinct and I start for home."

"And where's home?"

"Home is Marine Park."

"Okay. Continue."

"I saw the BMW when I left the precinct. I saw the kid driving it. Something looked a little suspicious to me. He turns onto Mother Gaston and so I follow him down. I don't know, I wasn't thinking of stopping him, I just wanted to get a feel for him, get a good look at the car, maybe run the plates. I figure we'd probably definitely come across that car again later."

"Alright, I'm going to stop you there, Brian," Pacheco interrupted him during the pre-interview. "Don't say you followed him from the precinct. Don't say you thought he looked suspicious. Surveillance footage will show that you did follow him, but you weren't, you just happen to be going the same way. You were just going home."

McNally nodded that he understood.

"Is that the way you usually take home?" Chang asked him, during the actual interview.

"I can take a couple of ways. Sometimes traffic is better on Mother Gaston, so I take that for a bit."

"Okay, go on."

"Yeah so, I'm driving, then I notice a BMW driven by a teenage black male pull over behind this other car."

"What kind of car?"

"It was a Nissan. Maybe ten plus years older. Kind of beat up."

"I'm going to stop you there again," Pacheco said during the pre-interview. "Just say the car was a Nissan. Don't go into how old it was or how it looked."

McNally nodded that he understood. "It was a Nissan," he answered flatly to Chang during the real interview and continued. "I see a white male, late twenties—thirties, get out the Nissan and get in the BMW. This looked suspicious to me."

"Why?"

"Because we're in Brownsville. You don't see that many white males like that in the area, and then to get into the car with a young black male, it looked suspicious. So, I pull over behind them and I watch for a bit and I see a sale go down."

"Now you we're off and you said you weren't feeling well, why didn't you just continue on your way home?"

"I found some wheat thins I left in the car from earlier and ate some and that eased the pain in my stomach for a bit. And yeah, I was off but I'm a cop. I see something going down it's my job to look into it."

"Okay," Chang said while taking notes.

"After a while, the white male gets out of the car and back into his. Both cars then pull off. They're side by side at the stop light. I'm a little behind them. The Nissan keeps going forward and the BMW makes a left. I turn and go after the BMW."

"Why stay with the BMW and not the Nissan. The Nissan was still going your way?"

"My instincts told me that the driver of the BMW was the dealer."

"Don't say that," Pacheco again corrected. "Say you saw the deal go down. Say you saw that the driver of the BMW was the dealer."

And that was what McNally told Chang, and he accepted it. "I put on my siren I flash my lights. I pull him over three blocks down. I park ahead of him."

"Why did you do that? That's against procedure. By parking in front of him you put yourself in unnecessary danger."

"He parked at the bottom of the block. The car didn't have a loud speaker for me to tell him to move up. I would have had to park in the middle of the street blocking traffic or on the previous block. The light was changing, and I was worried if I did, he'd use that opportunity to take off."

"Good," Pacheco said.

"Okay," Chang said.

McNally continued, "So I park ahead of him. I get out. I start walking towards him. He puts his hand out the window. I see a gun."

"You saw a gun? Are you sure?"

"I thought I saw a gun. It could have been a phone." McNally breathed. "I feared for my life. I fired off three shots."

"You fired off seven shots," Chang corrected him.

"What? No, it was three."

"No. It was seven," Chang said while looking through his files. McNally looked taken aback. "It's a high intense situation. It's easy to lose track. Continue," Chang said.

"I get to him. I see that he's bleeding. I tell him not to move. He doesn't. I ask him where's the weapon. He doesn't say anything. I call Riley, my sergeant. Then I called EMS."

"You saw him bleeding, why not EMS first?"

"Um," McNally stuttered a bit.

Pacheco answered for him. "There was a good amount of people outside. Crowd was growing, you feared for your safety and you wanted to protect the integrity of the scene, so you wanted back up there as soon as possible."

McNally told Chang exactly that, just that way. Chang didn't question him on that further. "I pulled the suspect from the car and handcuffed him. I then proceeded to search the vehicle, looking for the weapon."

"But you found no weapon?"

"No. Only what appeared to be an ounce of weed in his book bag. Within two minutes a blue and white pulled up. Within another five or so minutes Riley and the other officers in my unit showed up. EMS showed up after that. And that was that."

"Good," Pacheco said and nodded.

"Okay," Chang said. Well that seems sufficient. He hit the button and the recorder stopped. "I think we have everything. Thank you officer McNally."

"You're welcome, and thank you," McNally said to Chang, but first to Pacheco.

Pacheco shook his hand. "You're going to do fine, Brian. And don't worry. We got your back. You're going to get through this. You're going to be fine."

McNally exhaled.

21

Meagan Goodrich-McNally worked as a dance instructor at a studio in Park Slope, Brooklyn. She taught ballet, modern, hip-hop and Irish dance. She taught everything she used to do. She used to dance on and off Broadway.

She met a man, she fell in love, she had children, a boy now eight and a girl recently turned four. She got older; thirty-three now; younger dancers came in and she stopped getting chosen. She had no regrets. You make sacrifices for family. She loved her children; she loved her husband.

At five-nine, she was tall for a woman. Brian was an inch and a half taller, but comparatively she always seemed to tower over him, especially when she wore heels. She had strawberry blond hair and butternut skin that would freckle in the summer. She was lanky with shape. She had her Dad's prominent nose; not obtrusive but noticeable. If you were to draw a caricature of her you would highlight the nose. Through much of her adolescence she hated it and considered rhinoplasty too many times to count. It wasn't until Brian told her he loved her nose that she started to love it as well.

She never thought she would end up with a cop. Cops were all power tripping assholes—or so she believed. When she met Brian, he wasn't a cop, he was a cute bartender. He asked her for her number, and she gave it to him after two shots of tequila. He loved watching her dance and he'd come to as many of her shows as he could and escort her home. She felt safe and protected with him. He wasn't the biggest man, but it didn't matter. He always stood up for himself and her, and he had a firm grasp of right and wrong. He went into the academy a few months after she became pregnant with their son. Neither of them truly wanted him to do it, but he needed a job with security and benefits, and given his heritage being a cop seemed inevitable.

When you're a cop's wife, you're never truly at peace, which was not to say every minute you were a nervous wreck. You cope, you deal with it; being a bit on edge is your new baseline. But whenever he was on the job there was always an extra tick to her heart. She got a prescription for .5 mg of Xanax five years ago, after a suspect shot a bullet two feet in Brian's vicinity during a shout-out, and never came off it.

Every day you fear that dreaded call. Most nights it was near clockwork when he walked through the door at 12:35 am. If he would be late, he would call. He and the boys at times went for a drink after their shift. She didn't mind that. It was a stressful job. She understood they needed to blow off some steam. She just needed him to call. The police were always in the news, and mostly it was bad. Some cop in some part of the country did something and everybody hated cops everywhere. It troubled her terribly: the marches, the riots, the hatred. In recent years her anxiety had amped up that much higher.

The worst part was not even the worry but the loneliness. She felt like a single parent. He worked from four to twelve midnight, and on a good deal of holidays. Children grow in the day and sleep at night. He was missing their childhood. The job becomes the be all and end all for everyone. Everyone must sacrifice on the altar of the NYPD. He acted as if it was the most important thing in the world. He told her to join support groups, but she didn't want to learn how to better cope with it, she wanted it to stop. There was so much she could tolerate but there was one thing she would not—and she had packed a bag that night.

At 10:16 she got a call. It was from Daniels, one of the cops in Brian's unit. Why was he calling?

"There was a kid doing a drug deal and Brian pulled him over, and . . . he thought he had a gun," Daniels said.

"Oh my God. Oh my God. How . . . how is the kid?" she asked.

"He didn't make it. But Brian is fine. He wanted me to call you. He's going to be on his way home soon."

22

As McNally stepped inside, Meagan hugged him like she hadn't seen him in years. He held her as well but not as strongly. He couldn't muster the energy.

"What happened she asked?"

"I'll tell you. But not now. Now I'm tired and I just wanna shower and sleep." Even just speaking was like working a muscle to failure.

"Okay," she said and watched him walk off and head upstairs. After he had left, Meagan realized her shirt was blood stained.

Blood flowed down the drain. McNally had to keep reminding himself that it wasn't his. Blood gets everywhere. Even in places you least expect it. On his hands, in his fingernails, in his hair he expected—but there was blood on his chest, under his armpits, even in his pubic hair. How did it get there? Every time he saw it, he washed it away, but even after twenty minutes there still was a bit of red dirtying the water.

Meagan was in bed waiting for him. He came under the covers, held her tight, laid his head on her chest like a child, and she became mother and lover in one. She massaged his scalp as she ran her fingers through his hair. It was so comforting. It felt good to be loved. He could still hear their hatred ringing in his ears, like a song after a concert. He looked in her eyes, and they were wet and beautiful. He wanted to dive into those pools. He began kissing her and couldn't stop.

23

Steam filled the room. Water beat the back of his head and ran down his face like tears. However, he wasn't crying. He had cried so much in these last few hours already. He was tired of crying today. There would be time for that tomorrow. It felt unreal. He was awake and yet didn't feel altogether conscious. He felt like he was having a dream that felt so vivid you thought it was real but were certain it was a dream. How does a day change so abruptly? It was less than twenty-four hours ago that Desmond asked him to borrow the car. Bishop regretted that now. The world sees a black teenager driving a nice car and they think criminal. What a fool he was. *Oh God.* He pounded the shower wall. The porcelain tile cracked slightly and cut his hand. There was no waking up. This wasn't a dream.

24

Bishop came out the shower and found Diane sitting in the dark of their room crying alone. She had been distant since leaving the hospital. Did she blame him, he wondered? Was it because he allowed Desmond to drive the car? Or was it because it was his job to protect his family and by Desmond dying some-how, he had failed? Was it because he worked that night when he was supposed to be off? Was it because he drove by the street his son lay dying and he was too ignorant to know?

He approached her, she stood up and he held her. She cried in his arms, but she did not let go. They were as close physically as two people could be but there was this intangible distance. It would be imperceptible to anyone else, but they felt it. When you've been with someone for twenty years every hug told a story.

Diane pulled away like a partner on a dance floor who slowly retracted their body from yours. She went into the bathroom, closed the door and continued to dance by herself. He could hear her tears and prayers through the door.

Bishop felt impotent, like a half hard erection, like a muscle atrophied, like taking off his shirt in front of the mirror and seeing that his chest sagged and his stomach lacked definition. He felt less than the man he used to be. Another man had taken from him one of the three things that mattered most in his life and he felt powerless to do anything about it.

25

The Editor and five reporters sat in his office looking at a video of the shooting. There had been a few posted to social media already. The one they were watching was the best quality. It was captured from the playground across the street and showed the officer approach the car, open fire, pull Desmond from the vehicle and the aftermath. The video was from a distance, but the sound was terrifying. You felt the gunshots and the rancor of the crowd.

"Seven shots. Boy, he really lit into him," the Editor remarked. The video ended. "So, tell me what we know so far?" he asked.

"His name is Desmond Bishop. Went to Bishop Loughlin Memorial in Brooklyn. Pretty good athlete, decent student. He was supposed to be going away to school—Syracuse tomorrow, well today. He was going on the basketball team as a preferred walk-on. Mom's a vice-principal at a charter school in the Bronx, father's an MTA bus driver." This they learned from Desmond's social media and doing a google search.

"Record?"

"Should it matter?"

"It matters. It contextualizes things, and someone else will put it out so we might as well lead the story, instead of following it."

"He has no record."

"See, that's good. Alright, write it up."

They scoured his Facebook, his Instagram and his Snapchat. They were looking for a picture. How they wrote the story up would be one thing, but this picture would be the predominant lasting image of this boy. A graduation picture would work well. Fortunately, he had posted one. It wasn't the greatest smile, but it would suffice. It was the image used by the Daily News, Newsday, the New York Times, ABC, NBC and CBS. The New York Post used the graduation picture as well; however, it was printed two shades darker than the other outlets. It wasn't a garish difference and only noticeable upon comparison. They also included a photo from his Instagram from a year prior making his hand into a gun and pointing at the camera. Fox News used both images as well. Other conservative media eschewed the graduation photo and ran only the Instagram picture.

POLICE SHOOT UNARMED BLACK TEENAGER

OFF DUTY POLICE SHOOT UNARMED BLACK TEEN

NYPD SHOOTS AND KILLS BLACK MAN IN BROWNS-VILLE

NYPD SHOOTS SUSPECTED DRUG DEALER IN BROOKLYN

GANG BANGER KILLED IN POLICE SHOOTOUT

26

It was after eleven the morning after. It was just shy of eighty degrees and the sun was shining. It was a good day for a drive. They should be on the road right now halfway to Syracuse. The Rav4 outside was already packed with Desmond's things ready to go. Bishop sat at the kitchen table. There was a newspaper close by, sports-side up. Desmond was on the front cover. Bishop didn't dare look at it. He didn't want to read it. It felt too unreal. Bishop hadn't slept much—neither had Diane.

They had been on the phone with family for much of the night into the morning. He heard from relatives; his mother and father and her mother and father, and brothers and sisters, and aunts and uncles, cousins, nieces, nephews, and friends and friends of friends. Diane had called both of their parents and the word spread from there. Calls came from everywhere, Brooklyn and Queens, Miami and Fort Lauderdale, Virginia, Atlanta, Jamaica and London. With every call you tell the story again and you cry again, and you rage again, until you just can't do it anymore. You can't take any more calls. You literally can't talk. Cece had been doing her part with the calls, navigating through her contemporary relatives and her friends.

Diane's older sister Gabrielle lived in Queens and she was the first to come over. She was a godsend. She was the one taking most of the calls and relaying the messages. She was the one who brought the newspaper. They were being flooded with calls from the media as well. They gave no response. They didn't know what to say. There was so much they didn't know, and the grief was so fresh. How did they even know their numbers?

Gabrielle came to Bishop in the kitchen and brought him the phone. He looked at her dead-eyed and said he couldn't talk to anyone. "You should take this call," she said.

"Hello," Bishop greeted flat and lifeless.

"This is the Reverend Al Sharpton," the voice said, and it gave Bishop a shot of adrenaline. "I know what you're going through. This is probably the worst pain you've ever felt in your life. No parent should ever lose a child and especially not like this. A lot of things are going to come at you and you're going to need a support system to see you through. Now, I am pledging to you that I am in your corner. I am going to help you and fight with you. Now, I can help you directly or I can help you from the side, but any which way I'm going to help you, and support your family through this, and work to get justice for your son."

"Thank you, Reverend," Bishop said. "Thank you. We can use as much help as we can get."

27

His name was Luther Powell. Bishop had seen him on television, and the internet and social media. He had represented families in the most egregious and prominent police brutality cases. He was in his mid-forties but looked late thirties. He was light complexioned, not necessarily handsome but well put together and that made him attractive. He was made for television. His suit fit him well and he spoke assuredly.

He shook both Diane and Bishop's hands as he entered and Diane led him to the dining room, where they sat across from each other at the table. Cece sat in the living room and listened in. It was just the family present for this meeting.

"You have a lovely home," he began.

"Thank you," Diane replied.

"It's quieter now," Bishop remarked. "For the wrong reason."

"Yes, because Desmond should be away at school, and instead . . ." Powell trailed off.

"Yes," Bishop said.

"This is a daunting and devastating thing your family is going through," Powell said,

"It is," Diane said.

"I've been there beside many families, but I won't begin to think I know what you're going through. What I do know is, beyond the personal grieving that you're experiencing there is a whirlwind coming your way and I'd like to help navigate you through it."

"Thank you," Diane said.

"As you can see the press can be your ally or your enemy. Some will always be your enemy no matter what. That's just how they are designed. Some will make you think they're supportive but are trying to undermine you as well. There are a few that are truly genuine. How we handle them is crucial and making certain that the right messaging is brought out to the public," Powell said.

"Messaging. You make it sound like politics," Bishop remarked.

"In a sense there is a degree of politics involved as we are trying to present Desmond and yourselves in the best light to the public. Let's just be real, most white folk are just looking for any reason, it could be a D on his report card, to say, 'see criminal, he deserved it.'" Saying that, even rhetorically, upset Bishop and caused him to grind his teeth. "Even if he were a hardened criminal, he would not deserve what happened to him. But we know that, that is not the case, so it is our responsibility to show the real Desmond to the world. Have you been interviewed by the police yet?" he asked.

"No," Diane replied. "We do that tomorrow."

"Okay. I'd like to accompany you there. If you'll have me."

Diane nodded yes and held Bishop's hand supportively. "Yes," Bishop replied as well.

"Okay," Powell said. "Now let's get started."

"How will we pay you?" Bishop asked.

"Don't worry about that. You don't. I get paid when you get paid. When we make them pay."

28

The next day they met at the 65th precinct. Bishop, Diane and their attorney Powell were led to the interview room on the second floor. This was Diane's first time walking into a police precinct. It was like a municipal office and a prison mashed together. Like a hospital it gave you an uneasy feeling as soon as you stepped inside, as if whatever people had was contagious and if they coughed on you, you might get it and be carted off into a jail cell as well.

It was a hot day, but the room was cold—not literally. It just made you feel that way. There was no life to the room. The walls were painted a muted grayish blue, the ceiling was high just enough to accommodate a tall person. There wasn't a window and she noticed the camera in the corner of the room. It was antiseptic but made you feel dirty at the same time. Sitting on the chair gave her the creeps, imagining bugs crawling through the wood.

They met with Detectives Garcia and Monroe. Detective Garcia was a Latina in her early thirties. She wore a blazer and bell bottom slacks. Detective Monroe was in his early forties. He had washed out amber hair that was receding and a prominent gut in an otherwise slim build.

"First off, I just wanna say we are incredibly sorry for your loss," Garcia began.

"I'm sure you are," Bishop remarked with implied sarcasm.

"We are," Detective Garcia said. "It was a horrible horrible tragedy."

"Yes, it was," Diane said.

"So, we just have a few questions, this should go pretty quickly, and you guys can get out of here."

"Okay then, let's get on with it," Powell said.

"So, the car he was driving," Detective Monroe began, "current year baby-blue BMW 5 series. It's registered to you," he said to Bishop. Though it could have been a question.

"That's because it's my car," Bishop said.

"It's a nice car."

"It is."

"And you're a bus driver," Monroe kind of stated and asked at the same time again.

"I am," Bishop said.

"That must be a hell of a car note and insurance. Whoo. I don't envy your bill every month," Monroe said.

"I work very hard. We both work very hard. We get by."

"Shit, I need to start working for Transit," Monroe joked.

"You're a first-grade detective with seventeen years on the job. You're making at least a hundred thousand a year. You can afford the car," Powell pointed out.

"Yeah," Monroe conceded. "Maybe it's just my priorities, with a wife and two kids as well, you know."

"What's the fascination with the car?" Powell asked.

"No fascination. It's just the vehicle in question, so we're just trying to establish its history," Garcia said.

"I'm sure you already looked into it," Powell said.

"We did," Garcia answered.

"Great. So, let's move on."

"So, did your son sneak the car out that night?" Monroe asked.

"No. I let him use it for the night," Bishop answered.

"Really, you let your seventeen-year-old son borrow a 70,000 dollar car?"

"Would you ask a white parent whether they'd let their son drive their car?" Diane asked, not liking the insinuations being made.

"Race has nothing to do with it," Garcia said.

When it comes to white people, race has everything to do with everything, Bishop thought but bit this tongue.

"Black or white, I wouldn't ask it of a rich person," Monroe said. "They're a different species than us. But we're all working class people here, so I ask."

"He was leaving for school the next day and as a reward I allowed him to take the car out that night," Bishop explained.

"That makes sense," Garcia said. "It makes absolute sense. And where was he going?"

"He was going to hang out with his friends at his friend Garfield's house," Diane said.

"And where is Garfield's house?" Garcia asked.

"It's in Flatlands," Diane said.

"And you live in Canarsie?" Garcia asked.

"Yes," Diane said.

"Then why was he in Brownsville? It's not on the way."

Neither Diane nor Bishop had an immediate answer for that one. And though Desmond was dead they were both very angry with him for taking his father's car into Brownsville. "I know my son. I trust my son," Bishop felt compelled to say.

"It's not a reflection on you as a parent. It's the society we live in. We can be so much of an influence in our kid's lives, but they're just so many other influences outside. I mean sometimes we think we know where our kids are and what they are doing, and we don't," Garcia said.

"Like selling drugs in Brownsville, when we think they're supposed to be at a house party in Flatlands," Monroe interjected.

"I'm sorry but is my son being charged with anything?" Diane asked.

"Of course not," Garcia answered.

"Then why are his actions and the fact that Mr. Bishop allowed him to borrow the car in question?" Powell argued.

"Well as you know the officer involved in the shooting contends that he saw your son make a drug deal, which is why he pulled him over," Garcia said.

"My son is not a drug dealer."

"Maybe he is, maybe he isn't. But if he was, you wouldn't know, the same way you didn't know he was going to Brownsville that night and had an ounce of weed in his book bag," Monroe said.

Bishop seethed and if he could have punched detective Monroe and gotten away with it, he would have. "It's time to go. This interview is over." Powell said and rose to his feet and instructed his clients to do so as well. "I knew exactly how this would go, but I was hoping for once you guys would surprise me."

"We want the same things you do. We're just trying to get to the truth here," Garcia said.

"No, you don't. The truth is apparent. You're trying to find a way to justify murder," Diane said.

"Who's the officer?" Bishop asked, seemingly out of nowhere.

"What officer?" Garcia asked.

"The one who killed my son."

"His name hasn't been released yet," Monroe said.

"When will it be released?" Bishop asked.

"That's above my pay grade. I don't know," Monroe answered. "But it should be soon."

"We'd like to see him," Bishop said.

Diane was surprised to hear Bishop say this. He hadn't mentioned wanting to meet the officer before now. Still, she supported him in his request.

"Why?" Monroe asked.

"My son was murdered, and I want to look into the eyes of the man who killed him."

Neither Monroe nor Garcia liked the sound of that. "That wouldn't be possible," Monroe said.

"Why not?" Bishop asked.

"He's on administrative leave," Garcia said.

"Paid administrative leave." Bishop laughed. "He murders my son, and he gets a vacation. And you bring us in here, in the same room you interrogate criminals and try to prosecute my son. And this is what you call justice."

29

You can never know how another person feels until you see the world through their eyes. Perspective was the difference between sympathy and empathy. He'd seen many of these rallies for the families of the victims before. He always watched them at home on television or in front of his computer. Now, he heard Al Sharpton speak and it was not through a television screen but just three feet away.

He was much smaller in person, but his voice was bigger. It was loud—piercing. He heard him mention the name Desmond Bishop, and for a moment he thought that it was someone else's son, and he thought someone else had Desmond's name—but then he remembered. No, it's my Desmond. My son is dead. A white cop killed him, and his name was McNally. Brian McNally. The NYPD had just released his name.

They released the medical examiner's report as well. Desmond Bishop was shot seven times: one bullet tore off part of his right ear, another hit his right forearm shattering his radius, another grazed his right shoulder, another ripped through his liver, diaphragm and a lung before lodging in his spine—doing the most damage—another hit his left shoulder just below the clavicle, another tore through his left bicep and another went through his left pectoral. After which, officer McNally pulled Desmond out of the car and handcuffed his bleeding body and left him lying on the ground.

And we are here for, "Justice" someone yelled out, followed by another, "No justice no peace." Bishop felt disconnected as if his mind wasn't fully synced with his body as if he was seeing everything through some virtual reality headset, standing on that stage with his wife to his left and his daughter to his right, and the lawyer behind them. Seeing the uncanny valley in his eyes, Cece reached out and held his hand and brought things back to reality.

There were so many people there. It was a meeting hall, no bigger than a neighborhood church, packed to the rafters. He couldn't get an exact count, but he'd put it at well over 500. The room was so packed you could feel their breath. It was hot. There was no air conditioning. The room was cooled by large, very loud fans, one on the stage where they stood and four in each corner of the room. They were not sufficient. It was ninety degrees and humid. People made fans out of leaflets. There were people of all ages there, but mostly in their forties and older, and much older than that. There were elders in the front row; people who had been to so many rallies and heard so many speakers. Many had even heard Malcolm and Martin speak.

Sharpton finished speaking and invited the parents to the microphone. This was a toss up to either Bishop or Diane. They looked at each other nervously for a moment before Diane took the ball and went to the podium. It was good that she did. Diane was a vice-principal and before that an English teacher, and to be a good teacher you had to be a good public speaker. She was articulate, she was composed, she was dignified, she was beautiful. She represented the family so well. He was so proud of her, he held her hand tightly. He had never been more proud of her than in that moment.

That would have been the end of it. Diane said everything that needed to be said. Bishop didn't need to speak but a member of the crowd said, "let's hear from the father," and then other members joined in. And though Bishop did not wish to speak he felt he owed it to Desmond to do so, to show the world that he had a father, and that he was not another statistical product of a single mother household.

He got to the microphone and all he could do was breathe.

"Take your time," someone from the crowd said.

"My name is John Bishop, and Desmond Bishop is my— was my son. My wife, Diane, has pretty much said it all. I don't really have anything to add. I am not good at speaking. I do want you all to know that my son was not a drug dealer. Do not believe what they are telling you about my son. I know my son. I raised my son. I have always been in his life. From he left his mother's womb I have been there. And my son was not no . . . was not a drug dealer. They are trying to assassinate his character to justify murder. I just wanted to say that."

"Tell them what you want," someone else shouted. "What you demand."

"What do I want?" Bishop repeated, asking himself more than saying something to the crowd.

"Tell them you want Justice."

"Yes, yes, I want justice . . . but what is justice?" Bishop asked, and though he was not good at speaking, from somewhere unknown the words came. "Is justice the police officer who killed my son being arrested and charged for what he did, even though you and I know that hardly ever happens. Is that justice? Then yes, I want that, but that isn't enough. Is justice him going to trial and being found guilty of what he did, even though we know that just about never happens, then yes, I want that. But that still isn't enough. Is justice him spending the rest of his natural life in jail, though we know they will never do that, then yes, I want that, but that isn't enough. That won't bring my boy back. My beautiful, beautiful, black boy who was so full of love and life and had so much to offer to the world."

"What do you want brother, let 'em know."

And now Bishop spoke not to the crowd but to one person, and he spoke from the bowels of his soul. "What's his name? Brian McNally. Officer McNally. I wanna see him. I wanna sit him down across from me and look him dead in the eyes. I wanna look into the eyes of the man who killed my son. I want him to look into my eyes and see the pain, see what he has done to us, what he has done to my family. I want him to know what suffering feels like. I want him to know that who he killed was not some nameless brown boy you can easily throw away. His name was Desmond Bishop. He was our son and he was loved. And when you took his life you didn't just destroy one life you destroyed a family and we are suffering," he roared. "And it is time for you to suffer too. Do you hear me, Officer McNally? I want you to feel my pain. I want you to bleed. I want you to bleed like my son bled, when you shot him seven times—seven times—and then pulled him out of the car, handcuffed him on the street and watched him die.

"I want you to suffer. I want your family to suffer as mine is suffering. I want you to feel loss and agony and grief. I want you to want to bash your head into a wall and gnash your teeth so that the physical pain will take away from the mental anguish. You murdered my son. You killed my boy. My first born. You took my legacy. You have robbed me in a way that can never be recovered. And if it takes my last dying breath, I will let you feel my pain. Do you hear me Officer McNally? I will make you feel my pain. And even then, that will not be justice, but it will be a start."

Diane had been tugging at Bishop's hand for a bit now to get him to stop. Cece held him also crying uncontrollably. The Lawyer Powell and Reverend Sharpton held him by the shoulder. The audience at first was numb. They had heard many families speak before but rarely had it ever been so guttural. But every round of applause begins with one; one person, two hands coming together; a clap a release and then repeat. And after it began it was as if it would never stop. The applause came in vigorous voluminous cascades. There was a deluge of applause, a raw unfiltered outpouring of emotion. People cried, chanted and roared. It was cleansing. It was cathartic.

There was one man in the back. He stood tall—taller than everyone else. He was not the tallest man in the room, yet he seemed like a tower salient and singular. And though so many people were applauding, his applause seemed the loudest. It was distinct. It had more resonance and power. Each clap was a wave and an echo. It echoed in his face. His face beamed with appreciation. He smiled without teeth, but it was one of the biggest smiles Bishop had ever seen. Most of the room became a blur save for that one man in the back.

As the family was being ushered out of the building many people shook their hands and tapped them lovingly on the shoulder. And that distinct man approached Bishop, gave him a firm handshake and asked, "May I buy you a drink brother?"

30

McNally sat alone in his home office, the light from the monitor the only light source, watching the rally on his laptop. "Do you hear me officer McNally?" He heard him. He heard him in his teeth. They didn't chatter. It was more the effect of having a bad cold, and your teeth hurt even from just the air. "I want you to bleed . . . I want you to suffer." It stuck in his head like the refrain from a song he hated but couldn't shake. He turned off the computer, but it still played. He heard it in his sleep. He heard it in his dreams. There were no more good nights.

31

"The man should be arrested," the Pundit said.
"Seriously? His son was shot down unarmed by this police officer, and we're going to compound this tragedy by arresting him. Now I do agree, that he shouldn't have said some of the things he said, how he said them, but I can forgive a parent for expressing the immense pain that family must be going through," another Pundit argued.

"And what if someone takes up his words and decides to do something to this officer or his family? What then? Let's not forget that police officers have been killed. What Mr. Bishop did was inciteful, irresponsible and disgusting."

The attorney turned off the television and addressed Bishop

and Diane—mainly Bishop. "We'll need you to make a state-ment, stressing that you didn't mean what you said, you were only speaking out of emotion, that you're calling for everyone to be peaceful."

"This man kills my son and you want me to apologize to him. Who's lawyer, are you?" Bishop asked.

"I am your lawyer, and it is my job to represent you, and to protect you and that means even from yourself. Do you realize that because of what you said—"

"I was speaking for myself," Bishop interrupted.

"Yes, but other people heard you, and not everyone is stable. Someone might take you seriously, and if God forbid a cop gets killed, or there is a riot, you can be sued, or at the worst jailed. Do you understand?"

"I do."

"Will you make the statement?"

"I can't do that."

The lawyer sighed.

"I'll do it," Diane spoke up.

"Okay. And Mr. Bishop, it's probably best that Diane takes the lead with the public from now on."

"That's fine . . . that's best."

32

There was family everywhere. There was more family than Bishop knew he had; two large Jamaican families mashed together. There could have been three hundred plus people at that event hall. There was family he hadn't seen in years, fam-ily who traveled from overseas to be at the funeral. There were many here who would have been no matter how Desmond had died, but there were also many he believed were here because Desmond had become a *cause célèbre.*

The hall provided catering, but the family eschewed that. Whenever possible Jamaicans preferred to do their own cooking. The family on both sides had great cooks, aunties and cousins, and they had prepared a feast for the repast: mannish water (goat soup) and corn soup, and curry goat, and jerk chicken and fried chicken and brown-stewed chicken, and fish, escovitch, steamed and brown stewed, and rice and peas, and vegetable rice, and steamed vegetables, and macaroni and cheese, and potato salad, and rum cake, and fruit punch and sorrel to wash it down.

The food was good. He could smell it but couldn't bring himself to eat much. He nibbled at it here and there. He sat at a table with his Mother and Father and Diane's Mother and Father. Both their parents were in their late sixties and early seventies and still together. His mother held his hand. She held it throughout the entire service. Since she heard the news, she held him every chance she could. Most times she didn't say anything, she just held him. Parents don't like burying their children. They don't like seeing their children bury their children either.

Bishop was quiet mostly. He hadn't said much since the rally. He was afraid of what would come out of his mouth if he did. Bishop's emotions were like an ocean wave. They rushed in with anger and receded with sadness. Outwardly he was still. People moved around him, people said hello, they hugged him, they kissed him, they expressed their condolences, their love for Desmond, of how good of a boy he was, how much he had to give to the world, their anger with the police, their support for his speech, "Yuh talk the truth Johnnie, we tired of the suffering."

A few mentioned God and God's plan, and how God was good all the time, and God never gave us more than we can handle. Bishop wanted to hear none of that. God's name was bile. It was the rheumy saliva you taste in your mouth before you throw up. Bishop could not think of God without anger. The white cop killed his son and God let him do it. God let him do it. There was no other way around that, the way God had allowed countless atrocities to occur to black people. Bishop had a special venom for the Pastor of the service, who spent twenty minutes speaking about Desmond, then nearly an hour giving a sermon he could have given any Sunday. It was more promotional than elegiac. It took all of Bishop's restraint not to stand up in the middle of the service and stop his proselytizing, and he couldn't look at the Pastor now, eating food, without being pissed.

He looked around and saw Cece. She greeted and attended to everyone. Her friends were there as well. Josh was there and so were his parents. Josh was helping Cece as if he was part of the immediate family. Bishop thought, *Cece's such a good helpful girl—always had been. But she's doing so much—too much. But where is Desmond? Where is that boy? Why he have his sister doing all the work?* Then Bishop remembered, and the wave receded with sadness and rushed back in with anger.

Many of Desmond's friends were there, including Garfield and his girlfriend Sasha. They had both been interviewed by multiple news outlets. They were the ones who let it be known that Desmond was out buying and not selling drugs. Garfield was especially distraught, believing it was his fault Desmond died because he had urged him to get the weed for the party.

Diane spoke to Garfield and assured him it was not his fault. Diane was great. Diane was the family's ambassador. How she handled everything amazed Bishop. Women had an uncanny ability to organize and lead during tragedy. He was the man. He was the one who was supposed to be holding it together, but he was a mess. He felt impotent—castrated. It was a man's responsibility to protect his family, and when his family had been abused to avenge them. He imagined this was not that different from how his ancestors in bondage felt. They rape your women; they steal your children and you can do nothing.

There were children all around. There were cousins, nieces and nephews and children of cousins, nieces and nephews. He saw Desmond in every child. He saw a two-year-old waddling about. Desmond used to do that. He used to suck his two middle fingers just like that as well. He saw his cousin, her belly round, nine pounds pregnant. Desmond was like that. Desmond was born big, nine and a half pounds. People thought Diane was carrying twins. He saw Desmond's cousin Devon. He was seventeen—just nine months younger than Desmond. He was going into his senior year of high school and would be going to college the next year. Desmond should be in college right now.

This was all too much. He couldn't continue looking at them. Truthfully, he didn't want to be here. His escape came from his phone. It vibrated in his pocket. He pulled it out and saw he had received a text message. It was from an unknown number, but he recognized it none the same. "How about that drink my brother?"

33

"Yeah, I'm having a drink with a friend . . . no, no, I'll be home soon . . . yeah . . . yeah. Alright, I'll be home soon." Bishop hung up with Diane and turned to the man sitting a stool from him by the bar. They were in a lounge in Fort Greene, Brooklyn. He was the man from the rally. When he introduced himself, he called himself Soldier—that was all—and Bishop was satisfied with that. When he had asked Bishop for his number, Bishop wasn't sure why he gave it to him. He never gave out his number, especially now. But there was something very intriguing about this man Bishop found himself drawn to, and after burying his son today he wanted a break from his family and everyone he knew.

When he shook Bishop's hand, Bishop felt it in his feet. His hands were large, and his grip bore an unexpected intensity. Bishop had big hands as well, but they were enveloped inside of Soldier's. Bishop imagined Soldier could break a good many bones in his hand if he wanted to. He was six-foot three and two hundred and sixteen pounds of lean muscle. Even when relaxed his muscles were flexed. The vein in his biceps was like an anaconda stretching from his clavicle to his fingers. Bishop was still wearing his suit from the funeral, with the tie off and the top button of his shirt undone. Soldier dressed as he always did, wearing a t-shirt and loose fit jeans over black combat boots.

"Wife?" he asked Bishop about his call.

"Yeah," Bishop answered.

"She's a good woman."

"She's the best. Diane, she's the absolute best. Every time I think about what she's going through—y' know . . . as a mother. I see her crying, and I don't even know how to touch her, because I can't take the pain away. If I could, I'd carry all the pain for the both of us. I gladly would. In all this I feel so weak."

"How you're feeling is not an accident. It's by design. They want to weaken us and emasculate us. Kill our children and make us feel like we're powerless to do anything about it. Lower us in the eyes of our women. Lower us in the eyes of ourselves. Because black manhood is the greatest threat to them," Soldier said.

"Yeah?"

"Yes. That's why what you said was so powerful."

"Yeah, me losing my shit and screaming in front of the whole world," Bishop said.

"Hell yeah. I loved it. I felt it to the core of my soul. It was that righteous indignation that I've always wanted to see. So many times, when the loved ones of the victims come on camera, I get the sense that they feel like they gotta put on a show, and bite their tongues, because they're scared about saying the wrong thing. It's like even in our greatest pain from what they've done to us, we're still not trying to offend white sensibilities."

"I don't give a damn about white sensibilities . . . but I can't go off like that anymore. The lawyer says if I say the wrong thing, and someone does the wrong thing, then it can be seen as me inciting and I could go to jail or get sued. So, I won't be saying much anymore. I'll leave it to my wife. She's better at it anyway."

"That's probably for the best. Plus, you've already said enough, and whoever needed to hear it, heard it. I heard it." Soldier took a swig of his Red Stripe beer. "When you said you wanted the chance to sit before the cop who killed your son and look into his eyes, did you mean it?" Soldier asked.

Bishop was surprised he asked that. Of all the things Bishop said in that speech, that seemed to be a point that was lost on most people, but, "Yeah. I do. I asked the cops, even before I spoke at Sharpton's, and they told me no."

"Of course, they did," Soldier said, "but if I could give you that chance, would you want me to?" he asked.

Bishop looked at Soldier for clarification. What he got was a sobering stare. Bishop knew what he was insinuating and, "Yeah," he answered honestly but not truly taking Soldier seriously. "And what about you?" Bishop asked him.

"What about me?"

"What's your story?"

"I was a marine," Soldier said.

"You're a veteran." So, people didn't just call him Soldier for no reason.

"No. Not exactly. A veteran is someone who used to serve but doesn't anymore. I still serve. I just serve a different country and for a different cause now."

"And what country is that?"

"The country doesn't exist yet. It's more of an idea. The cause is the empowerment of our people. I'm about building us up. We're based in Brownsville. I know you drive a bus and your route goes through there. Have you seen the Change Brownsville Patrols we've been doing?"

"Yeah, I have seen them," Bishop said.

"I helped get that going. Brothers and sisters patrol the neighborhood in groups, and they're all armed, all registered, all legal. And they do it not just to deter and stop crime, but to make sure crime isn't being committed against us. They watch the police. They try to be there for every interaction people have with the police. We have eyes all over the hood and they radio them whenever anything is going down, and they get over there and make sure the police are always respecting our rights. We watch them, we advise and if an arrest is made, we follow the arrested person to the precinct, make sure they get there safely and that their rights are always being protected."

"Wow," Bishop said.

"And it's had an impact. In the last six months there's been a fifty percent drop in all the major statistics."

"That's amazing."

"That's a result of us coming together and doing for self."

"You're doing a lot of good work," Bishop said.

"So are you. You're a father and you're raising strong black children who love themselves. That is so important. I'm a soldier, my role is to defend us and do the hard things that sometimes need to be done. We all have our parts to play and they all matter."

He made everything sound so grandiose. "Are you from Brownsville?" Bishop asked,

"Born and raised," Soldier said. "It's funny. When I was a kid, all I wanted to do was get out of Brownsville. I never thought I'd be thinking the way I'm thinking and doing what I'm doing now."

"That's life. We grow up. Things change," Bishop said.

"Yeah. And Brooklyn sure has changed," Soldier said.

"Believe me, I know. I drive a bus. I literally seen it change day by day. At first, you'd never see a white person on the bus past a certain stop. Then one day I see a white guy get off, and I stop myself from asking him if he's sure this is his stop. Then a few months later, I see another one, I see them with bags from Whole Foods and Trader Joes, and in a few years, it is what it is. Some change is good. A lot of places are safer, more diverse. Some change is bad. A lot of people got pushed out of their homes. Hasn't really come to Brownsville that much yet though," Bishop said.

"Oh, they want to. But there's too much public housing," Soldier said.

"They'll probably start tearing those projects down and build condos where they used to be."

"You're right about that. Wanna know something?" Soldier leaned in to make his point more poignant. "Integration is one of the worst things that happened to black people."

That was surprising to hear. "How you figure?" Bishop asked.

"What do you think is the greatest problem facing black people right now?"

Given it was the thing most pressing on his mind, Bishop answered, "Police brutality."

"Police brutality is a problem. I can understand how significant it is to you, especially now. But to stop police brutality, we must understand it. It ain't a black and white thing. It's a power and powerless thing."

That sounded interesting. Bishop wanted to hear more. "Explain," he said.

"Human beings abuse whoever they think they can get away with abusing. That's human nature. It happens everywhere with everybody. Look at India. India is mostly just filled with Indian people. There's police brutality there. Guess who the police abuse—mostly the poor people. There's police brutality in China. You know there's damn near nobody but Chinese people there. Guess who the police abuse—poor people. There's police brutality in Russia. Guess who the police abuse?"

"Poor people," Bishop said. "You're right. There's police brutality in Jamaica. And it's usually the people in the garrisons getting abused."

"Exactly."

"But if it's just a poor people problem, what about middle class and even rich black people who get abused?" He thought of his son. "My son was middle class."

"He was also in the hood driving a nice car." Soldier could see how that struck a nerve with Bishop. "Look, middle class and rich black people get abused as well, not as much as poor black people but enough, because black is synonymous with poor and powerless throughout the world. So, they see black and think, I can automatically abuse you and get away with it."

"Hmmm," Bishop hummed to himself.

"Look at Arab people in this country. When was the last time you heard of the police killing one of them?" Bishop had to think on that. For the life of him, there wasn't a case that came to mind. "Now society sees them as terrorists and see us as thugs, but the police aren't killing them like they're killing us. Why do you think that is?"

"I never thought on that before," Bishop said.

"It's because they're together. They're organized. They are a community, as opposed to us who don't have a community."

Bishop had been following along with him but that sounded completely off track. "How are you gonna say that? Sure, we do."

"No, we don't. There's no black community. All we are, are a collection of people who look the same who live in the same area, but we are not a community because for the most part we don't own anything. You go to any community in this country, Korea town, Chinatown, Muslim, Indian, Jewish, Italian, what have you, as soon as you enter you know you're there because the buildings change, the signage changes, the language changes. They own and run the businesses in their neighborhood. Most of them own their homes. Most of us rent. When you're in the hood the only reason you know it's a black neighborhood is because you see more black people and shit looks more run-down."

"Hmmm," Bishop digested that one. He didn't want to agree with it but there was a lot of truth in what Soldier said.

"This is why we are abused, because we are not a collective unit fighting to make sure we are not abused. But we used to be. We used to have communities."

"Black Wallstreet," Bishop said, speaking of the early twentieth century African American community in Greenwood, Tulsa, Oklahoma, which had thousands of black residents, hundreds of black owned businesses, and several black millionaires, all achieved within fifty years of slavery's end. It was torn asunder in the Tulsa race riots of 1921, as white mobs burned it to the ground and killed hundreds of people under the pretext that a black man had sexually assaulted a white woman.

"Yup. But not just Black Wallstreet," Soldier said. "There was also Rosewood in Florida, and The Hayti Community in Durham, North Carolina, and Jackson Ward, Richmond, Virginia., and The Fourth Avenue District in Birmingham, Alabama. There were communities all over. Black people were progressing and then desegregation came and, in a few years, it was all gone."

"Why do you think that happened?" Bishop asked.

"Black people have a damaged psyche. We think everything white people do is better. So as soon as we got a chance, we abandoned ourselves and what we were building. So, you wanna live in a good neighborhood. You think to yourself, white people live in a good neighborhood, so let's go live where the white people live. Instead of thinking, let us work together to improve the neighborhood we live in. You think, I want my kid to go to a good and safe school, and you say white people send their kids to good schools, so let's send our kids to those schools. Instead of saying let's pool our resources together and improve the schools that we send our kids to. The whole fight for integration was wrong headed."

"I'm gonna have to disagree with you on that one. A lot of people sacrificed, fought and died so we could be where we are now. So, we could be sitting here, freely having a drink. You can't deny all of the progress we've made," Bishop said.

"What progress?" Soldier asked.

"C'mon man, look around. Look at all the things black people have accomplished."

"I agree, there's a few black people with some money. But it's not really their money."

"What do you mean it's not really their money?" Bishop said, taking exception to that.

"It's not really their money because most of them use it to

uplift themselves and not their people. I give you two hundred million, but then what do you do with it? You buy the house I sell you, you the buy the cars I make, my clothes, my jewelry. You don't seek to create anything of your own and create anything that will benefit your people. Basically, you're just spending my money for me, giving it right back to me, and sometimes you marry my daughter and give half of it right back to me. And when I'm ready I can pull your card and take that right back from you. And you will have no way to fight me because you did nothing to empower the people around you to help you fight against it."

"So, you're against integration?" Bishop wanted clarification.

"Not in principle. One of my best friends is white. We served together, and if that man called me right now and said he needed my help for anything, I'd be there. Still, I think the focus on integration was premature. It wasn't what we needed then."

"So, you're saying Martin Luther King was wrong?"

"I'm saying Martin Luther King was misguided. We were getting hosed and beat up and spit on. Why did we feel less than because we didn't drink from their water? Why did we want to shit where they shit? Why did we want to eat where they eat? We don't even like their food. We were fighting for the right to give people our money. What kind of nonsense is that? In the Montgomery bus boycott instead of boycotting to sit in the front of the bus, why didn't we pool our resources, create our own bus line and sit anywhere we damn well pleased?"

There was something logical in what Soldier was saying but it seemed so disrespectful to the movement so many people fought and died for. "I'm not sure if I'm buying all you're selling here," Bishop said. "And I think you're Monday morning quarterbacking a bit and criticizing things because you weren't living in that time."

"That maybe, but it doesn't make what I'm saying any less true. We keep on trying to make white people see us as human. Like this black lives matter movement."

"Alright, I'll give you that. There was always something about that that never jived with me. It's not that I'm against what they are doing, I just don't like the phrase."

"It's because it's based on weakness and victimhood. You say black lives matter, but who are you saying it to? Black people? Black people should already know that. So, you're saying it to them. It's like you're pleading to them. See me as human. Hands up, don't shoot. You're begging for them to change. You give them all the power. This whole integration movement has always been about begging white people to change the way they see us. Fuck how they see you. Fuck if they change. My life matters to me and that's what's most important, and I will do what's necessary to empower and protect it."

Bishop remembered a quote. "I remember Martin Luther King said: 'I fear I'm integrating my people into a burning house.'"

"Exactly. Martin Luther King had the wrong dream, and when he started waking up from it, they killed him."

34

The McNallys hadn't done this in a while, the immediate family gathering on a Sunday for dinner, not since two Christmases ago. There was nothing like a tragedy to bring family together. They met at McNally's house in Marine Park. They all hugged him tenderly when they entered. "Howya holding up, Brian?" His father, Edward, asked. His father was sixty with a round belly and strong arms. He still had his full head of hair and he had allowed his grey to show. He had worked as a longshoreman for years. He was a supervisor now and was soon looking forward to retirement.

McNally's mother, Patricia, hugged him and kissed him on the cheek. His mother was fifty-eight and still relatively slim. She took pride in that. She worked as a bookkeeper at a paper factory for most of her life, until the factory closed during the Great Recession. She now did real estate on the side.

McNally had an older brother, Joseph, who was thirty-six, who lived with his Korean wife and their three children in Santa Clara, California. Working in Silicon Valley, Joseph was the pride of the family. He couldn't make the dinner, but he sent his regards and his support, and told McNally if it ever came to court, he would be there for him.

His younger and only sister Jessie, short for Jessalyn was there. She was nearing thirty. She was a visual artist, and when that didn't pay enough, which was often, she bartended. She lived in Bushwick, Brooklyn, but McNally barely saw her. The family was more center right leaning politically. Jessie was different. She had always been the wild child. She was unapologetically progressive. And though her brother was a cop she often attended police brutality protest marches.

Riley came over as well. They invited Riley and the other members of the anti-crime unit over for dinner when McNally first joined the team. Everybody else came the one time. Riley kept on coming. Riley didn't have a wife and it wasn't unusual for him to stop in for a home cooked meal.

Meagan cooked, and she was a fair cook, but she wasn't good at traditional Irish dishes. She was better at Italian. She made lasagna and a kale salad. McNally's mother brought the Irish soda bread and the Irish lamb stew, her son's favorite, and a shepherd's pie. They sat at the table, McNally and Meagan together on one side, Edward and Riley together on the other, and Jessie and Patricia sat on opposing ends. McNally's children, Aiden and Sarah ate in the living room watching television.

"I just don't see why they had to release your name," Meagan said after they had said grace, and while they were sharing the meal.

"It's policy," McNally answered.

"But why so soon?"

"It's the Mayor. Politics. He's trying to shore up his base," Riley said.

"The family has a right to know," Jessie interjected.

"Okay, the family, maybe. But why put it out to the public. That puts Brian and his family in danger," Edward, McNally's father, said.

"Exactly," Meagan concurred. "Especially after what that man said." Meagan had seen the video of Bishop's speech and it had truly frightened her.

"Yup, with long time racist Al Sharpton, egging him on, never missing an opportunity to exploit a tragedy to divide people for his own profit," Edward said.

"I don't think the Father meant any harm. He was just in a lot of pain and he was just expressing it," Jessie said.

"You don't know that," Patricia said. "You don't know what's truly in his mind or in the mind of people who listened to him. Did you hear how those people cheered?"

McNally could see how this conversation was upsetting Meagan. "Okay, let's not talk like that. We're not in danger. I'm not in danger. I'm fine. We're all fine. They released my name because this is just the way it is. Okay," McNally said.

"I hate to say it, but they are very rude people," Patricia said, seemingly out of nowhere.

"Who are?" Jessie asked.

"Black people," Patricia said straightly.

"Mom?" Jessie shot back.

"Listen, you know how I raised you all. We don't see color and we try to treat everybody equally. But the truth is, you go around the city, and if you find people being loud, acting up, getting into arguments, whether physical or verbal, nine out of ten times they'll be black."

"That's not true," Jessie argued.

"It is so true—and it's not just the men. A lot of times it's the women. A lot of times they are even worse. They like to act as if people should be afraid of them. Like they just raise their voice and we should all cower. It's like, I'm big, I'm black, I've been oppressed, be afraid. It's like I'm riding on the subway, and this black lady is standing in the doorway blocking people from entering. An Asian woman is trying to get on and bumps into her, because of course she can't help it. And before she could even say sorry, though she shouldn't need to, the black lady goes off saying, 'You bumped me, you ain't say excuse me, you don't know me, you B. I'll F you up. I'm from Brooklyn.' It's a whole big scene she makes. And I can see the other woman is visibly upset. But I quietly tell her to let it go. That it's not worth it."

"So true," Edward said. "Then they always wanna play their music loud on the train. And it will be the most horrible rap song you've ever heard. There are children on the train, and he's blasting it out, with B and Hoe this, N word that. It's crazy. Absolutely no respect for the people around you. I mean, I'm on the train one day. This black guy stands next to a white man who is sitting down, and he literally puts his radio right beside the man's head and blasts his music. If a white person did that to a black person, they would be called a KKK card carrying racist."

"So, you've had an experience with two rude black people, and from that you want to indict the whole race," Jessie countered.

"No no, no. And the guy putting the boombox in the man's face is an egregious example. But you can't tell me, you haven't seen many of them playing their music loud?" Edward argued.

"And what about the kids dancing on the train," Patricia brought up. "For one, they're dirty, they smell and they're swinging around like you know what, very nearly kicking people in the face, and God help you if you move an inch when they're doing that. Then when no one gives them money they curse people out."

"True," Edward concurred.

"Then they walk around with their pants down, with their ass out. I'm sitting down, and this boy is standing in front of me literally with his underwear and his ass smack dab in my face."

"Black kids aren't the only ones who wear their pants sagging. A lot of white kids, and Spanish kids, and Asians and Arab kids, do it too. It's just youth style," Jessie said.

"Yeah, because they're following black kids. God knows why?" Patricia said.

"And so, all of this is to say, it's okay to kill unarmed black kids because they wear their pants down," Jessie said.

"No one said—no one said that," Patricia took objection. "And what are you trying to say? Are you saying that your brother is wrong? Are you saying you don't support your brother?"

"I do support Brian. That's why I'm here. But a seventeen-year-old boy is dead. Parents have lost their child."

"Yes. It is a tragedy. It is tragic. I truly feel for them. I do. But that kid was a drug dealer. And unfortunately, Brian was put in a very difficult situation."

"He was not a drug dealer," Jessie retorted.

"He had an ounce of weed in his car," Edward said.

"To go smoke and hang out with his friends on his last night in the city before going to college," Jessie said.

"And you need an ounce for that?" Edward asked. "What kind of smokers are these kids? What are they a reggae band? Back in my day, one joint fed all of us."

"He has no criminal record. By all accounts he was a good kid."

"There I have to stop you," Riley said. "Not having a record doesn't mean he's innocent, just means he's never been through the system." Riley turned to McNally "Remember that guy we picked up on the 3 line a few months back. Spanish . . . Dominican."

"Ecuadorian," McNally corrected Riley. "Yeah, I remember him."

"Yeah him. Clean as a whistle, no record. We were backing up Transit that day. Caught him walking through the trains. Pulled him off, ran his ID, about to give him a ticket and send him on his way. Something says, let me search this guy."

"So, you illegally searched him?" Jessie asked.

"I had just cause."

"Which was?"

"My instincts."

"Really?" Jessie said and looked at him with utter disdain.

"And he was wearing a large backpack in the subway system—random searches are legal. And it was a good thing I did. We found a brick of heroin on him."

"Yup," McNally added.

"Wow," Edward remarked.

"And that's not even the kicker. Took him in and ran his DNA. Turns out he was connected to three rapes."

"Oh, my Lord. Look at that," Patricia remarked.

"Yeah, there are bad people out there who haven't been caught yet. But that wasn't this kid. You cannot paint everybody with the same negative brush and judge a book by its cover."

"You know I hate that saying. That's one of the most cliché and wrong-headed sayings of all time," Patricia said.

"I can't believe we're arguing this. What's wrong with you?"

"I'm sorry, but it is wrong headed and unnatural. Of course, you should judge a book by its cover. The cover of a book is the way it markets itself to the world. It lets people know, this is what I'm about. You are your cover. You carry yourself the way you want the world to see you. When I pick up a book and I see Fabio on the cover I'm not expecting to read about quantum whatever physics. Ninety-nine percent of the time, how a person carries them self is the person they are."

"And if I wear a really short skirt, that means I'm asking to be raped," Jessie countered.

"Whoa—who said anything about rape? Where are you getting rape from?" Edward asked, aghast.

"That's where you're headed. That is if I dress a certain way, that's the person I am, and I deserve whatever happens to me."

"You think that of me?" Patricia asked her daughter.

"Mom, when I hear you speak, I don't know what you think sometimes."

"No one asks to be raped—ever. Okay," Patricia clarified.

"Thank you for saying that at least."

"Because obviously rape is something you don't want to happen. But—"

"Here it comes."

"When you dress a certain way, you are asking for attention."

"Attention? Oh my God, your views are so archaic."

"Yes. Attention. And it can come either good or bad. Listen. I wasn't born a mother you know. I used to be your age. And I knew what I was wearing, when I was wearing it, and why I was doing it."

"What's the point of dressing sexy, if you don't want people to see you as sexy," Riley said, and Jessie gave him the coldest look ever, to which he smiled flirtatiously.

"I'm for women's rights. I'm for women getting equal pay for equal work. I am for a woman president—hopefully not a Democrat. What it seems this new generation is for, is for women going around acting like sluts, doing whatever, and still being respected. And that's not gonna fly," Patricia said.

Jessie inhaled everything her mother said and then breathed it out. "Let me say this, women wear what they want for themselves. If I wear something it is because I like the way it makes me look and feel. And if it's attention I want, most times it's from other women. That does not make me a lesbian. I just value women's opinions more than men's. Mom, you are wearing pants and a form fitting shirt, a hundred years ago, people would consider you a slut for that." Patricia did not care for that analysis and gave her daughter a sour look. "See things have changed, and we had to fight for that—real hard. See you're happy to reap all the benefits of women who go out there and fight for women's rights, equal pay a woman president, but never want to do any of the fighting. Always choosing your sons over your daughters, forgetting that you used to be a daughter, and when you went out you just wanted to feel good about yourself without men's judgment or the threat of violence. And if a black man, or any man, wears his pants down, it is his choice, and it does not make him a thug and his life of less value."

"Jessie you are very smart. You get that from me. But sometimes you're too smart. And baby girl, you try to outsmart this world and it will bite you. So let me tell you this, you see a big black guy walking towards you with his pants at his knees, looking all menacing, don't play that, I don't wanna judge a book by its cover and seem racist, liberal, politically correct bs. You discretely walk the other way. Do you hear me?" Jessie said nothing. "Jessalyn Anne McNally, do you hear me?"

"Yes, I heard you," Jessie replied sharply.

Realizing things were at an impasse and might escalate into something worse, Edward intervened. "Okay, now that's enough of that. No more about the case. No more politics. Let's eat. Meagan and your Mother prepared a great meal and it's getting cold."

And then they ate.

35

At the end of the night they were all saying goodbye to Meagan and Brian as they were heading out. Patricia hugged them both. "I love you my son—and my daughter. I love you both so much." They hugged her back and shared kisses on the cheek.

Edward grabbed a hold of his son and held him firmly by the shoulders. "You're a good boy," he said. "You're a good man. Don't for a second believe any different. We're all here for you through and through. All of us. Right, Jessie?" Edward said and asked Jessie concurrently.

Jessie rolled her eyes and shook her head. "Of course, I am. You know that, right?" she asked McNally.

"Yeah, I know," he said.

They hugged.

"I love you, Brian," she said.

"I love you too," he said.

Jessie saw Riley and cut her eye away before hugging Meagan and walking out.

Riley approached McNally, smiling to himself, "I'm outside," he said to McNally. "Talk to me real quick before I leave."

"Okay," McNally said.

"And oh yes, I almost forgot," Edward came back and handed McNally a pair of keys.

"What's this?" McNally asked.

"It's the keys to your brother's cabin upstate in Indian lake. It's absolutely beautiful. He gave it to me to hold a year ago, and now I'm giving it to you. You kids, when you're ready, get away from here for a time. Detox. Get away from all this."

"Thank you, Dad," McNally said.

"I love you son. I love you both."

36

Jessie and his parents had driven off, and Riley was still parked outside. McNally entered the car and found him sitting silently listening to the radio—no music just words. "The white man is not allowed to be proud. Everyone else can be proud except the white man. You can be a proud black man, you can be a proud black woman—Spanish, Asian, Indian, Arab, what have you. You can even be a proud white woman. You can be a feminist fighting against the oppressiveness of white male patriarchy." He giggled. "But you cannot be a proud white man. Everyone else can be proud of the accomplishments of themselves and their forebears. But you go out there and see what the world says of you. You will be called a racist and a degenerate just for being white, male and proud. We built civilizations and cities the greatest the world has ever seen. We brought civilization to the challenged. We created the greatest and wealthiest nation in the world. We created automobiles and airplanes. We made man fly. Let me say that again. We made man fly. We mastered the oceans and beneath the oceans. We mapped the stars. We put a man on the motherfucking moon." There was applause. The speaker was speaking to an audience. "This world is our vision and we brought it to life. And every day we are made to feel ashamed for what we have done, for who we are. But no more. No more. I'm proud. I'm damn proud. Seig Heil." He finished and the audience repeated, "Seig Heil."

"What is this?" McNally asked.

"Just listen," Riley replied.

"Seig heil? Riley, why are we listening to some neo-Nazi shit?"

"Don't do that," Riley said wagging his finger. "Don't put labels on it and close your mind to it. All you gotta ask yourself is whether what he's saying makes sense. So, does it make sense?"

"Yeah, some of it," McNally said.

"Some of it?"

"Alright, a lot of it. But what would they say, if they found us listening to this? Me especially. Especially now."

"Nothing. Who do you think put me onto this?" Riley said.

"Who?"

"Reagan."

"Your rabbi?" McNally asked, sounding surprised.

"If you can call him that. Worst rabbi ever. Hasn't done dick for me. I had to work for everything I got."

With all the things on McNally's head he didn't have room for this Nazi diatribe. "I hear you and all but I'm not down with this Nazi shit," he said.

"Stop looking at the messenger and listen to the message," Riley said.

"I'm doing both. And I don't have the time or the energy to ingest any of that right now."

"You better make time, before time runs out." McNally looked at him, emotionally drained and shook his head. "Let me show you something," Riley continued. "I'm at the DMV the other day, had to renew my registration. I get on the elevator and I'm the only white person on it. You got this black guy talking some African, Haitian, baboon language, 'cause I swear all I'm hearing is: blablablabububaba—literally. You got a Spanish chick, Mexican or Guatemalan, the kind of ones who look Indian. You got this Chinese chick and some Arab looking Muslim, or he could be a sihk, I can't tell the difference between the towels on their heads. They're all talking on their phone, all talking loud as hell too—none of them speaking English. And I'm in the middle of this literally having my ear drums assaulted." McNally laughed picturing it in his mind. Riley began laughing as well. "I'm like get me off this elevator. It took every bit of restraint I had not to lose my shit. I'm like this is America? What the hell is happening to this country?" McNally continued laughing. "It sounds funny bro, but it ain't. This country is transforming into something real ugly in front of our eyes and we are sleeping on this shit. They are here man, and a lot more are coming. Soon this country will be no place for white men." McNally burst out laughing even more. "You keep laughing but I'm serious, bro. I can't even like rainbows anymore."

"If you think that way, what do you feel about Daniels? What about Roberts?"

"Daniels, I don't trust," Riley said.

"Why not? He's a good cop. I like Daniels."

"I know he acts like a good cop. But he feels more like a spy. He was forced on me. I didn't put him on the team."

"And Roberts?" McNally asked.

"We're cool. Roberts is my dog. I like him a lot. I might love the guy. And he's a good cop and that elevates him." He took a breath. "But he's still black."

"And what does that mean?" McNally asked.

"It's the natural order. Man was meant to rule woman and the white man is meant to rule all other men."

"I'm not buying that," McNally said.

"That's alright. It's like air. You ain't gotta buy it to breathe it." McNally chuckled uneasily. "I see you're stressed though, and I feel it for you. But I want you to know you're not alone in this. The whole department is behind you. You're gonna be alright, man," Riley said bringing the conversation back to the most pressing issue.

"Thank you," McNally said.

"So, how about you put in a word for me with Jessie?"

"What?" The non-sequitur took McNally completely by surprise. "No. No."

"Why not?" Riley asked.

"Because she's my sister and I see how you treat women."

"Yeah, but that's because they were all hoes. I'm tired of these badge bunnies. I'm ready to settle down and get a good woman and get a family like you."

McNally earnestly replied, "Hell no. Plus Jessie hates you."

"No, she doesn't."

"Yeah, she really does."

"But she looks at me with so much intensity," Riley said.

"It's intense disgust."

"Yeah, but it's intense though. If it was bland then I'd think I'd have no shot. But she's got some fire for me."

"You guys have absolutely nothing in common," McNally said.

"Why—because she's a liberal? That's only because she hasn't gotten any good dick. Them soft latte drinking lumberjack wannabe gender neutral pussies don't know how to put it down. She gets with me, trust me, I'll bang the liberal out of her."

"Alright, that's my cue to go. I'm gonna wash that image out of my head."

"Hey, I love you man," Riley said as McNally exited the car.

37

Bishop got dressed in his MTA blues (light blue top and navy bottom) and headed off to the East New York Bus Depot. Normally he would drive but his car was in an NYPD impound lot in the Brooklyn Navy Yard, shot to hell and stained with his son's blood, and Owens his co-worker who he would carpool with was off today. Diane offered to drive him, but she worked in Bronx and it would take her too far out of the way. "Why don't you take the day off?" she asked him.

"We both already took a week off. You gotta work. I gotta work. Life goes on," he said. She agreed and headed off and he headed to the subway.

As he walked to the subway station, he heard the voices of young men calling from the side, "Sour, sour." Sour stood for sour sativa, a common strain of cannabis. Bishop was surprised they were selling it so openly. Was that how Desmond got into smoking? Was one of these boys the first to sell it to him? Bishop had an ill temper towards the drug, as it had played some role in his son's death, and it upset him that people were making his son out to be one of these boys selling weed on the corner.

He walked by them and approached the station entrance. There was a gathering of men, dressed in black pants and embroidered purple tops. They were Black Israelites. He had seen them before. In the nineties they used to be a staple on daytime talk shows. The black man was the true Israelite and the white man was the devil. That was their message. They quoted bible verses to prove it and would debate anyone, vehemently, who disagreed with them.

Bishop walked by them and down into the station. At the base of the station before going through the turnstile was another set of black men. They all wore the same hunter green suit with a collar-less blazer and matching kufi hat. They were called Nuwaubians and they were followers of Dr. Malachi Z. York. They preached his work and sold his books. They were calmer than the black Israelites, but their message was essentially the same. The black man was God and the white man was the devil, though they came at it from an ancient Egyptian astrological perspective. They attempted to get his attention and Bishop politely refused and walked by.

Just before he got to the turnstile there was a group of white people, men and women, from teenagers to people in their forties, dressed in white button-down shirts and khaki pants. They were Mormons. *A long way from Utah,* Bishop thought. They were preaching their gospel. They didn't say what color their God was. They didn't have to. It was presumed. A young girl tried to hand Bishop a pamphlet and again he politely refused.

Bishop walked through the turnstile and before he got to the escalator leading to the track to catch his train there was a lone man, Haitian, Bishop believed from his thick accent, preaching the good old-fashioned gospel. He railed against fornication, homosexuality and transgenderism—and masturbation for good measure. "Repent," he chanted. "Repent, for Jesus is coming." Bishop was forty years old and for as long as he could remember people had been preaching that Jesus would be coming—soon—yet and still soon never came.

At the subway platform there was a man dressed in a gray suit and bowtie selling newspapers. He was with the Nation of Islam and he was selling their newspaper the Final Call. Bishop was about to politely refuse again when he saw that Desmond was on the cover. Curious to see how the Nation had written about him, Bishop bought a copy. The member of the nation thanked him for his support and that would have been it, but then he recognized Bishop. "Praise be to Allah, you're the father." Bishop nodded affirmatively. "Let me shake your hand, brother." They shook hands affectionately. "I am so sorry for your loss. And I want you to know that the Nation supports you and your family, and we are with you."

"Thank you," Bishop replied.

Bishop got on the subway and took a seat. There was a man sitting across from him. He was homeless and filthy. He reeked of piss and shit, of many days without a shower and wet mildewed clothes. Driving a bus Bishop didn't encounter the homeless as much but the subways were filled with them; every train, every car. New York was the richest city in the world, and it was rotting from the root. His eyes were agape, and his mind was gone. The smell was too much. Bishop had to move.

38

Bishop settled into the bus and began his shift. It had only been a week yet, so much had transpired, it seemed so much longer. Usually muscle memory took over and he operated as if he and the bus were one symbiotic machine, but today he had to remind himself what to do. It's like not riding a bicycle for several years. You regain the hang of it but you're a bit wobbly for the first few meters.

Bishop received a lot of sympathy from his fellow coworkers when they saw him. Transit was a family. Even the ones you hated you still loved because of your shared struggle. Many were surprised to see him back to work so soon. "My bills ain't taking off, so I can't," he said.

His coworkers weren't the only ones who expressed their sympathy and support. The video of him at Sharpton's went viral. At last count, Cece had it at over fifty million on Facebook. That was to say nothing of YouTube and Instagram and any other number of social and traditional media. When fifty million people have seen you speak you start to get recognized.

At times, he noticed people on the bus whispering. "Yo, is that him?" "I think that's him." "The father, right?" Then they would check their phones to verify. "Yeah, that's him." Some people discretely videotaped him. Some were less discrete. Some did a live stream and he could hear them talking to their followers. One of them was particularly obnoxious and took the bus for their own personal reality show, performing for the camera, speaking loudly. She even tried to get an interview with Bishop while he was driving, to which, Bishop simply replied, "Back behind the white line, please."

Most people who recognized him simply nodded supportively. There was this one elder woman, Mrs. Johnson; she had ridden with him for years. He took her from her stop by her building to the senior center. She told him come here and meant for him to get out of his chair, and when your elders speak to you, you listen. She hugged him like his grandmother used to. "I'm praying for you and your family. I'm so sorry for what you're going through, but Jesus will see you through." It was a beautiful moment and he appreciated it, and of course someone decided to videotape it.

39

At the end of his shift before he left for the day Bishop was called into his supervisor's office. Mr. Jacobs, the head of the Transit Workers Union was there. Bishop had never had a private meeting with any of the Union heads before. However, he had never had a child killed by the police before. He imagined he was here to express his sympathies and support, and he did. However, that was not the reason they called the meeting.

"John, why don't you take some time off," Baptiste, his supervisor, said.

"I just took a week off," Bishop said.

"We know, and we don't think you're ready to come back yet. We think you should take some more time."

"Did I miss something?" Bishop asked. "Did I have an accident or fail to do my job properly today?"

"No. Like always you did great," Baptiste said.

"Then, I'll continue to do my job."

"But you are becoming a distraction," Mr. Jacobs said.

"How so?" Bishop asked.

"People are live feeding while you're driving." *Damn, things moved fast in this world. How were they aware of that already?* "It could lead to an accident."

"But it didn't," Bishop said.

"But it might. And I'm just going to be straight with you. The police unions are not very happy with you at this time," Jacobs informed him.

"What the hell does the police union have to do with me?" Bishop asked.

"You called for a police officer to bleed and suffer."

"I called for the man who killed my son to bleed and suffer."

"Who is a police officer and part of their union—and you are a part of ours. And as they are upset with you, they are by extension upset with Transit as well," Jacobs explained.

"What?" Bishop didn't get how the connection was made.

"Look John, you know all the city unions stand together," Baptiste said. "And because of this issue with you and the PBA, it's affecting other drivers. On nine occasions today when our drivers called for police assistance, the patrolmen showed up either extremely late or didn't show up at all."

"Really? The police would do that?" Bishop asked.

"They're doing it," Jacobs said. "And I was told on good authority it's because of what you said about the cop. We have to take you off John. Just for a little bit, for this to blow over."

"You working right now is putting other drivers in danger," Baptiste said.

"I'm putting other drivers in danger, and not these crooked, petty ass cops?" Bishop argued.

"Look you're part of the Transit family, and we feel your pain and stand by and support you," Jacobs said.

When Jacobs said that in the beginning of the meeting it

sounded more genuine. "Yeah, right?" Bishop replied.

"But you've been on the job long enough to know that all city unions, TWU, TFA, UFA and PBA support each other. And we're in a contract year and we're going to need the support of the police unions for city hall to give us a new and better deal, which will benefit you and all transit workers."

"Look John, you have a good deal of vacation time. Take it and be with your family," Baptiste said.

"No," Bishop said assertively. "You guys want me to take time off then fine. But I'm not using up my vacation days. You will pay for it. That cop, McNally, is on paid administrative leave, then I can be on paid leave as well."

Jacobs and Baptiste looked at each other and considered it before Jacobs nodded yes.

40

"I want you to consider that you may never drive a bus again," the attorney, Powell, said to Bishop and Diane in the living room of their home. He came over after Diane had informed him of Bishop's forced vacation.

"Why would that be?" Diane asked.

"You'll always be Desmond Bishop's father. What you said will always be there. Police unions have a long memory and they hold grudges. I don't think they'll ever be okay with transit taking you back."

"So, then what happens?" Diane asked. "They're going to fire him?"

"No, they can't do that. They'll force you into early retirement. But we'll negotiate a settlement and make sure you have your full pension. And with the roughly seven million you'll get from the city you guys should be secure financially."

The seven-million-dollar figure was news to Bishop. "Seven million? Where did that come from?" he asked.

"It's an estimate of what the city will payout from the wrongful death suit we'll file," Powell said.

"And where does seven million come from?" Diane asked.

"From my experience with these cases," Powell said. "Now we'll file a notice of claim for seventy-five million. We won't get that, but that's what we'll sue for. The city won't make it go to court, and they'll settle for anywhere between six and nine million. I'm saying seven to be safe."

"And how does the city boil it down from seventy-five to seven?" Bishop asked.

"Well they base it on what they assume would have been Desmond's future earnings." Bishop looked insulted. "Like I said, it could go up to nine. But seven is still on the high end with these settlements. Some families have only gotten a million, a million and a half."

"My son could have done anything he put his mind to. He played basketball. He could have made it to the NBA. He could have been a billionaire. And when I get the money, this seven million, a million for every bullet I'm guessing that's what you thought was fair, what do I do with it? Do I buy a big house with a big TV and have everyone come over and watch football on the TV my son's blood money bought?"

"I understand how you feel. How do you qualify your son's life in dollars and cents? It's offensive to even think about it," Powell said. "But aside from a criminal suit, which as you have said, rarely goes in our favor, this is the only way to make them pay for what they've done. You don't want the money, don't spend it. Do good with it. Start a foundation in Desmond's name or a scholarship. Do whatever you feel best but make them pay."

"Oh, they're going to pay. And what will you do with your settlement?" Bishop asked.

"Excuse me?" Powell said.

"Your thirty-three percent of the roughly seven million?"

Powell seemed offended by the question. "I'll use it to keep on helping other families like yourselves."

"It's a good gig you got going here," Bishop said.
"I know you're upset Mr. Bishop, but I am here to help."
"Okay . . . yeah."

41

You meet your wife. She's the girl of your dreams. You fall in love. You have children. You have a house. You have a life. You don't need more. You shouldn't want more—but you do. You meet another girl. She awakens something in you, something you didn't know had fallen asleep, something you haven't felt in years. You fall in . . . and it is bad . . . and it is good . . . you feel guilty . . . yet you persist. She texted him. He had been ignoring her, but this was something McNally couldn't put off anymore. He had to deal with it. He had to end it.

McNally said bye to his wife and kids as they went off to work and school. He had been staying home. It had been a month since the shooting, and he hadn't left the house much since his name and picture had been released. He would have to leave today, however. In the afternoon, he got in his Buick and drove off—and unbeknownst a Honda followed behind him.

42

Bishop was home alone. Diane was at work and Cece was back in high school. He was already going crazy from his forced vacation. He had been mostly staying in. He didn't like going outside much anymore. His speech at the rally hadn't made him famous but he was no longer anonymous. Every time he went out someone would eventually recognize him, and come up to him and tell him how sorry they were and how much they supported him, and it was all very nice, but after a while people constantly telling you they support you just gets cloying.

Being home all the time wasn't much better. There was no escape from the emptiness you felt from losing someone you loved. So often he sat in his chair watching television and seethed . . . and then his phone rang. The number wasn't familiar, but he remembered it.

"What's up Soldier?" Bishop greeted. It was good to hear from him. He enjoyed the conversation they had.

Soldier got to the point. "Do you remember when we spoke, and I said that I might be able to give you that opportunity you said you wanted?"

Soldier was purposefully vague—no doubt because they were speaking over the phone. It took Bishop a moment to intuit what he meant, but he did. "Yes," Bishop said.

"Well, I might be able to give you that opportunity."

Suddenly something that before seemed like absurdist fiction became very real. "How?" Bishop asked.

"Don't worry about that," Soldier said. "I just want you to confirm that you would want this opportunity, understanding fully what it means . . . everything that it means."

His words were vague, but his point was very clear. Everything became dark and heavy. So many thoughts and emotions rushed through Bishop's mind at once. The question sat in his diaphragm, churning in acid, bandying between doubt and resolve, before bubbling to the top, and he answered with the only word his mouth would allow him to utter, "Yes."

43

"I know you're upset," McNally said.

Shannon swallowed her sigh with a giggle. "Upset. Upset is just the tip of it. I'm pissed. I'm disappointed. Mostly I'm sad," she said.

McNally had driven from his house in Marine Park to her apartment in South Ozone, Queens. He had been in her apartment a few times now. Usually it had been at night. "I'm sorry," he said.

"So am I," she said. "I see your picture on the news. I find out that you killed some black kid. And on top of that, I find out that you're married." She heard it when the head of the union was speaking about what a great police officer and family man McNally was.

"I wanted to tell you," McNally said.

"No, you didn't. You had three months to tell me, and you never did."

She leaned against her kitchen sink. She had just washed the dishes and her shirt was a bit damp, creating a sense of translucence. He could make out slightly the outlines of her pink bra.

It was only meant to be one-time. Meagan had taken the children to visit her parents in Vermont. He couldn't get the time off. Not that he was keen on spending two weeks with her side of the family, not that they were bad people, but Vermont people were always a little off. He went out drinking with Riley and the other boys after their tour. This was something he couldn't do much when Meagan was home. She worried and always wanted him home right away. McNally told her, though the job was inherently dangerous, statistically it was one of the safer jobs out there. The death and injury rate with construction workers was far greater. This did nothing to assuage her. And she worried even more whenever there was a police officer involved shooting anywhere in the country. He came home straightaway most nights. He didn't mind much. He loved his wife; he loved his children—but he liked her.

She pulled her auburn tress behind her ear that night as she smiled with her friend at the bar. She had freckles on her cheeks and her shoulders. It was a scene that often replayed in his mind. Riley was the one who approached them. Riley was good and bad for that. McNally saw her smile and felt it in the inside part. He hadn't seen a woman who immediately turned him on since he first saw Meagan. Sometimes he thought he liked her more than Meagan. After being with someone for so long there was a routineness to everything that took away the passion. Shannon was very passionate in ways Meagan wasn't. Still he knew whatever he felt for Shannon was just passion and nothing more. He loved his wife, now more than ever. Here in his darkest days she was his rock. He couldn't bear the thought of her finding out and the hurt she would feel. Truthfully, he feared hurting Meagan more than the thought of losing his job and potentially going to jail for killing that boy. He had to end it. This couldn't come out now. "You lied to me," she said.

"I didn't. You assumed I was single, and I let you," McNally said.

"Don't give me that. You didn't wear a ring." Not wearing his ring that night was at Riley and Roberts's insistence. They didn't want any wedding rings raising any unwanted questions.

"You're right. I was wrong. I am wrong," he said.

"You realize that now after you've killed some kid and the whole world knows your name. Are you worried that I might go out there and say something?" He just looked at her. "Is that why you finally answered my text? Is that why you came here? Don't worry. I don't want that kind of attention."

That was very good to hear, but, "That's not why I came," he said.

"Yes it is. And it's okay. I know who you are now. Now just go," she said.

He got up to leave.
"I really liked you, Brian."
"I really liked you too."
"Oh well," she said.

44

It hurts when you hurt good people. McNally broke it off with Shannon, but he still liked her. If he hadn't met Meagan, he believed he could have loved her, and built a life with her. He still desired her. He fought every impulse not to take her, right then and there, if she would have had him. But it had to be done. He hated hurting her. He dreaded hurting Meagan. It had all been too much to deal with. His head was a bit clearer now. He could devote all his mind to his family and this, "—What the fuh—" he blurted. There was a sudden jerk, like getting kicked in the ass, and McNally had to quickly regain control of the car. A back tire blew out. He pulled over at the side of the road and got out to investigate.

45

He was patient. Being a sniper teaches you patience. You wait hours, sometimes days, for the right moment—and that was all it was, just a moment. And if you weren't ready it would be lost. The Buick turned onto the road, the one with little traffic and a non-functioning surveillance camera. Soldier had selected this road as he followed the Buick to South Ozone Park. He hoped the Buick would take this path coming back—and it did. This was the moment. He attached the silencer, took aim, took a breath and let his finger slide. The back tire blew out.

A few meters down the car pulled over. The Target got out to investigate. Recognizing he had blown a tire, the Target popped his hood looking for his spare. Soldier pulled over and got out as well. He walked over under the guise of helping. "Hey, do you need a hand?" The Target turned about and before he could even accept or refuse, Soldier gun butted him on the right temple. It knocked him back falling into the trunk. The Target was unconscious, but he wouldn't be out for long. Soldier covered his mouth and nose with a chloroform rag. Then other men, in the car Soldier came in, pulled up beside them. Soldier quickly handcuffed the Target's hands and took him from the trunk of his car and brought him to the trunk of the theirs. The other men drove off. Soldier stayed by the Target's car. He changed the tire and drove off seven minutes later.

46

Where the gun at? Where the gun at? Voices: many, hushed, angry, simmering, shouting, cursing—couldn't understand them, but felt them—felt like hatred. *Where the gun at? Where the gun at?* McNally began to open his eyes. Whenever he opened his eyes after a long sleep, he always expected to open them in his bed. It was always discomforting when he didn't. His eyes cast down. He saw his hands through the rheum. He was wearing silver bracelets. *What?*

He woke up like coming out of anesthesia. His body ached; the side of his head throbbed. He attempted to rub it, but when he lifted his right hand his left hand lifted as well. He saw that he was handcuffed, and the chain of his hands were handcuffed to an old cast iron rusted radiator built firmly into the ground. He jerked it and realized he couldn't move. He was a prisoner. It was coming back to him. He went to see Shannon. She was angry; she was hurt. He was driving home. His back tire blew out. He went to examine it, a man approached, and then darkness . . . and then here.

He looked around. It was a room, average size, lit by sunset; looked like what used to be an office; empty except for an old flat square desk in one corner and four shovels in another. The floor was tiled and cracked and had become the color of dirt. There was a small hole in the floor and a mound of gravel beside it. The walls were paint chipped and mold festooned like floral wallpaper.

There was a folding chair by the adjacent wall. There was a man standing by the wall looking out a small window. He stood so still he blended into the room. Was he real? "Where am I?" McNally asked to see if the man was alive.

"Somewhere in Brooklyn," the man replied.

Brooklyn. Where in Brooklyn, McNally thought, but didn't ask, gathering the man had been ambiguous for a reason. "How did I get here?" he asked instead.

"I had help," the man answered and turned and faced him. "Do you know who I am?" John Bishop asked.

McNally had never met this man, but he knew his face. I want you to bleed. I want you to suffer. Before those words had hit him in the chest, now he felt them in the pit of his stomach. "Yeah . . . I know who you are." Bishop looked at him waiting for him to say more. "You're the father." Bishop kept looking at him. "Desmond Bishop's father." Bishop took the folding chair and dragged it across the floor, to the center of the room, so that it was on the same sagittal plane where McNally sat, roughly six feet between them. "What are you doing?" McNally asked him. "You're making things worse."

Bishop took a seat. "Oh, I think things are already way past worse." Bishop had been looking forward to and dreading this moment for some time now. This was the man. This was the demon who killed his son. He was of average height, average build, altogether unremarkable. It was kind of like meeting a celebrity. You build them up into something preternatural and then after a minute your eyes adjust and they're just human. He looked disoriented and afraid—and he should be. Bishop spent a minute just looking at him, trying to read him and, partly not knowing what to do next.

For McNally there was something unnerving about the silence. Bishop just sat there staring at him, his eyes dissecting him like an x-ray. McNally felt like the silence could erupt into violence at any moment and he would be at a great disadvantage. Someone should speak. "I never meant for any of this to happen," McNally said.

"No, and what did you mean to happen when you shot my boy seven times?"

Every time McNally was reminded it was seven shots and not three something felt wrong, like saying the sky was green. *I thought it was three.* "I thought he had a gun."

"No, he didn't."

"I thought my life was in danger."

Those words burned Bishop's insides like biting into a pepper while eating your meal, and he had to choose whether to spit it out or bear it and swallow. He spit. "And your life is so much more precious, that just the hint of a possibility that it might be in danger and you felt you had the right to take my son's life."

McNally didn't know what to say. Everything he said seemed to come out wrong. "You're his father. I don't expect you to understand."

"Oh, I understand," Bishop said. "You stalked my son, you shot him seven times and then you watched him die."

That all sounded so wrong to McNally, as if he was describing some other set of events completely. "No, no . . . that's not what happened."

"I've seen the video. I saw what happened. You stalked my son, you shot him seven times, and you watched him die, and all because," Bishop raised his hand showing his skin.

"No, that's not true, that's not true. I don't see color."

That upset Bishop—the blatant bullshit said with such sincerity. Bishop couldn't tell if McNally was lying to him or to himself. Either way it was a lie. Bishop had been restrained, keeping his emotions in but that pissed him off. He reached behind his back and pulled out a gun, a black Glock 9mm. Bishop pointed it at McNally, braced his elbow on his knee and leaned forward. "You know, I brought you here so we could have an honest talk, man to man. You lie like that to me again and I swear I'll put a bullet right in your eye."

Now there was another character in the room, something else for McNally to contend with. McNally had had a gun pulled on him before. He had been shot at before. The gun made the threat of death more immediate, but it also made the situation more familiar. Strangely, the gun made him less afraid. "Alright, alright . . . you want the truth?" Bishop waited. "With all due respect sir, the truth is your son was a drug dealer."

"No . . . he was not."

"I am sorry sir, but your son was a drug dealer."

"Don't tell me sorry. And don't tell me who my son was. I know my son. I raised my son. I know my son. My son was not a drug dealer," Bishop said.

"You're right, I don't know your son. All I know is what I saw. And I saw him pull over and I saw him make a deal with my own eyes."

"You don't know shit. You thought you saw a gun too, when he put his hands out the window to show you, he didn't have one."

He put his hands out to show he didn't have a gun. McNally had heard that explanation before. It always struck him as an odd thing for the boy to do. Criminals who have had many run-ins with the police do that, not regular civilians. Doing so, would put McNally less at ease not more. "It was a tragic and unfortunate set of events, but my actions were justified," McNally said.

"Justified? Justified?" Bishop repeated. It was such an insidious word; vile and bilious. It was justice corrupted. "You call shooting an unarmed boy seven times, pulling his bleeding body from his car, handcuffing him to the pavement and watching him die justified?"

When he said it like that, it sounded so much more horrific. "Like I said, you're his father. I don't expect you to understand."

"You're goddamn right I don't," Bishop yelled.

McNally again recognized that violence could erupt at any moment. He was strategizing what to say to keep himself safe when four men walked in the room, all wearing all-black Yankee caps and surgical masks. Bishop couldn't make out their identities except for Soldier. He knew him by his build.

McNally had been scared enough contending with Bishop and the gun. The abrupt appearance of these men raised his anxiety considerably. This must be the help Bishop spoke of. The largest and apparently oldest of them came forward. He greeted Bishop with a handshake.

"Sorry for the interruption but there's something we have to take care of." Bishop didn't know what this something was, but Soldier ran this show, and he moved as such. He approached McNally and squatted so they were at eye level. "Hello Officer. How are you doing?" he asked calmly. McNally didn't say anything he just looked at him, his breathing heightened as if he were doing a light jog. "I understand you're a bit out of sorts right now, but there's something I need you to do for me."

"What?" McNally asked cautiously.

Soldier took a phone from his back pocket and showed it to McNally. A video was playing. It showed the outside of a house and children playing in the lawn. It took McNally a moment to recognize what he was looking at, and who the children were. His eyes opened wide. The video continued. The camera panned from the house and the children to the inside of a car. A man sat in the driver's seat, and in his lap sat a gun. Seeing that gun filled McNally with equal parts dread and rage. "I know what you're feeling," Soldier said. "But right now, I need you to be calm and collect yourself, and I need you to call your wife and tell her you won't be home tonight. To be safe, tell her you'll be away for a few days."

"What?"

Soldier began again, "Call your wife—"

"I heard you," McNally interrupted. "But she's not gonna believe that I just got up and went away for a few days without telling her."

"Make her believe it," one of the other men said.

"She won't," McNally stressed. "She knows I haven't been leaving the house. Especially after my name got put out there."

"But you did leave today," Soldier reminded him. That stung McNally in more ways than one. He was already hating himself for going to see Shannon. His actions had put his life and now his entire family in danger. "Think of something to tell her."

"There's nothing I can tell her that she won't question."

"Tell her, you leaving her for your new bitch," one of the other men said, and the others laughed. Soldier raised his open palm slightly and they stopped. It hit Bishop then the reality of what he was in. This truly was a kidnapping and everything that entailed. This wasn't just a meeting between two men, one the offender the other the aggrieved; it involved threats, and violence and families.

"I need you to think of something . . . otherwise," Soldier didn't elaborate. He didn't need to.

McNally kept thinking where he could tell her he had went that would satisfy her. It also occurred to him that abating Meagan's anxiety may deter any chance of him being found. However, at this moment, keeping his family safe was paramount to his own safety. Thinking about his family, he thought about his father and then it hit him.

"We have a cabin upstate. I can tell her I went there," he said to Soldier.

"How far away is it?" Soldier asked.

"Indian Lake. It's a good four-hour drive."

"That will work." Soldier put away the previous phone and took another from his pocket. McNally recognized this one. It was his. "Now, I want you to take ten minutes to collect yourself. Think about exactly what you're going to say to your wife and how you're going to say it. Think about how she might respond and how you'll respond to that." McNally nodded he understood. Soldier gave him the ten minutes to collect himself. During that time the three other men spoke to themselves and Soldier spoke to Bishop.

"How are you doing?" Soldier asked Bishop.

"I'm good," Bishop replied. He wanted to ask Soldier if threatening McNally's family had been necessary; wisely, he didn't.

"How's it been going?"

"It's been going. Nothing much yet."

"Yeah, that's how these things are. But give him time, he'll break. They always do."

After ten minutes, McNally indicated he was ready. Soldier returned to him and handed him his phone. "Now don't lie. Don't give any nonverbal signals, anything to make her think you're under duress. This is about you. Let's keep it about you. Let's not get your family involved."

There was such a calmness and professionalism to this man, that even though he had kidnapped him, McNally was certain he was the man who had knocked him out earlier, and was now threatening his family, McNally believed he could trust him; at the very least trust him to do as he said he would. "Okay," McNally said.

McNally made the call, and within two rings Meagan answered. "Brian, where the hell are you? I've been calling."

"I know. I'm sorry my phone battery died."

"Well why aren't you home? Where are you?"

"I'm up at Indian Lake. I'm at the cabin my Dad talked about."

"You went to the cabin, today? Without me—without the kids?"

"Yeah, I'm sorry. It was spur of the moment. I was going stir crazy being inside."

"So, you just got up and left without telling me?" she asked.

"I'm real sorry. I've just been going through so much lately, with everything. And I just needed to be away . . . and alone. I just needed to be alone for a bit and deal with all this."

"I understand that you're going through a lot. But I'm going through it too you know. We're going through it together."

"I know. I know. I just felt like I needed a few days by myself, to detox and get my head right. Please understand."

After a weighty exhale, "I understand," she said.

"I love you, okay. I love you so much."

"I love you too. Do you wanna talk to the kids?" she asked.

Soldier shook his head no and gestured with his finger for McNally to wrap it up.

"No. My battery is dying. I left without my charger. I barely had enough juice to call you. I'll buy one tomorrow and call again when I do. Okay."

"Okay."

"Bye." He hung up.

"Good," Soldier said and took the phone from him.

McNally was of two minds about his conversation. In one hand he was hoping Meagan bought it, and that this man bought it as well, in order to keep his family safe. And in another he was hoping she didn't altogether and maybe would try to locate his phone and she would see that he wasn't in Indian Lake. Soldier broke McNally's phone in half with his bare hands. There went that hope. This man, this leader, he was smart. This was obvious. There was a conviction and confidence in him that only comes from experience. He began walking away, and McNally had to ask, "How are you doing this? How did you know where I lived?"

Soldier replied simply, "Black people know how to use computers too." He then called to Bishop, and he and the other men walked off and left McNally alone in the room.

Outside the room and out of earshot of McNally, Soldier said to Bishop, "Go home. His mind is all over the place right now, especially after that call to his wife. He's no good to you now. Give him a night to sleep on it. He'll tell you everything you want tomorrow. You get some sleep as well, come back in the morning. He'll be hungry. Bring him food. He'll be grateful. He'll start talking then."

Bishop looked at the mask and hat Soldier was wearing to conceal his identity and wondered, "Should I have been wearing a mask?"

"No. That wouldn't serve your purpose," Soldier said.

"Then why are you guys wearing masks?"

"Because he needs to believe he has a chance of getting out of here. If he saw all our faces, he wouldn't, then he wouldn't give you what you needed."

"Yeah, that makes sense," Bishop said. Soldier began walking away when Bishop felt compelled to ask, "Have you done this before?"

"I've done a lot of things for this country," Soldier replied.

47

Bishop returned home that night. Diane asked where he had been. He told her something about getting a drink, which was odd because he rarely drank, had never been the pub going kind, and didn't smell of liquor. She let it go. She knew they were both stressed and was fairly certain he hadn't been with another woman. She told him the lawyer called and had some new details about the case to go over. He heard her but didn't listen and nodded at the parts he felt were appropriate. Diane didn't need to know his exact comings and goings, but she didn't like speaking to a robot. "What's going on? Where are you?" she asked. It took Bishop an extra second to come out of robot mode and try to give an answer, which was more robotic than if he had remained in autopilot. Diane shook her head and walked away. In the other room, he heard her say, "I can't do this all by myself you know."

Bishop laid in bed that night. He heard Diane crying in the bathroom. It broke his heart. He wanted to comfort her but didn't know how. He heard her praying as well. She had been praying a lot more since Desmond's death. Bishop couldn't bring himself to pray. Every time he started he became upset.

Diane came to bed, put the sheet on and turned her back to him. He wanted to touch her, but it was as if he had forgotten how to, and maybe she would be mad if he did. A part of him wanted to tell her what he had done, maybe she would be proud of him taking initiative and doing something; but another part of him wanted her to have no parts of this. He had embarked on something there was no turning back from. He had looked into the eyes of the man who killed their son. He was holding him prisoner, chained in the bowels of an abandoned building at this very minute. He knew he wanted something from him. He however, didn't know what that was exactly. It was more of a feeling he supposed, and when he felt it, he would know it.

48

There was a train. He heard it stop. He heard it pull off. Five minutes later he heard it again, and roughly five minutes after that. He heard it in his dream, like falling asleep to a song, and the song becomes a part of the dream. Or was it the dream that made him hear the song? McNally dreamt of the shooting as he had done every night. He heard the voice of the people. He heard the roar of the train. He smelled something foul. He opened his eyes and there were eyes looking back at him. There was a face four inches from his.

He was black, looked homeless, looked haggard. McNally jerked back. The man began speaking what could only be described as madness. "The world is round but when I walk all I see is flat. Flat, flat, flat. Sunny day, planes fly, strange clouds in the sky." He had been kneeling ass to grass to be eye level with McNally. "Look, look." Suddenly he stood up. He was tall, six feet plus. He was skinny—not skin and bones but close. He was in his thirties but could be younger, homelessness adds at least ten years. He wore a red shirt and baggy black jeans, no belt. He held his pants up with one hand. The clothes hung on him like a hangar. He had an afro uncombed, unkempt. He pointed to the window. "Clouds but not clouds. Look." Of course, McNally could not see outside. He could only see the room, lit by the morning sun, and this man.

It was a hell of a thing to wake up to. McNally had barely slept. The floor was his bed and the radiator his pillow. There were rats scurrying about, and when he didn't see them, he heard them in the walls. It was hard to sleep in such conditions. He was finally able to fall off two hours ago and now this.

"No see?" The man asked.

McNally felt compelled to answer, "No see."

"White devil, no see or no want see?"

"What the hell is this?" McNally whispered to himself.

Bishop walked into the room, and the crazed man turned his attention to him. "The world is round but when I walk all I see is flat. Flat, flat, flat." Bishop looked just as bemused to see this man as McNally was. "Sunny day, planes fly, strange clouds in the sky. Look, look." He pointed to the window and gestured for Bishop to look out.

Bishop knew he was, as Jamaicans would call him, a madman. As a boy in Kingston he remembered seeing them walking around town, talking to themselves, brushing away flies that weren't there. He was taught from a young age to tread lightly. He didn't know what this man was on, but he was quite adamant to show Bishop something.

Bishop obliged to keep him calm. He followed him to the window but kept him always in his peripheral vision for any sudden movements. The man pointed out the window and had to kneel and crane his neck to see the sky. Going along, Bishop did the same. "Look," he said. "Clouds but not clouds." Bishop at first couldn't see what he was supposed to be seeing. But when he looked closer, he noticed the clouds did look different—unnatural even, like they were sprayed on. "See, see?" The man asked.

"Yes, I see," Bishop said.

The man seemed very pleased by this. "White devil no see," he said. "White devil no want see." They both looked at McNally and McNally looked back at them, eyes wide, as if they were both crazy. Bishop looked at the man and saw how haggard he looked. Bishop was carrying plastic bags with food, sandwiches and waters, he got from the deli. "Are you hungry?" he asked the man.

The man turned calmly. "Yes, I am quite hungry. I have not eaten in days," he said so lucidly, it seemed like a different person. Bishop gave him a sandwich and a bottle of water. "Thank you very much for your kindness. I truly appreciate it." He took the sandwich and water and began walking away but then he saw McNally looking at him and he did not like the look of it.

"What the fuck you looking at?" he shouted with rancor and bass. "You don't know me, nigga. You don't know me. I'm from Brooklyn, Fort Greene, Bedstuy, Crown Heights—what?"

Seeing him agitated, Bishop calmed him down. "It's okay," Bishop said. "It's okay." And Bishop was able to lead him out while the man kept looking at McNally the entire time.

49

"Jesus, Mary and Joseph, what the hell?" McNally blurt-ed. McNally had never said that out loud before. His mother had plenty of times. Especially when he was growing up and she had been upset with either him or his brother. He always hated when she said it and often mocked her. "Is this hell?" McNally asked after the man had left.

"If this is hell, hell is not that bad," Bishop said. "Trust me, you haven't seen hell." Bishop walked over to him and placed a bag in arm's reach. "Here."

"Thank you," McNally said as he took the bag. There was a sandwich in it and there was water, a large gallon and two smaller bottles. There was also a toothbrush and a small tube of toothpaste. McNally took it out. "Thank you," he said again.

"That's for me, not you. I can't stand bad breath."

McNally nodded with a slight smile and began brushing his teeth. He washed and gurgled with some of the water. He took out the sandwich. It was turkey on a roll. McNally hadn't eaten in going on twenty-four hours and was quite hungry. Bishop was his captor but after the long miserable sleepless night, and waking up to that crazed man, he was quite happy to see him. "What's your plan?" McNally asked after taking a bite. "What do you want? What's your endgame?"

Bishop took his seat, left in the same spot it was last night. "I don't think you wanna get into that."

"Okay, I just don't know what I'm doing here. I look at you, and from what I see, you seem like a good decent man. You work hard, you have a wife and a daughter—"

"And I had a son," Bishop said.

McNally swallowed. "I am sorry for what happened to your son. I truly am."

"You say that like something just happened to him. Like you

had nothing to do with it." McNally was about to say something but caught himself. "What were you about to say?" Bishop asked. "Were you going to say that it was justified again? Or were you going to say it was an accident? Like oops, I killed your son. Sorry, it just happened. Oops your son is dead, but it is a tough job."

"It is a tough job," McNally said.

"And shit happens," Bishop joked.

"All due respect sir, but you have no idea what we go through, putting our lives and the security of our families on the line on a daily basis. I killed your son in the line of duty, and I understand you're angry. You have every right to be. But you don't understand what we go through, and the split-second decisions we have to make."

"I understand just fine. You killed my son, like police been killing black men for years."

McNally was visibly irritated. "You wanna judge me, but I'm out there every day saving you."

"Saving me?" Bishop said with objection.

"We deal with the worst of humanity, the drug dealers, the gang bangers, car jackers, rapists, people who break into your house and kill you, the ones who have girls, chained up in project apartments only feeding them McDonald's, while they got a string of dudes coming in on them every day. Young girls, girls your daughter's age."

"Don't you mention my daughter," Bishop said, his ire raised. "You don't ever mention my daughter."

"Fine. Fine, I won't. But you don't see it, because you don't have to. You can close your eyes to it and drive your bus. But it's my job to see it, to look at the ugliest shit every day and take it down, and you wanna judge me. There are these people out there and they'll kill you as soon as they look at you. You know it. You might not wanna say it, but you know it. If it wasn't for the police, they would eat decent people alive."

"What's decent people?" Bishop asked. "You killed my son. Are you saying my son wasn't decent?"

"I didn't know your son, but I know what I saw."

"Say he was a drug dealer one more time," Bishop said and pointed the gun at McNally. McNally was silent. "You know what," Bishop began again, "say he was a drug dealer. Say I give you that. What's the sentence for selling an ounce of weed?"

The question took McNally a bit off guard. "I don't know off hand," he said.

"Is the sentence death?" Bishop asked.

"No," McNally said.

"Then drug dealing don't have shit to do with it. You killed my son because he was black and because you are a racist."

"You think I'm a racist?"

"I know you are a racist."

"You think all cops are racists?"

"Most."

"You think we're just here to kill black men. You want us gone. There's an easy solution. Stop committing crimes. How about that? You commit less crimes, there's less reason for us to come into your neighborhoods, less cops, less chance of something unfortunate happening."

"Something unfortunate happening. You gotta sweet way of saying murder."

"You know why I'm here, why I'm working in the hood? I asked for this assignment. I did. Because this assignment is a gateway to a promotion. Because the hood is where most of the action is. This is where the crime is. Because black men, fifteen to twenty-five, commit seventy-five percent of homicides in the city, and they're mostly killing black people. I'm not making this shit up. These are facts. So, I come here to get my arrests up, get my promotion and then get the fuck out."

50

"White people, I tell you. You're so full of shit. You make it sound like we'd tear each other apart without you, like we need you. We don't need you. You know black people lived together and lived good, long before white people ever came. If you, racist police, weren't here I think we would do just fine. I think we'd do better."

"Then do better," McNally said.

Bishop restrained himself from pistol whipping that smug look off his face. "Those neighborhoods with the most crime that you're talking about, those are also the poorest neighborhoods, right?"

"In New York City standards, yeah they're poor."

"See what you don't see, what you don't understand is, it's not black people killing black people. It's poor people killing poor people."

"What . . . what . . . I'm sorry sir but don't give me that," McNally rebuffed.

"You know, I used to think like you, a little bit. Wondering why black people can't come together without some shit happening. We always never go to clubs or lounges in Brooklyn, because, some shit would always pop off."

"Exactly. You see what I'm saying."

"I used to. But then in the summer they have all these festivals, celebrating African culture, black pride. My wife and kids always go. I go too, if I have the time off. For years, they've been going. Thousands of black people show up, every year. Not one incident of violence ever happens. None."

"And all of these people at these festivals are middle class or rich. Is that what you're saying?"

"Most are working people. Some are rich. Some are poor."

"So, what's your point?" McNally asked.

"I drive a bus, and I run into a lot of people. I've run into my share of poor white people, and you should see how they act. They're drunk, they're high, they're loud, they curse. When I first saw it, it kind of surprised me, because I was like, they're acting like some poor . . . you know."

"No, I don't know," McNally said—but he did. He knew family members who acted like that.

"Poverty makes you loud and more aggressive. You're born rough and you grow rough. Poor people are always defensive because everybody steals from the poor. The poor steal from the poor because it's who you can touch. And the rich steal from the poor, because though we're poor together we're rich."

"You're not poor," McNally said.

"I was born poor."

"Yeah but you're not poor. We're the same."

"We're not the same," Bishop said.

"You own your home. You're driving a nice car."

"Why you keep asking about the car? Black people can't drive a nice car without doing something criminal? You killed my son because he was driving a nice car?"

"I never asked you about the car."

"Yeah but your people did."

"My people?" McNally asked.

"Yeah, your people, at the precinct."

The conversation had digressed. "I'm sorry I mentioned it. But my point is, you guys don't have a monopoly on poverty. You got poor people everywhere. You said it, they're a lot of poor white people out there, and they're not killing each other like you are. You got white people, up in the Appalachians, poor as hell. People so poor they're buying pepsi with their food stamps and trading that in for money."

"Glad to hear you know white people are on food stamps too," Bishop remarked.

McNally ignored that point. "I'm saying these people are just as poor, and probably worse off than most places in the hood, definitely in New York. And they have crime, but they don't have anywhere near the killing you have. So, it has nothing to do with just being poor."

"How do they live up there, in the Appalachians?" Bishop asked.

"Fucked up."

"That's not what I'm asking. Is it a city, suburbs, farm, what?"

McNally thought for a second. "Mostly, mostly country, small counties."

"See in Jamaica, most of my family lived in Kingston. Kingston is a city. My grandfather though lived in Clarendon, that's one of the other parishes. He never took well to city life, hated it. Sometimes we'd go there in the summer to visit him. And I liked it because we'd swim in the river. The people in the country are poorer than the people in Kingston. I mean real poor, living in shanties, zinc roofs. And there ain't no food stamps or government subsidies. But country had less crime, much less killing. Because there were less people, and the people were more spaced out. In the city, they're so much people, and everybody is packed in. Here in the projects, you're literally on top of each other. It ends up being like crabs in a barrel. My grandmother would always say that about people. Them act like them a crab in a barrel. Each crab keep tearing the other down so none of them can get out. The thing though I never thought about is that crabs aren't supposed to be in barrels, nothing is. And if you pack any living thing in a confined space with limited resources, they're gonna stifle each other to survive. Step on each other's necks. Even plants and trees. My grandmother had a garden in her backyard in Jamaica, and she'd teach me how to plant, peppermint, scotch bonnet pepper, tomato, and she'd always stress that you can't plant them too close together because their roots will stifle each other. They need room to grow. It's the same with people. Living things need space. When you're that close to each other, breathing each other's air, you got one of two choices, you're either gonna fuck or you're gonna fight."

51

It went straight to voicemail. 'This is Brian McNally. I'm not in. If I feel like it or if I ever check my voicemail, I'll call you back.' It was 10:34 in the morning. Brian most likely hadn't had a chance to get a charger for his phone yet. Meagan would give it another two hours then call again. Still something about all this didn't feel right. It was so sudden and abrupt. It was unlike Brian to leave on his own without first telling her. Then again, he had never killed someone in the line of duty before, much less an unarmed black teenager, and being reviled by half the country. He was going through so much. She could see the strain it had put on him. He had hardly been sleeping and ate barely.

Part of her wondered if she was doing something wrong or if she wasn't doing enough. Was she not supportive enough? Was that why he felt the need to get away from her as well as everything that was going on? She shouldn't think that way. She was making it about her. God knows there were times she felt the need to be away from everyone. Everything was fine. He just needed time away. She would call again in two hours.

Meagan was looking for a mop in the hall closet, when a baseball glove fell and hit her on the head. It was her son Aiden's glove. He broke a window playing catch two weeks ago, and she took it from him and put it in the back of the uppermost shelf. She was putting the glove away again when she saw something that caught her attention. It was a leather samsonite pullman luggage. It was the kind that could carry a good deal but still fit in the overhead compartment of a plane. It was Brian's go to bag whenever he went on a small trip. She looked right at it . . . for a good half-minute. Ten minutes later she called him again. It went straight to message. 'Hello this is Brian McNally . . .'

52

"You know, before, I wouldn't have guessed you were Jamaican," McNally said.

"That's the thing with us Jamaicans, we're out of many one people. We're not all the same."

"I been to Jamaica. Went there for my honeymoon. It's beautiful. We went to Ocho Rios. We went to, um, Dunn's River Falls. I almost busted my ass trying to climb that thing," McNally chuckled. "My wife though, Meagan she was great. She used to dance on Broadway. She teaches dance now. Still has those great legs. Great balance. She went up the whole thing no problem. We had a great time. Beaches were beautiful. And I loved the food. Had jerk chicken. Guys were selling it outside in this kind of grill, looks like it's made from a steel drum."

"Pan," Bishop clarified for him.

"Yeah, that. It's so good. I had it for lunch every day. And curry goat. I fell in love with curry goat. I'm Irish and we have a lot of lamb dishes. So I can relate. When we got back, I tried to get Meagan to cook curry goat. She got the recipe online. Didn't work out too well." McNally laughed to himself. "It was terrible. Every once in a while, I'll go into a Jamaican restaurant and I'll order the curry goat, and people will look at me like, white boy what are you doing here?"

"What do you think you're doing?" Bishop asked.

"Hmm?" McNally replied.

"Why you telling me all this fuckery about Jamaica? I don't care how much you love jerk chicken and that your wife can't cook curry goat."

"I'm just talking, man."

"That ain't what we're here for," Bishop said.

"What are we here for?" McNally asked frustratingly. "What are you doing? Have you, seriously, thought this through?"

"Believe me I have."

"Then what do you want?"

Bishop smiled slyly, "I want justice."

"This isn't justice, man."

"And what is justice? What is justice to you? Hmm? Should I thank you, for your service? Maybe I should just understand. You saw a black kid driving a nice car, so you followed him, you shot him seven times, and you watched him die, but you know you do a tough job, and you had to make a split-second decision, so it's okay. You tell me sorry and I shake your hand and that's it."

"I did not kill your son because he was black, not everything is about race," McNally said.

"When it comes to black and white people everything is always about race."

"You're so focused on race, you won't allow yourself to see anything else. Black people kill more white people than white people kill black people, do you know that? It's true. Is that about race? Wouldn't that make black people more racist than white people?"

"Black people can't be racist to white people."

"What—what? Don't give me that," McNally said. "Some of the most racist people I've met are black."

"Listen, a black person can dislike you. They can even hate you, but they don't have the power to institute their views to hold you back, and to benefit from that. That's racism."

McNally had a look as if he wanted to cry bullshit before surrendering the point and moving on to another. "When you have a gun in your hand, isn't that power?" He waited a moment for Bishop to say something. He didn't. "When those black people killed white people, they had power over them then. You have more power over me right now," McNally said. "And you have prejudged me because I'm white, are you not racist?"

"It's not a one on one thing. It's about institutional power," Bishop answered.

"Power is power."

"Then what's a racist to you? You tell me. You define it." Strangely, McNally had a clear concept of what he believed a racist was but couldn't quite articulate it at that moment. He knew what he wanted to say but couldn't find the exact words. Bishop smiled. "I bet you think, just because you're polite enough not to call black people niggas to their face, that you're not."

"There goes that word again," McNally said shaking his head.

"What word?"

"Nigga," McNally replied while looking away.

Coming from McNally that word cut like a knife through the air. Bishop at once went for the gun behind his back and held it down by his side. "You tread real lightly now, McNally."

"I don't mean any offense," McNally said.

"No. I'm not trying to hear that word from you again," Bishop warned.

"You won't. It's a vile word. It's ugly—hateful. But what I don't get, for the life of me, is why you guys say it? I mean you can't get two black guys together without hearing it."

"You're not around enough black people. I hardly ever say it, neither does my wife."

"Really? You guys must be the exception, because I'm around black people every day, and it's just about all I hear. In fact, if it wasn't for black people, I think the word would be obsolete by now."

"Yeah, because you never use it," Bishop said sarcastically.

"Honestly, I don't. And most white people I know don't."

"Yeah, I believe that," Bishop said.

"I'm not saying they never use it. And there are some who use it a good deal, not as much as someone black, but they do use it. But for the most part, most of us, it's just not something we say."

"And that irritates you, don't it? You wanna say it so bad."

"I don't. But I'll admit it is hard to get through a rap song. And yeah, I listen to rap."

"A little bit too much, maybe."

"Maybe. But it makes me wonder why you guys are so bent on keeping this word alive."

"You don't need to worry about that. You just need to keep that word out of your mouth," Bishop said.

"Then it occurred to me, maybe it's a subconscious thing. Maybe it's because you never want anyone to forget about how guilty we should all feel about what happened to black people, about slavery and everything. As if black people are the only people anything bad ever happened to. So, whenever you see a black person, you have to hear that word, again and again and again. And the word triggers you to the past, and it's a past black people don't want to let go of, don't want to move on from. So, you say it, again and again and again. And then as soon as someone else says it, it's time for holy war."

Bishop would have to admit he himself didn't fully understand why so many black people used the word. He didn't remember the first time he ever heard it, but he did remember the first time he heard one black person call another that word. He was a child in Jamaica watching a movie, it was something from the seventies, some black exploitation movie. He heard one black man call the other that word, and he said it with venom. At the age of five, Bishop was confused. Why would he call him that? It just didn't make sense. In Jamaica it was not common to hear black people call each other that word. When he came to America that all changed. He heard black people call each other that word all the time. And as he assimilated into African American culture, he learned to find the word less offensive when said by another black person, but he still found it offensive. He never liked being called it, even when said affectionately.

"No, it's slang," he said to McNally. "It's slang that's reserved only for a certain people. They're women who call each other bitch, and they mean no offense to each other when they say it. I've even heard women call each other cunt. But if a man were to call a woman that it would be offensive. Some white people call each other rednecks. Sometimes I've heard them say it proudly. But if I were to call that same person a redneck that would be offensive. It's like I have a brother. And I might curse my brother out. I might say it affectionately or I might say it with real intent, but that's between me and my brother. But if someone else said those same words to my brother, it's going to be war. Because he don't have the right. This is something all people do."

"That maybe. But I think you guys took that word to a whole other level," McNally said.

"Well you don't need to understand it. You just need to understand that you can't say it."

"I don't need to say it. And I'd prefer a world where that word didn't exist."

"You keep getting caught up on the word, but what does it matter if the word exists if the meaning of the word still exists?" McNally looked at him a bit confused. "You say you don't say the word, and I'll take your word for that. But you still feel the word. You don't call black people that word, but you feel it when you see one. You felt that word when you saw my son, and you followed him, and you pulled him over, and you shot him seven times, and you watched him die."

Every time Bishop repeated that refrain it raised McNally's blood pressure. It was untrue. It was a bastardization of the events. "That's not what happened. And I get it. You want me to say that I killed your son because he was black, because maybe that will make you feel justified in doing whatever it is you wanna do. But I can't do that. I can't. Because that's not true."

Bishop looked at McNally and was still trying to determine if McNally was lying to him or lying to himself. Perhaps he had said the lie so much he had forgotten that it was a lie. Perhaps he was addicted to the lie. Maybe the lie was like alcohol and its pull was so strong it seeped into your DNA and you passed it on through the generations. "You know, when I think about white people, I remember this thing this dread said to me one time, years ago, in a barbershop—and I never forgot it. He said you were like a family at a dinner table. Big family. Mother,

Father, lots of kids. And the family has a main business, and the business basically is crime—robbing, murdering—like the mob. Call them a mob family. Everybody in the family knows about the business, but you talk about the business like it's this honorable thing, or you mostly don't talk about it at all, and you act like all the money that comes in comes from all your legit businesses, acting like the legit businesses weren't funded from the dark business, and isn't just a way to wash the dark business money. Mom and Pop found the business but now you have the older brothers and sisters who are running it, getting their hands dirty. Then you have the middle kids who aren't involved in running it but are in support of the family business. They run the legit businesses and wash the money. You have other middle kids who are just happy to be in the family and act like they don't know anything about anything. You have some middle kids who will talk up about the family from time to time—but they still mostly fall in line. Then you got the younger kids, who are at the other end of table and they're upset about the family and they're always telling the family how messed up they are, and they protest the family every chance they get. They make family dinners interesting because they are always arguing with the older kids, while most of the middle kids they stay quiet. But the one thing with the family is, whether they support the business or not, whether they stay quiet or not, when dinner is served, everybody eat . . . everybody eat . . . except for one kid. Call them the black sheep of the family. They could be an old kid, middle kid, young kid, they can pop up anywhere. The family disown this kid and they don't invite this kid to dinner anymore because when they come to dinner, they don't eat . . . they turn the table over. They don't make anybody eat." Bishop let that sit for a second. "Unfortunately, they're not that many black sheep out there."

53

Race was never formally brought up in McNally's home when he was a child. It was like learning your first language. No one really teaches it to you. They just speak it around you, and you absorb it. At three years old he already knew that he was white and that it meant something good. He couldn't remember the first time he saw a black person, whether it was in person or on television. He remembered, though, always having an upsetting feeling when he saw or thought of them. The word black was disconcerting in and of itself. It evoked feelings of the night and darkness and things that were scary. Most times he saw black people they were doing scary things; getting arrested for robbing people, killing people, raping and selling drugs. Then there was always an aggressiveness in how they spoke. And when a black person was in the news, his mother would always sigh and shake her head, as if she was always holding herself back from saying something.

He would hear the word 'nigger' flung about here and there, usually by a male relative or friend of the family—and it could have been said positively like, "Boy, that nigger can run." But his mother would always admonish them. "We don't use that word in this house." Sometimes he'd hear the word monkey referred to a black person. McNally read a book on Irish American history once, and he saw newspaper cartoons from the 1800s where the Irish were drawn in a simian fashion and were openly compared to monkeys. They used to have Vaudeville minstrel shows where Irishmen were portrayed as illiterate, drunken and lecherous and prone to abandoning their families as well.

He remembered being around six and watching boxing with his father and his father's father, and an announcer said Muhammad Ali was the greatest boxer of all time, and his grandfather balked. "The greatest—that draft dodging bastard. A man who dodges his duty to his country gets no respect from me."

"He didn't believe in the war," McNally's father said, more so playing devil's advocate than opposition.

"Who believes in war? Nobody believes in war. You go to war because it's your duty, because your country demands it, because it's where you lay your head and reap your sustenance."

"Maybe he didn't feel it was his country."

"It's not his country—but he's happy to make his money in America and become a millionaire. And I bet if they kicked his black ass out, he'd fight like bloody hell to get back in. No, that loudmouth gets no respect from me. The first and still the greatest heavy weight champion of all time . . . John L. Sullivan. Seventy-five rounds in Mississippi heat with Jake Kilrain. No gloves. No judges. You fight till the other man gives up or dies. That was a real fighter. That was a real man—c'mere Brian," he said to young McNally and McNally walked over, and his grandfather shook his hand. "Now you've shook the hand of the man who shook the hand of the man who shook the hand of the man who shook the hand of the man who shook the hand of the great John L. Sullivan." McNally looked at his grandfather utterly perplexed, and his grandfather and father laughed.

When McNally was ten one of his best friends was Jeffrey Morgan. Jeffrey was black. They were on the same little-league team and became close. Jeffrey used to come over after games and they'd play Super Nintendo. McNally's parents were fine with Jeffrey coming over and treated him well when he did. But they never wanted Brian going over his house and Brian would always have to come up with an excuse as to why he couldn't. His friendship with Jeffrey eventually faded away. That's how it was with black friends. He would meet them through school or work, and they'd be cordial and sometimes close, but it was never lasting.

Brian remembered when he watched the mini-series Roots. It was in middle school and it was during black history month. He was shocked by the brutality in it; the whipping scene and the foot chopping scene particularly stood out. And the over-seer on the plantation, he seemed to have an Irish accent. Brian was truly disturbed. When you watch a movie, you like to see yourself as the good guy, but all the white people seemed so bad. "Why did they do that Mom? Why did they treat them like that?" he asked his mother when he came home from school.

"Let me tell you something, it's sad and it's horrible, but you don't feel any way for that. You didn't do that. We didn't do that. That was a long time ago. And the history of the world is a history of people doing horrible things to each other. Look at the Jews, they've been oppressed for centuries, look at the holo-caust. You've seen pictures of the holocaust. The gas chambers. Look at the Irish and what we've been through. Eight hundred years of oppression by the British, and all we suffered when we first came to America. But you pick yourself up, you pull together and you move on and you move up. Black people never want to move on that's why they don't move up. They just want to keep talking about the past to hide their failures in the pres-ent."

"And I tell you, as bad as slavery was, you can argue they are better off for it. Look at them now compared to the rest of Africa," his father chimed in.

What his father said made sense to Brian. All he saw of the people in Africa were huts and starvation. Black people were doing much better in America. When they had finished watching the mini-series, they had a discussion in class about it. The black students dominated the discussion. When it came time for him to say something, Brian attempted to make the point his father made that maybe slavery wasn't all bad because black people were doing so much better than if they stayed in Africa. The looks and the verbal lashing he got for that one. He barely sur-vived. He learned a lesson. Never talk about race again. Black people didn't really want to talk to you about race anyway. They just wanted to talk to themselves and talk down to you.

McNally never dreamed of becoming a cop—though in the back of his head he always knew he would. The Irish have a long tradition in law enforcement. In the 1840s, during the famine years, close to two million Irish made their way to America. For many, the only work they could find was dangerous and low paying. They gladly took positions in the police and fire departments, as it provided a means of income and acceptance into American society. Ironically the police departments in Boston and New York were first created to contend with the unruly Irish immigrants. Police cars were pejoratively called paddy-wagons; paddy a shortened form of Patrick and a slur for Irishman. Once Irish policemen began having families, their children and their children, would follow suit in law enforcement. In many large cities, New York, Boston, Philadelphia, Chicago, the Irish dominated, and bagpipes became the staple of funeral marches.

McNally had two uncles, one on each side of the family, who were cops, one in Boston and one in Philadelphia, and he had a cousin who worked out of Midtown South. There were friends who he grew up with who went into law enforcement as well. His family always supported the police, the way you would support family, because they were family. When a police shooting happened, you defended your boys. There were times it looked bad—very bad. But you had learned not to rush to judgment and wait for the full investigation. Because though they may err and make terrible mistakes, you knew they were always operating from a place of good.

As much as law enforcement was familiar to Brian, it wasn't his first choice or his second, but he always knew it existed as an option. Like teaching for many, he saw law enforcement as his fallback. He wanted to be a baseball player first, and a lawyer second, but he was a middle child and seemed to be middling at everything he did.

His older brother Joseph was brilliant and always had a knack for computers and now worked for Google writing code—whatever that meant. His little sister Jessie was a great artist. Mom bought her a watercolor painting set when she was five and she never put the brush down. Brian was a fair student who was ecstatic whenever he got a B in school. He had some athletic ability and took to baseball at a young age—loved Derek Jeter—but was never good enough to go beyond his college team. He figured he'd study law but spent most of his time at SUNY Binghamton getting shit-faced at parties. He got shit-faced so much he figured he'd give bartending a go.

He met Meagan while bartending in Manhattan. She was a dancer. She made the chorus on a few Broadway plays. She had great legs. Beyond her smile that was the thing that drew him to her most. He worked on the docks with his father for a time but hated the work. Afterwards he gave construction work a spell; then Meagan became pregnant and he knew he needed something steady and secure with benefits. At twenty-six he turned to the thing he had been trying to avoid his adult life, and at thirty-four he killed a black teenager in the line of duty.

54

The afternoon sun shined through that small basement window. The day was not terribly hot, but it was humid, which felt worse. His sweat stayed on him like an extra layer of skin, then he sweat again, and another layer would come. To say nothing of the filth and the mold in the room. He became accustomed to inhaling must with every breath. A day plus without a shower, McNally could smell himself. He was rancid. He felt miserable, his ass was sore, his back was sore and, "I need to piss," he said to Bishop.

"You got water bottles," Bishop said and turned away and walked to the corner of the room where the window was.

McNally, sitting on the ground, awkwardly placed the opening of the eight-ounce bottle at the head of his penis and began relieving himself. It was an effort not to make a mess. He finished and screwed the cap back on the bottle. "What happens when I need to take a shit?" he asked Bishop.

Bishop turned back to him. "There are extra napkins in the bag."

"Napkins, that's thoughtful. But how am I supposed to wipe my ass?" McNally lifted his handcuffed hands.

Bishop hadn't considered that but, "I'm not taking off your handcuffs so you're gonna have to figure that out. Having a nasty ass is the least of your problems." McNally looked at him disgusted. "Imagine how bad it was for people during the middle passage."

"The middle what?" McNally asked.

Bishop looked at him as if this was something he should know, when he realized, no he wouldn't. "It was the part of the slave trade when Africans were brought across the Atlantic in the bottom of slave ships, and they were chained together laying down, and they had to eat and piss and shit in the same place. Millions of people died during the middle passage."

"Okay," McNally said. McNally knew that slaves were brought on ships, he didn't know that part of their journey had a specific name. He had just learned something and felt like imparting a bit of knowledge himself. "The Irish were once slaves too you know." Bishop looked at him crossly. "It's true. They called it indentured servitude, but it was pretty much the same thing. You were treated the same, you had a master and you had to work for your freedom.

"During the famine, landlords were kicking people off their land and shipping them away to America in these things they used to call coffin ships because so many people died during the trip. Conditions sounded a lot like that middle passage you were talking about. Then there were the Irish that came and had nothing and had to do whatever jobs they could to survive. And they had the Irish doing jobs slave owners wouldn't even have their slaves doing, because their slaves were their investment. But they didn't care if the Irishman got sick and died, just get another Irishman, hundreds were coming every day. We were disposable."

Bishop had a look of dumbfound incredulity.

"The Irish faced great oppression too. We were at the bottom of society. No Irish need apply, that's what they used to put in the want ads. And they wouldn't hire you or rent to you if you had an Irish sounding name. We had to scrap and fight for everything. And in two generations we pulled together and pulled ourselves out of the muck."

"Are you trying to tell me, you're not white?" Bishop asked.

That question seemed out of left field. "No—I'm white," McNally said assertively.

"Are the Irish then some lesser white? Are you sub-white?"

That offended McNally. "No—we're white," he said with a bit of vinegar.

"Then what the hell are you talking about?"

"I'm talking about real oppression."

"Real oppression? As opposed to what?" Bishop asked.

"The British robbed us of our wealth and resources and made us subsist on mainly potatoes, and when the famine came, they left us to starve, hundreds of thousands. When the Irish came to America, they didn't come in chains, but they didn't have much of a choice either."

"Were you sold and auctioned off?" Bishop asked.

"No."

"Were you chained?"

"No,"

"Were you whipped?"

"Sometimes."

"Did they take your language from you?"

"Partly."

"Did they take your religion?"

"They tried—believe me they tried."

"Did they take your children?"

"No."

"I don't know much about Irish people and everything you went through, but how are you gonna tell me that it compares in anyway shape and form to what black people went through?"

"I didn't say it was the same. I said we suffered too."

"And how many generations you said it took you to get out?"

"Two," McNally answered.

"Two generations compared to four hundred plus years. You see when you tell me that, you're telling me one of two things. Either you're telling me that you are better than me or you were less oppressed than me. Which one is it?" Bishop leaned in and looked squarely at McNally. "Are you better than me?"

"No . . . I'm not better than you," McNally said. "And no, the Irish weren't slaves, but we faced great oppression, and we didn't choose to sit and wallow in it."

"I tell you, you people," Bishop began saying.

"Yeah, *you* people too. You always have an answer don't you. For everything there's an excuse. It's slavery, it's poverty, it's living conditions. It's the white man. Four hundred plus years and it's the same thing. You're like a comic book with a super villain you can always put all the bad shit on. I dropped outta school, the white man did it. I ain't got a job, the white man did it. Got my girl pregnant and I'm not taking care of the kid because of the white man. I sell drugs because the white man sent me the drugs. I shot a man. The white man made me do it. The white man made the gun. Who made me pull the trigger? The white man in my head."

"You are the greatest murderer, robber and rapist this world has ever seen. Everywhere in this world you have gone, you have brought destruction. You think you're strong but you're weak, because you don't know how to be at peace. You want all the riches in this world—and you're so full of your own shit, you even want all the blame. White man, I ain't gotta put shit on you, you ain't done, because you've done enough."

"And when are you going to start taking responsibility for the shit you do?"

"You murdered my son. Take responsibility for that," Bishop roared.

"Believe me, I am sorry. I wish to God I went straight home

that night. You think I wanted any of this? You think I wanted my entire life upended. My name and face splattered across every newspaper and website. People writing vile things about me. Sending death threats to my wife and kids. My son and daughter—"

"Man fuck your sob story. You're not sorry you killed my son and destroyed my family. All you care about is what it did to you and yours. You know what it feels like to see a video of the boy you raised since he came out of his mother's womb dying on the street, and to watch that woman cry herself to sleep every night? No, you don't, you can't because you still have your son. What's his name, Aiden? How old is he, eight?" Bishop saying McNally's son's name and knowing his age raised all the hairs on McNally's body. He remembered that video of the car outside of his house with the man with the gun while his kids played, and his blood boiled. "Yeah officer McNally, I know who your son is. I debated it. Maybe I should have taken him instead. Maybe, I still should."

"Don't you fucking touch my kid," McNally raged, and tried to get to his feet but the chains would only permit him to get to his knees.

Bishop pointed the gun at him. "Sit yo' bumboclaat down," Bishop said commandingly. McNally stared at him menacingly before receding to the floor. "Look at you. Look at the fire in your eyes. That shit burn don't it? Just the thought of it. It burn real bad."

"Fuck you," McNally said. "I swear to God if you touch my kid, I will kill every single fucking one of you."

"Oooooo. Now we getting somewhere. Now I'm seeing the real you, McNally. Just the thought of your kid getting hurt and you're ready to kill everybody."

"And I see the real you," McNally shot back. "You would threaten an innocent child."

"What about my child? My child wasn't innocent?" McNally was silent. "But don't worry though. I'm not like you. I don't kill children. But now try and imagine my everyday reality."

"I don't give a fuck about your reality."

"Don't give a fuck. Why? Is your anger worth more? Is your pain worth more? Are you more human? That's it isn't it? Deep down inside you still think you're better."

There was an extended moment before McNally answered, "No . . . and yes. When a white person dies, I care more than when a black person dies. I do. And so do you, in the reverse. And don't lie and say different."

"I'm not telling you to love my son like I love my son. You can never do that. But I'm asking, no I'm demanding you respect my son, because his life was precious, and you don't just take it, just because you decide to feel threatened."

"Yeah, life is precious," McNally said. "So how about the six-year-old girl who was killed in that drive-by? Or the three kids who were killed at the basketball game uptown. Or the old woman coming home from church? Were their lives precious too?"

"Yes."

"So where are their killers? Why don't you have them handcuffed so you can preach to them just how precious life is?"

"Because they didn't kill my son. You did," Bishop answered.

"Oh, so you only care about your son. Or you only care that a white cop killed your son. Because you damn sure don't care about all the other killings going on," McNally said.

"I care about it."

"Really, because I never hear any black people talk about it."

"You're not listening. We talk about it all the time. They constantly have stop the violence rallies," Bishop said.

"Oh those, those are bullshit," McNally said dismissively.

"They're not bullshit."

"They're bullshit, they're bullshit. I've been to them. I was assigned to a few when I was a uniformed officer in my first five years. The parents of gun violence are there, maybe a few of their family members, a few politicians who wanna get their name in the press show up, and like a hundred other people at most. That's it. A six-year-old girl was killed and that's it. Half her head is spilled on the playground and that's it. A cop kills someone, who a lot of times was probably a gang banger, one of the same ones who would have shot that little girl, and not given a shit about it, and you raise holy hell. Thousands of people show up. You riot for days. The only time black lives matter to you is when someone white takes it. That's why no one takes you seriously. And this is not just a cop thing, or a black and white thing. I've been around other people, Asian, Indian, Arab, even Hispanic, and a lot of times they see shootings and they just roll their eyes. They tell me we support you. They tell me, it's just black people being black people. In and out of uniform people tell me these things. I'm telling you, no one takes you seriously. They don't. Because you want people to treat you better than you treat yourself and shit don't work like that."

"Well shit's about to change," Moses said to himself as he stood outside the old office in the boiler room of the abandoned building listening to McNally and Bishop go at it. He enjoyed listening in on them. Part of him felt like joining in. However, he had more important things to get to.

Saquon, one of the young men, who had helped him kidnap McNally approached him. 'We're all upstairs, Soldier," he said.

"Good," Moses replied. "Let's go over the plan again for tomorrow."

55

Robert Ford Moses was born and raised in Brownsville, Brooklyn. He lived in a four-bedroom house three blocks from Marcus Garvey Village. His family had lived there before there was a Marcus Garvey Village, before many of the housing developments were built. It was his mother's mother, Mary's, house. She and her husband Edwin bought it in 1963 just as the last of the Jews and East Germans were moving out. They had four children, three boys and one girl, Moses's mother, Karen.

Edwin worked for sanitation and Mary worked as a grade schoolteacher. They worked hard, kept their children out of trouble and were exceedingly proud on the day they paid off their mortgage. Edwin had a stroke and died a year later. All the boys became men and moved away. Karen married Jerome Moses, a brick layer, from Bedstuy and being unable to live on their own, they moved into her mother's house. It became their house when Mary like her husband died from a stroke. Karen and Jerome had three children in a five-year window; a girl, a boy, a girl. His father died when Moses was five years old. He worked construction and worked very hard to get on a union job. He was one of the few black men on the site. He died after a cinder block fell on his head from three stories up. The casket was closed. Her parents had worked hard to own their home outright. However, Karen had to take out a mortgage on the house to make ends meet, as working as a nurse's aid wasn't enough to take care of three children on her own.

Moses had vision. All his life he had exceptional eyesight. He could see things, yards off, most people couldn't. Most of his childhood and adolescence he didn't pay much attention to it, as people, beyond his mother didn't pay attention to him. He wasn't the most handsome boy. He was by no means ugly, just unremarkable. He had a sullen disposition and rarely smiled. He was one of those black boys who walked about with their lips slightly pout, unknowingly sour. He wasn't great at sports. Even when he shot up past six feet the summer after ninth grade. He had large hands but couldn't dribble a ball if his life depended on it. He had a lengthy phase of being lanky. He was skinny and wore size thirteen shoes that looked like boats on his feet.

It was hard growing up as a boy in Brownsville. Coming home was a challenge. You try to avoid other boys your age and older at all costs. Moses remembered the first time he got robbed. It was fifth grade and he was riding home on the bus with two other friends. They were in their own world talking about video games, when he felt something in his pocket. It was a hand, but it wasn't his. He looked to his left and an older boy, a teenager, bigger than him, had put his hand in his pocket. He did it casually, with no announcement or imminent malice. He did it simply as if it was his pocket, but with a sense of pride and glee as he talked to his friend.

Moses was shocked. He was too shocked to resist or even say something. He simply looked at the boy as if to say what are you doing, and the boy looked back at him, as if to say, "yeah, I'm robbing you, and you can't do shit about it." He stole two dollars, forty cents and Moses's bus pass. Then he and his friend got off and went on their way, as if this was simply what they did. Moses's friends saw, but they were just as shocked and quiet.

When Moses got off the bus, he cried all the way home. His friends couldn't console him. He had that two dollars and was going to buy a slice of pizza and a soda. He had been looking forward to it all day. He felt violated. The worst part was how helpless he felt to stop it. He wished he was a superhero, or a villain, it didn't matter. He just wanted power. He wished he was Wolverine. He wished he could heal from anything and had adamantium steel claws. He would find those boys and anyone like them and tear them apart.

He hated them—young black boys—not all of them, not

boys like himself, but the ones who were in gangs, and those that weren't in gangs but acted like it. He hated how they walked, he hated how they talked, he hated how they dressed, he hated how they breathed. He hated Hip-Hop, he hated Tupac, he hated Biggie. He never listened to anything they said. He saw how they looked. They looked like the boys around the way terrorizing him. They celebrated those boys. What about boys like him? Boys who weren't in gangs who didn't celebrate thug life but were into comic books and video games and anime. All he wanted to do was go to school and come home safely, without the ever-present anxiety of what might happen today.

He hated Day Lights Saving time, because it stole an hour from the day. It was dark by 4:30 from fall to spring, and he never left his house when it was dark. They were even worst when it was dark. Like wolves he could hear them outside the house, howling, laughing—gunshots. He went straight to school and came straight home, that was his life. Karen saw her son's sadness but was happy at least he stayed in the house. Boys in the house aren't getting into trouble outside.

His mother bought him a pair of Jordans for his fourteenth birthday. He had begged her, and she saved up and got them. Moses didn't think he could have loved an object more than he loved those Jordan XIs, white with the patent leather black trim. He looked at them all night. He would breathe them in, and the smell, the leather, the newness, would intoxicate him. He wore them to school the next day. His friends were amazed. People who never looked at him before looked at him, even girls, even the pretty ones. His exuberance ended on his way home. A group of boys encircled him.

"Yo, he got the new Jordans." "Yo, those are dope, son." "Can I see them?" "No." "C'mon just take them off for a bit, I just wanna see them." "No." "Whatchu scared?" "Whatchu scared for?" "Ain't nobody trying to take your shit, we just wanna see them." "No." There were four of them. Moses paid too much mind to the two in front. One of the boys behind him threw a punch connecting to the back of his head and the side of his left ear. It stung. Moses stumbled and they all ravaged him, throwing punches in all directions. He felt like falling, he felt like crying. He remembered being in fifth grade and how that boy took his money, and he let him, and how he had agonized about that. A voice inside said, hit back—hit back. He threw a punch without looking, it was wild, but it had force and it connected. One of the boys was staggered. Moses surprised them, he surprised himself. He threw another punch and connected with the sternum of another boy. Moses was skinny but there was power in his large hands—and he let them fly. This was a fight and not a massacre, but they were four and he was one. They overcame him, they knocked him to the ground and kicked him repeatedly. Two of them grabbed each leg and pulled the sneakers from off his feet. They were pissed to find out his shoes were size thirteen and didn't fit any of them. One of them threw them back at Moses, and another stepped on them when they walked away laughing. They left Moses on the ground, bruised and beaten but not crying—not crying. He picked himself up and hobbled home.

His mother and sisters were distraught when they saw his swollen face. His mother bemoaned what had become of Brownsville and she wanted to call the police, but Moses wouldn't let her, and he wouldn't tell her who the boys were who did this to him. Moses just wanted to go to his room and rest. He looked at the Jordans. One of them had a large footprint stamped across its face. They were defiled and the thing that he had loved so much the night before, he now hated. He threw them in the closet and never wore them again. He never wore Jordans again period. He developed a hatred for the brand.

Three days later Moses went back to school. His lip was still swollen, his body was still bruised, he hobbled when he walked, but he walked with his head up, and paid no mind to the chatter around him. On his way home he saw those same boys, and he walked right by them. He saw in their faces that they were bruised too—not as badly—but he had got them, he had got them. They said nothing to him, he said nothing to them. They laughed after he had walked away but that didn't matter. He got them and he felt proud, and consequently they never troubled him again. These were the hardest days of his life.

When he graduated high school, other than getting out of Brownsville, Moses didn't know what he wanted to do. He wanted to go to college, but he didn't have the money or the grades to go away—not even to a state school. The best he could do was a city college, but that wouldn't get him out of Brownsville. An army recruiter was at the subway station and he called to him one day. Moses had seen him before and had always passed him by. Moses didn't know why he stopped that day, but he did, and it changed his life.

56

Circumstances do not make the man they only better reveal the man to himself. Moses discovered a talent he never knew he possessed. He could endure, mentally, physically, just about anything. You don't know this until you're pushed to your very limits, pushed your muscles to failure and that place beyond failure. The Marines did that. Three months of recruit training, in Garden City, New Jersey, then three months of infantry training at Camp Pendleton in California, then seventeen days of negative eighteen degree temperatures for cold weather training in Hokkaido, Japan; digging a hole in the snow to make a bed to sleep, using his body heat as a radiator; fighting off hypothermia and frost bite, learning to ski, not for fun but simply to be able move; melting snow for water, living off the land. Hell is not hot, hell is cold, and after completing cold weather training, Moses knew he had the will to survive anything.

The first time a bullet went by him in live combat it sounded like the pitch of a steel mosquito. He was slightly shaken and asked himself what was that? Was that what he thought it was? Yes. And a few inches over and that would have been his head, that would have been his ass. That was how close death was. The 2nd battalion, 4th Marines had deployed to Ramadi, Iraq a month earlier, planning to win over the people by restoring government services and economic activity disrupted by the 2003 invasion. However, people don't take too kindly to being invaded. It's akin to raping someone then trying to be their friend afterwards.

Insurgents kicked off a jihad in the beginning of spring. Moses was in the middle of it. There was an uncanny sense of focus like he had never experienced. His vision got better, his hearing was more precise, but more aptly how he gathered and processed information improved. He had a talent for handling chaos. He saw through it. He could see the order in it and focus with a clear head on what needed to be done. They fought street by street for four days. By his count he killed at least four insurgents. Twelve marines in his battalion died, one of them just a few feet behind him, exactly where he was seconds before.

57

Your first enlistment contract with the Marines is for essentially eight years. The first four years is active duty, the second is inactive. You are home but can be called up whenever needed. He was home but it didn't feel like home anymore. Moses had always been a shy and sullen boy. He had never been good at talking to girls, even the ones he didn't like, and he was mortified around the ones he did. He remembered in high school the feeling he got trying to speak to a girl, and she looked at him, as if to say, "how dare you think you can talk to me," and how she laughed with her friends when he walked away. That look, and their laughter, traumatized him. He never forgot it. Going to war and coming back didn't change that. He was a bigger man than he was before he left. Physically he was bigger, roughly fifteen pounds, all muscle. Mentally he was smarter and more confident. However, all the skills he had acquired weren't applicable at home.

At home he was still shy sullen Moses, that's who people expected, and he didn't know how to act differently. He didn't know how to laugh with them and fully speak his mind like he did with his brothers in the corps. He hated who he was when he was with them and by extension, he hated them. His mother could see that. He sounded happier when she spoke to him by phone when he was away. She mentioned him going away to school. He could afford to go now. The Marines would pay for it. However, that seemed so utterly useless. He was beyond college. He had seen and learned more things in his four years than most college graduates would learn in a lifetime. His choice was clear—he re-enlisted.

58

Each Marines battalion selected infantrymen at the rank of lance corporal and above for sniper training. Because of his great marksmanship, Moses was recommended and accepted into the scout sniper screener. The course was known for having a high wash-out rate. Of the forty-nine marines that started the course, twelve remained after the first day. By the end of the course, ten completed the screener and nine were selected to join the platoon.

"Everyone wants to be a sniper until it's time to put out," his instructor always said. Sprinting in ninety-degree weather with full gear; wading through a pig pond (a fetid pool of muddy water and rotting vegetation); doing pushups till failure drenched in muck and sweat; being up two hours before dawn to be ready to shoot on a range as soon as the sun rose; learning how to camouflage equipment, building your ghillie suit, a living piece of camouflage made from plants native to the location; learning to hide from people who are hunting you; stalking your prey by laying prone, head to the ground and using your elbows and knees to move. This was the hardest thing Moses had ever done, but he was determined that it would not break him. This was where he went from being a PIG, Professionally Instructed Gunmen, to a HOG, Hunter of Gunmen. He received his Hog's Tooth, a single bullet, 7.62×51mm NATO round with a 550-nylon cord through it to wear around his neck. He never took it off.

A Scout Sniper Platoon was composed of eight to ten scout sniper teams. Typically, each team had two members, a sniper and a spotter. The sniper carried a long-range, specially-made sniper rifle, such as the M40 along with his side arm. The spotter had an M4 Carbine rifle along with a high-powered spotting scope to spot targets and follow-up shots for the shooter. The shooter-spotter relationship was not always set; some platoons had designated shooters, others had team members switch off. Such was the case with Moses and Caleb. Caleb Joshua Jones was white and pale and would turn red in the hot desert sun. Caleb was from Jefferson City, Missouri. Moses and Caleb couldn't have come from two different parts of the country, but like any great spotter-sniper tandem they became great friends.

59

After fifteen years in the corps, Moses had risen to the rank of staff sergeant. He had two bronze stars with valor, and Caleb and he had eighty-one confirmed kills to their credit. There were many more unconfirmed but only God knew that number. Moses imagined there would be a proper accounting one day. Moses had put on weight throughout his years of service, each year adding another layer of muscle, and the skinny kid who had joined the Marines was now a formidable man.

Moses had every intention to make the military a lifelong career, but Caleb decided not to re-enlist. They both survived an IED explosion—and it was their third. Fortunately, the third time wasn't the charm, but how charmed could they be, how long could they cheat death or dismemberment? After collecting the remains and viscera of their friends for the umpteenth time Caleb had had enough. A feather had fallen. He couldn't bear this weight anymore. He also had a wife who was close to leaving him and three kids who he had barely seen grow up. Moses had no such attachments at home, but he felt attached to Caleb and once he was gone serving just wasn't as much fun.

Then the call came. His mother was sick. She had stage four pancreatic cancer. Pancreatic cancer was one of those that didn't reveal itself until it was damn near too late. It had only a twenty percent one-year survival rate. There was a sliver of hope, however. There was a new drug that could stop the spread of the disease. It wasn't a cure, but it could halt the progression enough to buy her time. It could buy her years even. It was FDA approved but Medicare didn't cover all of it. They would have to pay out of pocket roughly three thousand a month.

Both his sisters had families of their own and were just keeping their heads above water with their own bills. It was an egregious amount of money, and Moses couldn't fathom why they would charge so much for something that could save someone's life. It was unconscionable. But there was no one in the world he loved more than his mother. Moses didn't have a family and had saved most of his fifteen years of service pay. He agreed to pay for the treatment. For six months things were good, and his mother was doing well.

He was out in the field training new scout snipers when he was told to return to barracks immediately. It was his sister. "Mom is gone," she said. Moses was stunned. He had spoken to her a week before and she had been doing well. But it wasn't the cancer that killed her. She was killed during a drive by shooting in Brownsville, where she had lived all her life, right there on Mother Gaston Boulevard; named after Rosetta Gaston, the matriarch of Brownsville. She was an activist, and a contemporary of Carter G. Woodson and Mary McLeod Bethune. She founded the Brownsville Heritage House in the public library. She taught all who came to her about black history. Mother Gaston had taught Moses's mother as well. Moses was heartbroken, devastated to the point of being demented. Those same boys who had harassed him growing up, who he left and joined the Marines to get away from had killed his mother. They had taken the one thing he truly loved—and he hated them even more.

60

A few days after he buried his mother, Moses took a flight and met up with Caleb who had settled with his family in Winston Salem, North Carolina. After consoling his friend, over drinks at a local bar, Caleb revealed that he was helping run drugs and guns for a Mexican cartel. Moses couldn't stop laughing until he realized Caleb was serious.

"Veteran Affairs sucks ass," Caleb said. "You give so much to this country and this is how they treat you. The politicians, the bureaucracy, it's all bullshit." It was US policy there were no troops in Yemen in 2007. Caleb and Moses knew that was bullshit, because they were there. "We bombed that place every night for two weeks straight. I didn't believe in the mission anymore. All I cared about was my brothers over there. But then we would lose brothers, and more would come and we would lose them too, and it was a never-ending cycle. All for what? I can't think of one good, lasting thing we've done. What did all those men die and get maimed for?

"And now I can't stand being around regular people. I'm sitting here, listening to them talk about the Bachelor. These people have no clue what's going on in the real world. America is in this bubble that's one big reality show. And they're all liars, Democrats, Republicans. They have their heads so far up their asses, and I got tired of all the lies. I didn't want to become a cop or a fed. I was tired of the bureaucracy, and my skills don't translate well into the private sector. I didn't know what to do with myself. I was depressed for a while but then a few months ago me and Rodriguez met up and had drinks like we are now. You remember Rodriguez?" Moses nodded yes. He was another member of their scout sniper platoon. He had left the Marines three years prior and had been working with the Cartel for two years. "He brought me in," and now Caleb was offering Moses the same opportunity. "We do what we were trained to do. We take out Targets that need to be taken out and cover our team when deals are going down—and get paid a shit ton more for it, with way less risks." This was all very overwhelming for Moses, and with the recent death of his mother, he told Caleb, his head wasn't in the right space to do that kind of work right now. Caleb understood and told Moses he was there for him whenever he needed him.

61

"How you want it Soldier?" The barber asked, as Moses settled into his chair.

Moses smiled. "What gave it away?"

"You're a big man. You don't get that big unless you been in the forces or you been away. And you walk and sit too straight for that."

"I could be a cop."

"Nah. You don't read like it. Cops always act a little superior. And you never have to figure them out. Whenever they talk, somehow or another they'll bring up they're a cop—always. Few times I cut army boys, I don't get that. They're usually real chill with it. Never bring it up." Moses was amazed at how astute the barber was. "So how do you want it?" the barber asked again.

"Just cut it real low," Moses said, and closed his eyes.

The code on the street was no snitching. The police had no clue who his mother's killer was. However, if you're in a barbershop, at the right time someone might reveal things to you, without you even asking. Two young men walked in and took a seat on the padded bench.

"They was straight "whylin', yo,"

"Yo, they lit the block up, and didn't even get ma dude."

"Yeah, he grabbed big girl, and used her as a shield on some straight bitch shit. She took two shots and still lived."

"Yeah, that old woman wasn't so lucky though."

Moses eyes opened. Did he just hear what he thought? It had to be. The circumstances were too similar. He looked in the barbershop mirror and could see the two young men behind him. They both couldn't be more than nineteen.

"What caused it though?"

"I heard they was beefing on the gram, going at it for a while then shit popped off."

They? They. He knew who they were. That one, the one on the left, with locks, and the black hoodie and the Jordan ones, he knew.

Moses got his cut, tipped the barber and left, but only to go across the street to the pizzeria. He sat on a stool that gave him a view out the window at the barbershop. Over an hour and five slices later, Jordans and locks and his friend came out the shop. Moses left the pizzeria and followed them from across the street and half a block down. He followed them for six blocks until they got to one of the NYCHA complexes. They greeted their friends in the courtyard. "Whud up Q?" Someone greeted him. That was his name. His friend from the shop remained in the courtyard and Q went inside the nearest building. This was where Moses would lose him. Moses looked too conspicuous to follow him inside. He would wait for the right moment and get him alone.

The right time came three days later. Moses bought a NYCHA baseball cap he saw selling on eBay. He also bought a tool bag and stuffed it with a bunch of tools. He sat in his mother's car outside of Q's building waiting for him to appear. When he did, Moses left the car and followed him inside. With the hat and tool bag, Moses looked like a maintenance worker. Two women in the lobby asked him if he was coming to fix their apartment. They talked about moldy pipes and water damage in the ceiling. He asked for their apartment numbers and told them he would be up shortly, while keeping an eye on Q who was waiting for the elevator. The elevator arrived and Q got on and Moses got on with him—just the two of them.

After two flights Moses pushed the stop button. "What the fuh—? Yo, ma dude, whatchu doing?" Q said. Moses said nothing. He turned and faced him and gave Q a moment to absorb what he was getting into. "Ma nigga, what's good?"

"The shooting on Mother Gaston, two weeks ago, who did it?" Moses asked calmly.

"What? I don't know what you talking about." Q tried to push the button to get the elevator moving but Moses blocked him.

"You know," Moses said.

"I don't know shit you talking about. Now move, I ain't trying to be stuck in this elevator."

"We'll move once you tell me what I need to know."

"Yo, yo, yo. I don't know who you think you is."

"Good."

"But you don't know me, yuh heard. You don't know who I run with."

"I don't give a shit. Shooting, Mother Gaston, two weeks ago—who?"

"What are you, a cop?"

"It doesn't matter. Mother Gaston, two weeks ago, who?"

"I told you, I don't know shit." He tried to push past Moses and push the button, but it was literally like trying to move a brick wall. Moses put his hand on his chest and moved his 155-pound frame and slammed him against the wall, pinning him there with one hand. Q was astonished he couldn't move. He hadn't been held against his will like this since he was a child.

"Mother Gaston, two weeks ago?"

"Yo, I'ma fucking kill you. You put your hands on me."

"Are you threatening me?" Moses asked.

"Hell yeah. I'ma—" Before he could finish Moses gave him a slap with his large hands flush across his face.

It was like getting an electric shock. Everything lit up. His eyes opened wide. "Oh shit. Oh shit. Yo, yo, yo, you are dead, ma—"

"That sounded like another threat," Moses said, and slapped him again, harder this time, so hard his entire face was on fire, and the electric currents went throughout his body, and it took all his intestinal fortitude not to pee himself. "Do you wanna threaten me again?" Moses asked.

Q didn't say anything, he just huffed and seethed.

"Good. Now Mother Gaston, two weeks ago, who?"

"I told you, I don't know."

Moses became enraged and grasped his throat, with his other hand, under the jaw squeezing his larynx, cutting off his air. "I'm getting tired of this shit." He loosened his hold to allow Q to answer.

"Yo, you can't do this to me. This ain't right. I got rights."

"You got the right to breathe also, how's that working for you right now."

Moses was about to grip his throat again, when Q gave in. "Alright, alright. It was them CMK niggas," he said.

This sounded foreign to Moses. "Who?"

"CMK. The ones over at K house. Moses still looked confused. "McKay Houses. Claude McKay projects."

Now Moses understood. "Good. Who did the shooting?"

"I heard it's the one who runs it now. Saquon."

"Good. Good." Moses released him. "Thank you," he said.

"Damn, you almost ripped my throat out."

"Remember that feeling, because if you're lying to me, I'm coming back for you."

Moses pushed the button allowing the elevator to move,

when Q said under his breath, "Not unless I come for you first." Moses heard that and turned back to him.

"You don't have to come for me. I'm right here. Is there something you wanna do?" Q was trying to look hard but was silent. Moses put his hand behind his back and gripped his Colt 1911 under his shirt. "Just give me a reason," he said. "Just one. I want to, so bad."

Looking at the intensity in his eyes, Q realized this was no idle threat. "We good man, we good."

"Good." Moses replied. "I think you'll know to keep this to yourself. Don't let me come back for you." The elevator arrived at the next floor and Moses walked out as other people, angry with the elevator being delayed, got in.

The next day, Moses drove to North Carolina and met with Caleb. He needed guns. Caleb asked him why he needed them. He told him he had found his mother's killers, and Caleb told him to kill them all.

62

The Claude McKay Houses existed on two square blocks located between Livonia and Riverdale Avenues and Powell and Sackman streets. It was built in 1956 during the public housing boom. It was comprised of three buildings; buildings one and two which were fourteen stories tall, and building three which was sixteen stories. The buildings had been in severe disrepair for years. Especially building three, which was a recurrent fixture on local news as an example of the failures of public housing. After Hurricane Sandy building three went from disrepair to disaster and it was closed, fenced off and boarded up. Only buildings one and two remained in the complex. All the members of CMK crew lived in either buildings one or two.

They were all in the courtyard, roughly twenty of them. They were roughly two hundred and fifty yards off. Moses was on the roof of the building two blocks over. He had them in his sights, his eye behind the scope of a modified AR-15 assault rifle. He imagined he could kill ten of them, at the very least five; Saquon first, then at least four others before they all scattered. He knew who Saquon was. He had been scouting the crew for days now, getting a sense of their movements and had heard him answer to that name many times.

The cross hair hovered over the back of Saquon's head. Moses took a deep breath, steadied his aim and was prepared to pull the trigger when a group of women with young children came into the courtyard. They might get caught in the crossfire. If that happened, Moses would be no better than his Target. He recognized this strategy was inherently too risky, and there was no way to account for who might walk into the courtyard once he had begun firing. Saquon would live for another day.

Moses bought a used black sixteen-year-old Honda Accord he saw at a gas station with its price and owner's number written on the back window. It was 2,100 dollars and had near 150,000 miles, but still drove well, and still had a kick when it accelerated. That was good. Most importantly it was nondescript and unremarkable. No one should see it coming and should forget what it looked like if they ever did. He didn't put plates on it. If the cops pulled him over, he'd tell them he had just bought it and was driving it home. Flashing them his military ID should take care of the rest.

A day later, he was following them. Saquon and another gang member were driving in a car. He had been following for a half hour now. He had his pistol at the ready and was just waiting for the right opening to do it—one shot one kill. Their car pulled over and Saquon got out and bought a bouquet of flowers from one of the street side vendors. *Oh, he has a girlfriend,* Moses thought, how sweet. It didn't matter. If he went to see her, Moses would put a bullet in his head right in front of her. He would kill the driver as well and then peel off.

Saquon got back into the car. Moses followed them as they turned onto Mother Gaston Boulevard. They stopped beside a store front, and Saquon got out with the flowers. There was no one else around. This was the moment. Moses would pull up, hit Saquon, then the driver and then peel off. He was just about to when he saw Saquon stoop over and place the flowers he bought on the ground. That was odd. Why would he do that? Then Moses recognized that Saquon had placed the flowers by a street side shrine, a shrine for someone who had died. Then he realized where he was. This was where she died. This was his mother's shrine. He watched Saquon kneel for a moment. What was he doing? Was he praying? He looked mournful. Was he crying? Moses couldn't be sure, but in the seconds he spent ruminating he lost his window. Saquon got back in the car and drove off, and Moses let them go.

He pulled over across the street and went to inspect the shrine. There were the flowers, along with three other bouquets just like it that had withered and turned black. Had Saquon been the one placing these flowers here? Moses didn't quite know what to make of this. He was both mad and meditative. Meditation won over. He would think on this. He saw a flyer for a meeting at the local church across the street stapled to a tree. It started in a half hour.

63

It was held in the church basement. There were stale bagels and donuts and bad coffee on a table in the back. Nevertheless, they were edible and the few people who attended the meeting ate them.

There were enough chairs set up to sit a hundred people. There were only about twenty-five there by Moses's count. Most were seniors in their late sixties and up; a few were in their forties, and fewer still in their late thirties, and that was it.

The week before they held a fashion show and the room was packed with a lot more people in their teens and twenties. Today they were discussing the educational crisis in the community. The speaker, Yalitza Noel, was in her late thirties. She was half Haitian half Dominican and all black, she joked. "My mother is a Dominican woman, my father is a Haitian man, they met on the same island, they had six children and we ranged in the spectrum. I fell somewhere in the middle. Every shade under the sun came from a black woman," she said.

She was a financial adviser, author and a historian, and she had grown up in Brownsville. She worked on Wallstreet and now wanted to use what she had learned to turn the neighborhood around. She spoke at a podium into a microphone, which was abysmal, sometimes screechingly loud and other times too low to hear anything. Eventually she ditched the microphone and projected with her natural voice and asked everyone to come forward and sit closer.

"In this country, in their lifetime, one in three black men will find themselves caught up in the criminal justice system. That is an astounding figure. But I want you to flip it. It also means that two out three black men will never be caught up in the criminal justice system. So, with all the forces and factors working to criminalize black men the vast majority will succeed. And believe me there is a system out there designed to criminalize black men, all black people, but our young men especially.

"In an average year the city spends some two hundred million dollars in police brutality settlements. This is to say nothing of the millions spent in overtime pay and for property damage incurred during protests whenever there is an unjust shooting. And this is more expensive in New York City because everything is more expensive in New York City, but this is a cost police departments throughout the country incur. Yet we see time and again police officers are not sanctioned for their actions. In fact, we have many officers with multiple complaints on their record, who've cost the city hundreds of thousands of dollars, working still. Now, don't you think given the hefty price it cost that someone would say, hey let's start punishing these few bad apples, as they like to call them, in order to dissuade this kind of behavior in the future, not because it violates people's civil and human rights but, because it's messing with our bottom line. But no, because it's much more important that they maintain this social order, and black people remain criminalized.

"These cities want to get tough on crime. We know that there is a direct connection between unemployment and crime. As unemployment goes down crime goes down. So, jobs fight crime better than cops. The city spends roughly 170,000 a year to jail one inmate. That's one phenomenal paying job. That's two great paying jobs. That's four good paying jobs, that's seven to eight jobs. That's men and women, working, taking care of their children, keeping them out of the system. That's roughly seventeen students put through one year of college. Now tell me, which do you think is a better allocation of taxpayer dollars if we truly wanted to stop crime? Exactly. The goal is not to stop crime. The goal is to create a pipeline of black people into the prison system to become essentially slave labor. More black men are in the prison system right now than there were at the height of enslavement. And it all begins in the schools. Seventy-five percent of people in prison are functionally illiterate. If you are behind by the time you are in third grade your likelihood of ending up in the system increases tenfold.

"We live in a society that doesn't celebrate intelligence. In fact, we shun intelligence. If you're smart, you're called a geek, a nerd, a weirdo. If I were to ask you, who will be the number one draft pick in the NBA this year many of you would know. But if I asked you to name me the student who aced his SATs and got into every Ivy League school, I'd be surprised if one of you knows. I know because I make it my business to. Now there's nothing wrong with acknowledging what we can do athletically, but if we only celebrate what we can do with our bodies and not what we do with our minds we remain reduced to beasts of burden.

"Eighty percent of our teachers are white, and most are liberal. Now most of us will take liberal over conservative, but that's like trusting the good cop over the bad, forgetting that both are trying to put you in jail. Being liberal doesn't mean you've given up your white privilege. Gentrification hasn't fully taken root in Brownsville yet, but it has throughout the rest of Brooklyn, making Brooklyn the most unaffordable place to live in the country. The majority of the gentrifiers are white and liberal. Do they care that they've priced the previous people out of anywhere decent to live leading to a spike of people living in the shelters and on the streets, which is why we have more homeless people now than we did during the great depression. No, they don't. They are the first ones to call the police on you. Knowing very well how perilous an encounter with the police can be. They move here but they don't send their children to the local schools, because they know the schools are abysmal. There are schools that only have five percent of their third graders passing math and an even more abysmal three percent in English."

"The system is failing them," someone shouted.

"No. I'd say the system is succeeding. It is doing what it was designed to do. The teachers don't believe in our children's ability to care enough about them. Their idea of educating our children is stepping on them during black history month and handing out pieces of cotton for them to touch, to remind them of what enslavement was like. Our children don't need to be taught what it was like to be enslaved, our children need to be taught what it was like to be great. They need to know that black people, African people, built some of the greatest and richest civilizations the world has ever seen. To accomplish greatness, you must see greatness. If as a child all you see is drug dealing and gangbanging all around you, you'll think that's all I can do. But if you see astronauts and mathematicians around you, you'll think I can go to the moon and beyond. Most people do as they're told, they do what they see, they live up to expectations, however high or low.

"But the true blame for all of this falls on ourselves. You can't expect your oppressor to properly educate your children. They never intended for us to learn how to read. And many of us are unfortunately functionally illiterate. You, we, must do that.

And we haven't been. We need to celebrate our intelligence. We must read to our children. We must teach them. It takes a village to raise a child and we need to become a village again."

After the meeting people approached Yalitza about her talk and shared their own horror stories about the education system. She listened attentively and took pictures with them. They also promised to come to her next meeting and bring more people.

"Especially the youth. They need to be here to hear this."

Moses waited until everyone who had wanted to speak to her had. "I enjoyed your presentation," he said.

"Thank you," she said.

"I didn't know a lot of what you said."

"Most of us don't."

"Are the schools that bad?"

"Yes, too many of them are."

Moses wanted to say more but his issues with talking to women crept back up. "Well thank you again," he said awkwardly.

"You're welcome." Moses began walking off. "And come back," she said. We'll be having these once a month.

"I will," he said.

64

Moses sat up in his mother's bedroom that night. It was his bedroom now. It was his house now. It was hard to sleep. He had been of such a single mind before. He wanted to kill Saquon; and was very happy to kill as many of the other boys in his gang with him. Then he saw Saquon place flowers at his mother's shrine, and he heard that woman speak, and his mind was a mess. Things didn't seem so simple anymore. When he finally went to sleep, he had a dream, more like he relived a memory.

Moses was an exceptional sniper, but he was not perfect. He

was in the Helmand Province in Afghanistan, prone on a dusty rooftop, in the Musa Qal'eh District, his eye behind the scope of his M40, his target, five hundred yards off, a known producer of IEDs. He was getting out of his car and about to get into a building. The window was tight but Moses had made shots like this before. Caleb gave him the go and Moses took it, and the wind shifted ever so slightly, and the target saw something on the floor and bent his head to look, and the bullet whizzed through his hair and into the head of the woman who had been walking behind him. She died instantly. Moses saw himself placing flowers at a shrine for her at the very place she died. He never did that, but he had never forgotten her—and she was not alone. He awoke.

Moses had never been one of those pro black people. He had as much praise as he had issues with his people—boys in gangs especially. Boys like Saquon, who killed his mother because he was out to kill another boy like Saquon. Funny. Those boys hated each other just as much as Moses hated them. Where did this hatred come from? What was this drive to see yourself and want to destroy it? Something that woman said kept reverberating. Most people do as they're told, they do what they see, they live up to expectations, however high or low.

He still wanted to kill Saquon but admittedly not as much as he had wanted to the day before. Today he wanted to know more about him. He was the head of the CMK crew, the Claude McKay Killers. They were a gang onto themselves, unaffiliated with any other. Ten years young, born where they got their name in the Claude McKay Houses. A few years ago, the Brooklyn District Attorney had led a raid and many of the older members had been arrested, along with their previous leader, and founder, Saquon's brother.

65

There were mostly women waiting for the bus. Many of them had young children. They were mostly black, then brown, one white and one man. His sex made him stand out. His size made him remarkable. The women would steal glances his way; not out of fancy, just fascination. Who was this man? Men hardly took this bus.

They waited at the stop across the street from the famous Junior's Restaurant in downtown Brooklyn. The prison bus was supposed to arrive at nine PM. It didn't show until a little past ten. The women bemoaned but they didn't argue. There was no one to argue to. They simply tried to keep their children occupied. Moses sat in the back of the bus. It was cramped but the military taught him how to deal with uncomfortable situations. He read a book on the nine-hour ride to the Wyoming Correctional Facility. It was called Wyoming, but it was in New York State and adjacent to the more infamous Attica prison. Moses was processed and then he waited. It was two hours before he got to see him. The visiting area was like a school cafeteria with round tables and chairs.

He walked out in his prison khakis looking around not knowing who he was coming to see. He was brown skinned, a bit lighter than his brother (different fathers), bigger than his brother too, bigger than he looked in the video Moses saw of him being arrested. Moses saw him and ushered him over to his table. He walked over cautiously. Marcus had agreed to the visit not knowing who this Moses man was, but he was curious and happy for a reason to leave his cell.

"What's up?" he asked as he took a seat.

"My name is Moses." Marcus looked at him as if to say, and? "I'm a former Marine."

"Yeah. Good for you. What is this, some veteran inmate program?"

"Something like that," Moses played along.

"Cool. So, you been in Iraq?" Marcus asked.

"And Afghanistan, and Yemen and Libya and Syria, and Pakistan."

"Damn, you been in a lot of places. You must have seen a lot of shit."

"And done a lot of shit," Moses said.

"Tell me about it."

Moses shared war stories and Marcus listened. Marcus was riveted and revealed he had considered joining the military years ago. He imagined how different his life would be at this moment; twenty-seven years old with no possibility of getting out for another ten years. "Not all of us get to choose the part we play, you know what I'm saying. Most of us just gotta make do with the part we get." Marcus told him stories about being inside and what men must do to survive. It wasn't unlike growing up in Brownsville, he said. "You have to crew up, otherwise you're gonna get eaten."

Marcus had been in three years now and rarely got visitors anymore. His girlfriend, now just his baby's mother, used to come, but she had moved on, and taken his baby girl with her. Moses left a hundred dollars in his commissary and said he would like to come again. "Yeah man, cool." Moses left him a book to read. It was the same book Moses had been reading on his ride up. He had bought it a week ago from a street side vendor.

On the ride back Moses meditated on everything. Marcus was one of those boys who would have robbed him when he was a kid, and who had beaten him up for his Jordans. He admitted as much, doing dumb shit with his friends, things he thought was fun at the time, things he looked back on regretfully now, playing the part he thought he was supposed to. But sitting down, talking to the man who he was now, Moses liked Marcus.

Moses came back, once a week, and every time he did, he

brought a new book and it was always about black culture and black history. The street side vendor fed Moses and Moses fed Marcus.

"Damn, black people was here before white people came here. So, we're like Native Americans too."

"Yeah," Moses said. That had tripped Moses out as well. "Columbus himself wrote about black people already being here."

On another visit they discussed how the slave patrols were the first police. "The more things change, the more they stay the same. They're doing the same shit right now," Marcus said.

"Yup. And they created a war on drugs before there was any drug problem, then they sent the drugs to the hood, crime rate shot up, then they used it as a reason to lock us up again."

"Mansa Musa. That's ma nigga right there, though. Richest man in the world—ever. Why didn't they teach us this in school?"

"You know why," Moses said.

"Yeah but if they did though, we would have been more interested in learning. All they teach you about black people is slavery, Abraham Lincoln, Harriet Tubman, Rosa Parks and Martin Luther King, and all of it is depressing as shit. People don't wanna hear that."

Moses had a revelation. Things had to change and, for the sake of his mother and all the other mothers who had gotten caught up in this fruitless war these young men were engaged in, it would require direct action. Moses saw that now. Moses had made in-roads with Marcus and that was good but to effectuate real change he would need to get to the boys in the gang directly. He was steadily formulating a plan.

Moses whispered to Marcus on his next visit, "I have a connect. He's my boy, former marine, he's in with this cartel. They have quality shit coming through. They have a foothold in Chicago, they want street level distribution in New York as well. I thought of CMK."

Marcus was surprised to hear Moses say this and a bit disappointed. Moses didn't seem the type and had never mentioned doing anything criminal before. He wondered for a second if Moses might be an agent and if he was trying to entrap him. But why go through all of that? And CMK were legends in their own minds but were barely known outside of Brownsville. Why would the FEDs go through all this trouble for them? Also, over the last three months, he had grown to like Moses a great deal and to trust him as well. He had learned more with Moses in these months than he had in his previous twenty-six years.

Two weeks later both Moses and Saquon came up to visit. Marcus made the introductions. Saquon was twenty-one at the time and had a slim build and a cool dark complexion. He was quiet for the most part and just listened. It was awkward for Moses to sit next to the man who had killed his mother. His baser instincts still wanted to kill him. However, there was something much bigger at play now. Moses broke down the details of the deal then stepped aside and gave the brothers privacy to talk. Marcus assured Saquon, he wouldn't stare him wrong, and having never had a reason to not trust his brother, Saquon agreed.

Moses called Caleb and set everything up. Saquon and three of his lieutenants came. Caleb asked Moses about his mother's killers. Moses told him they had been arrested and sent up before he could get to them. These young men, were members of a gang along with his cousin who was currently doing time. His cousin offhandedly revealed to Moses that they were looking for a new connect, during a visit, and Moses thought of Caleb, and decided to broker the deal. Caleb accepted his explanation and didn't question him further.

The deal took place in Americus, Georgia and went off without a hitch and everyone was happy. They did three other deals over the next three months and all went well. Then Moses revealed the next part of his plan to Marcus.

"You wanna join the gang?" Marcus asked looking gobsmacked.

"I think we can do something great with them. I think we can make them like what the founders originally envisioned when they formed the gangs, to protect the community instead of preying on it."

"I don't know about that. It's hard for a man to see past the shit when he's deep in it, and it's all he knows," Marcus said.

"I know, and I know I can't change things from the outside. I have to get in the shit with them," Moses said.

"But you grown. You done a lot already. You can leave and do whatever you want. Why, why you wanna do this?"

"I feel like it's my purpose. I don't know, I just feel like it's what I'm meant to do. Even when I was in the corps, even though I was a great soldier, I was just doing it because I was good at it. I never felt like what I was doing had purpose or meaning. I never believed in it. I do now."

"You wanna join, you got my blessing," Marcus said. "They could use your guidance. But shit won't be easy. They hard-headed. But I'll talk to Quon."

66

Over the last three months from deal to deal, Moses developed a working relationship with Saquon. He was the leader of the gang, but he wasn't boastful or overly belligerent. He was quiet and introspective, and considered things a great deal before doing it. He didn't seem like the type to recklessly go after a rival on a busy street. Maybe the shooting had changed him.

Saquon's opinion of Moses was cautious. They were making good money with Moses's connect but why was a former marine doing this—and why CMK? Marcus's trust in him put Saquon at ease but his guard was not fully down. He accepted him for what he was, but then Marcus said Moses wanted to join the gang. Saquon was stunned at the request, and even if he were inclined to let him in, he knew the rest of the boys wouldn't like it. However, Marcus vouched for him, and Marcus was one of the founders. They agreed to give Moses a shot. Still, if he truly wanted to join the gang he would have to be initiated. His initiation took place at the Claude McKay Houses behind building three.

Building three had been rotting from the inside with lead poisoning, mold, no heat and rats for years. It had a litany of problems exacerbated tenfold by Hurricane Sandy, after which it became wholly unlivable. NYCHA, the New York City Housing Authority, began relocating the tenants. Many residents left after signing a deal under a plan called HOPE VI.

The deal offered residents temporary townhouse styled housing while they were told their apartments were being renovated. Many of these residents were instead given vouchers to alternative Section 8 housing. NYCHA would later suspend the project. The problems were too plentiful to fix, and in fact it would be more cost effective to simply tear the building down and build anew.

However, the Claude McKay Houses consisted of three buildings, not just one, and tearing down one building, given their proximity, the dust, fumes and debris, would deleteriously affect the other two buildings in the complex, essentially making them unlivable as well. And the other two buildings, though in bad shape themselves, were much better off than building three, and they had nowhere to relocate the hundreds of people living in them.

Building three was shuttered. They boarded it up and built a chain-link fence around it, until they could work out moving everyone out of the other two buildings, then they could bring all three buildings down together. Many community leaders fought against this move, seeing the imminent destruction of the houses as the harbinger to gentrification; as what would be built in the future would be vastly more expensive than what many in the community could afford.

Building three had been boarded up for going on six years and no further action seemed imminent. This allowed the CMK crew to essentially take it over and use it as a base of operations. A good many homeless people had taken up shelter in the higher floors of the building as well. The police hardly ever came back here. It was hard to control. They would run them off but they would always come back.

67

It was the middle of January. Night came at five in the evening. It was winter but it was fifty degrees. It drizzled instead of snowed. They stood in a baseball diamond patch of unkempt brown grass and weeds, surrounded by concrete. It was here, Moses was to be squared in. He was to take on four of the strongest members at once, Saquon explained to him. Moses took off his jacket, wearing only a tank top; all his muscles and veins were visible. Some of the members let out a silent, damn.

"That's okay. All of you can join in," Moses said.

"Join in what?" Saquon asked.

"I'll take on all of you at once," Moses said calmly.

"You suicidal, nigga?" Gucci, one of the lieutenants in the gang, remarked. Gucci was Puerto Rican, twenty-two, had tattoos covering both arms and extending up to his neck, and liked to dress in a lot of—Gucci.

"Yeah we ain't taking shit easy on you. You might die in here," Demarius said. He was another lieutenant and, at twenty-three with a stout build, he was their best fighter, and he hated the idea of Moses joining.

"Yeah, you ain't gotta take on everybody just to join," Saquon said.

"I ain't come here to join you. I came here to lead you."

"Lead what? What the fuck you think this is? You ain't leading shit," Demarius said.

"Well if anybody has a problem with me leading, step up."

There were twenty-three of them. Twenty of them took part in the initiation. Saquon, and two others abstained. One of them was videotaping the event on his phone, the other was a recent recruit who was recovering from his own initiation. "Quon, you ain't in this?" Gucci asked.

"Nah. Marcus already vouched for him on his life, so I'm good." Also looking at Moses, Saquon had no desire to get hit by him, and as improbable as the one on twenty odds seemed, Saquon wouldn't bet against him.

There is a rush you get when you're in combat. It's unlike anything else. No other high compares to it. Knowing that your life is literally in the balance brings you a focus like you can't experience otherwise. Moses welcomed that rush of blood in his veins. He hadn't felt this focused since being at war.

They ensnared him and began steadily creeping closer, arms ready. These were boys, and barely men, ranging from sixteen to twenty-three. All of them were smaller than Moses but they were many and he was one. Most were waiting for one person to start it off. The way these initiations went, they rush in, you're savaged, you defend yourself to the best of your ability, you take your licks, maybe you deliver a few licks back, but eventually you submit, you fall, badly bruised, bloodied, sometimes bones broken, but then they pick you up, it's over, you're in, you are family. But what they don't expect is for you to strike first.

Moses rushed in, grabbed the smallest one in the center, draped him by his coat, lifted him off his feet and swung him around and threw him back into the pack, knocking back five other members in one swoop. There was a collective, oh shit. Moses pressed his attack. He connected a straight right on the temple of a stunned member. Moses had large hands and his fists were almost the size of the boy's head. The boy staggered out of the brawl. After the initial surprise the others rushed in, all at once. Blows came from every direction. But they were wild and undisciplined. Many of their blows cancelled each other out, as there were just so many of them, they blocked each other. Moses went into a peek-a-boo boxing stance, forearms up and closed tight around his head. He cared mostly about protecting his head. His torso was made of pure muscle hardened over years. He absorbed the blows. It was like a wave of punches.

But he didn't so much feel pain as more so the concussive force. Fortunately, while the boys were swinging wildly, they were not defending themselves.

He threw a straight right and it landed flush on a member's face just below the orbital bone. Kareem, twenty-two years old and second generation Haitian, had been in many fights in his life and this was the hardest he had ever been hit. He stepped away to make certain his eye was still in place. Moses rushed forward pushing back three members at once. He pinned one against the wall and gave him two successive uppercuts right under the chin. He bit his tongue—damn near bit it off. Another member saw an opening and swung at Moses, he dodged that blow, but caught another to back of his ear. It stung and the others rushed in and there was another wave of concussive blows. Moses's biceps were big, so were his forearms. They blocked most of the blows, but a few got through. He kept his back to the wall so no one could come behind him. He bobbed and swung, bobbed and swung, getting hit but always connecting and his punches hurt more. Usually after a member had been hit once, he had enough.

After two minutes, there was a lot of wailing, and members bent over, holding their sides, and their faces, gasping for air. There were only three men left standing, Moses and the gang's two best fighters Gucci and Demarius. These were the only members to take Moses's punch and come back. They were all wet from sweat and drizzle. Demarius had his hands in the position to strike, Moses moved in, swung his arms over and down, like doing a breaststroke, hitting Demarius's arms, breaking his guard, then moved in, grabbed him by the back of the neck with both hands and delivered a headbutt to the bridge of his nose. Demarius's nose broke, blood spurted, and his knees buckled, falling backwards. Moses then turned to Gucci, who after seeing Demarius go down and feeling a taste of Moses's power had had enough. "A'ight. Stop. Stop. You hit too hard, ma nigga. You hit too hard. You good. You in."

"I'm not just in. I run this shit . . . you listen to me now."

Many of them wanted to object but were in too much pain to say anything. Except for Demarius who was struggling to get to his feet.

"Fuck you. You think you can just come in here from no-where and takeover." He got to his feet, wiped the blood from his nose and put up his hands. Moses respected his heart. He swung at Moses and caught him square on the jaw. Moses shook off the hit and slapped Demarius. Demarius was staggered but still determined and swung again, Moses dodged, and delivered a right hook in a downward motion, right on the cheek, drop-ping Demarius to his ass. Still Demarius would not stay down. He struggled to get up, grabbing on to Moses's pant leg as a crutch.

Moses grabbed his hand, pulling him up and gripping him at the same time. "I respect your heart. You're a fighter. But you can't win this. You're out matched. You think you're a man. But you're not a man. This is what a man feels like." Moses intensi-fied his grip and squeezed almost to the point of breaking. De-marius hollered feeling the most pain he had ever felt in his life. He felt it in every bone, orifice and cell. If Moses had held on any longer Demarius would have urinated and defecated himself simultaneously. Moses let go and Demarius fell back looking at his hand as if it were mangled. Structurally it was fine but felt like pure hell. "I run this shit now," Moses declared. "Anybody else have a problem?" No one said anything. "Good," he said and walked away.

When Moses returned home, and the adrenaline had left his body, the pain came. Nothing was broken but everything hurt, even places he hadn't been hit hurt. In that two-minute span he may have been hit over a hundred times. The cumulative effect was now taking its toll. He took two pain pills and eased himself into bed. Whatever he was doing, it was very real now.

68

The next day everyone met again in the back of building three. Everyone in the fight was still bruised and aching from the beating the day before. Demarius had to go to the hospital and had a large bandage over his broken nose. Saquon walked around having a laugh at their expense. Most laughed along as well, except Demarius who had a very sour temper. Moses came carrying a large duffel bag. He dropped the bag at their feet and called them to attention.

"New rules. No robbing. No banging. No scamming. Just drug dealing." He let that sit and they were silent, listening but not fully absorbing. "No civilian harassment. No fighting. No congregating in front of buildings. Residents come and go without obstruction. When you see them you're polite."

"What's wrong with hanging out in front the building?" Saquon asked.

"Do you have a sister?" Moses asked. Saquon nodded yes. "I'm guessing a lot of you do. Ask them if they like walking by twenty dudes every time they have to get in and out of the building. I have sisters and they used to talk about how much they hated having to walk by a group of boys."

"Why?" Gucci asked.

"If you can't figure that out, I don't have time to explain it. Just don't do it. And it's not just girls and women you make feel uncomfortable and unsafe it's everybody. And if the people see you as a menace, they don't care about you, and will happily snitch on you."

"Fuck how they feel. We a gang. We run this. They just have to deal with it. And people don't snitch on us," Demarius said.

"Yeah. Tell that to Marcus and the other members who got arrested. In the war our intel came from the people sometimes living right next to the insurgents, and they gave them up because as much as they hated us, they saw the insurgents as a greater immediate threat. Now do you wanna make money smart or do you wanna be terrorist? And believe me, you don't want to be a terrorist. I've seen how they handle terrorist."

"You said, no banging. We don't bang unless we have to," Kareem said.

"You don't have to. Whatever beefs come about from rival gangs comes to me first and I'll handle it. No violence. Violence is a cancer. That's what brings down all the heat."

"How you gonna have the dealing without the violence?" Saquon asked.

"Like I said, any beefs arise, come to me and I'll deal with it. If we are attacked, we will defend ourselves. But you don't seek conflict. You don't initiate it. No more interactions with rival gangs on social media. In fact, go through your social media, everyone. Scour that shit. Any posts you have making any reference to being in a gang get rid of it. All of it."

"You turning us into a bunch of pussies yo." Demarius said.

"No, I'm trying to educate you and keep you outta jail. There's this thing called a predicate act. You sell weed." He pointed to one member. "He killed somebody." He pointed to another. "You're in the same gang. You the weed seller get caught up in a RICO charge as conspiracy to commit murder. How do they know that you're in the same gang, because you're all over social media bragging about it." They were silent, a few mumbled to themselves. "Drug dealing is enough. We're going to do it smarter. We're getting our shit pure from the cartel. Most of it we won't cut. We're gonna sell it to other dealers. We'll be their connect. We'll move more and move it faster. You're going to make more. So, we're cutting out all the other nonsense that gets you into trouble."

Moses was giving commands, but the boys would look to Saquon for his reaction. He was so far giving a slight nod of approval. Saquon truthfully never wanted to be the leader. Leadership was foisted on him after Marcus and many of the older members were arrested and everyone started looking to him. He was curious to see where this experiment with Moses was going, knowing whenever he wanted to, he could cut it off and retake control. "What's in the bag?" he asked.

Moses opened the bag and took out basketballs, football helmets and baseball gloves. They all started laughing. "What are those for? You turning us into a rec league, ma nigga?" Gucci asked.

Moses smiled as well. "No. Anytime three or more of you are walking together, you walk with a basketball. Some of you will walk with football helmets, some with baseball gloves. That way if cops see you, you look like you're part of a high school team and not gang members."

"Oh shit, that's smart," Kareem said and the rest of them seemed to agree.

"Now there's another problem. You all look like drug dealers," Moses said.

"Like you just said, we are drug dealers," Gucci said.

"Yeah, that doesn't mean you wanna look like one. You look exactly like how they say a drug dealer is supposed to look. See, white boys sell more drugs than you do, but you got the look."

"What am I supposed to do about that?" Gucci asked.

"For one, pull your pants up."

Many of them waved him off with their hands as if to say, here we go again.

"Why are you looking at my ass, ma nigga?" Gucci said.

"I'm not looking at your ass but why are you showing your ass?"

"Because that's me. That's how I like to wear my shit."

"Let me ask you something, how many times have you been stopped by the police?"

"I don't know."

"Just give me a ballpark figure. Less than five, more than five."

"I told you I don't know."

"Look at that. It's happened so much you lost count."

"We live in the hood. You Puerto Rican, you black, cops gonna harass you," Gucci said.

"Yeah they do. But they harass some black and brown people more than others. When a cop pulls you over, he documents it, and he has to give probable cause for why he stopped you. One of the reasons for stopping someone is because they suspect them of having a gun or drugs. Now, how does a cop know someone has a gun? He doesn't definitively, but he uses his cop instincts. One reason they use is saying that guys walking with a gun on them are constantly fidgeting with their waistbands, always pulling it up, and when you wear your pants low, what are you always doing?" They knew the answer but couldn't bring themselves to say it. Moses said it for them. "Exactly. So he may see you and think, he keeps messing with his waistband, I think he has a gun on him, or maybe he thinks you have some drugs, or maybe he doesn't and he just wants to stop you, run you through the system, see if you got any warrants on you, if you don't hopefully you do something stupid and give him cause to bring you in for resisting and add to his quota. And you've given him the excuse all because you don't wanna wear a belt."

"I am wearing a belt. It's Gucci," Gucci said.

"It's nice but it ain't doing what it's supposed to."

"Look, I seen mad people get beat down by the police, people in suits and shit. Martin Luther King, Malcolm X, all they did was wear suits, they still got killed. Dudes today, who ain't got nothing to do with the game get stopped, get killed, whether they wearing they shit down or not. And bitches get beat down all the time. It ain't got shit to do with what you wearing."

"You're right, black folk get harassed by the police. We ain't arguing that. But you get harassed the most. You need to ask yourself if you like always being at the bottom of the totem pole. And you do it too, if you go out looking for a rival. You looking at how he dress, at how he walks, and when you see it, it's a signal saying that's an enemy combatant."

They all thought for a second on what Moses said. "Fuck that shit," Gucci blurted then sucked his teeth. "I'm Gucci, yo. You ain't killing ma style. I like how I look. Ma Moms been saying that shit for years, and if ma Moms ain't change me, you ain't changing me. Old heads always got shit to say. But ya'll use to wear your shit too. Used to wear bell bottoms and shit, and zoot suits back in the day. This is us. We good." Whatever impact Moses had been making on them, after Gucci spoke, none of them seemed to listen.

A week later an anti-crime unit stopped Gucci coming out of a bodega. Fortunately, he had nothing on him. He had been stopped and frisked before, but he had never directly related it to how he wore his jeans, not until Moses put the idea in his head. As he left them and headed home, he unconsciously pulled his pants up, about halfway, and buckled his belt a notch tighter. Without acknowledging it he never wore his pants down to the levels he did before again.

Gucci was the de facto fashion leader of the crew. Other members wouldn't acknowledge it, but they took things Gucci did and merged it into their own style. Gucci began wearing his pants closer to his waist, and throughout the weeks, steadily it permeated to the rest of the crew.

69

Saquon and a few of the boys along with Demarius, Gucci and Kareem were in the park by the basketball court. It was a pleasant spring day and Saquon sat on a bench taking everything in. Gucci and Kareem stood by the fencing talking to two girls walking by in the street. It had been three months since Moses had taken over.

Demarius had a sour look on his face watching a group of middle schoolers who were on the court playing ball the same time the crew was there. He found this blatantly disrespectful. A few months ago, these kids would have never dared being on the court in the gang's presence. They wouldn't have used the court period for fear the gang would find out. A kid could get stomped out for that. Things had changed, and not for the better, in his eyes. It was all Soldier's doing and Demarius was sick of it.

"Yo, why you let Soldier just come and take shit over?" Demarius asked Saquon. "We used to run this. CMK is our shit. Now everything go through Soldier."

"CMK is Marcus, and Bilal and Tony. They founded it and brought everybody together." Tony had gotten killed in a gang shooting six years ago, and Bilal was serving twenty-five years in Texas. Essentially Marcus was the only OG left. "Marcus decided to let him in. That was his call. And it wasn't like dude just strolled in and ran shit. Remember that ass whooping he gave you. He gave all of you."

"Yeah, except you."

"Because I didn't need it. Plus, what are you complaining about? We more organized. We getting shit done. And we making more money than we did before," Saquon said.

"Yeah but look at these little niggas on the court while we out here. We used to be feared in these streets. Now they just look at us and just smile and shit. We turned into a bunch of bitches, yo. We need to take the K out our name and put in a B. We be CMB. Claude McKay Bitches."

"That can be you then. You can be the bitch if all you care about is some little kids being afraid of you."

"It ain't just them. The other crews don't fear us anymore either," Demarius said.

"That ain't what I heard. And let them come test us if they want to. I'll take my chances going to war with Soldier."

"Soldier, Soldier, Soldier. Everything is about Soldier. You changed man. Where my dog at? The Quon, I know, would have never let this shit go down."

Saquon took a moment before saying, "That old woman died, man."

"What old woman?"

"You know." Demarius had driven while Saquon did the shooting. "And she could have been my grandmother. I see a picture of that woman and I swear I'm looking at my grand-mother. I see them in my head and they're the same person. And that woman raised me, raised me and Marcus, and we broke her heart with all the shit we did." She died from complications with diabetes three years ago. "And I killed her."

"She wasn't your grandmother, bruh," Demarius said.

"Nah, but she could have been. And I killed her. And I gotta live with that."

"That's how war is. Innocent people day all the time. Sol-dier was in war. You think he ain't kill no innocent people," Demarius said.

"Maybe. But who we warring with, and for what? For what?" Saquon asked.

Demarius didn't have an answer and could only blow air out of his mouth.

Saquon turned to Gucci and Kareem. "Yo Gooch, Kareem." Gucci and Kareem turned away from the girls and walked over.

"Whud up?" Gucci said.

"Yo, ya'll got a problem with Soldier?" Saquon asked.

"At first, I wasn't really feeling him. But I ain't gon' lie he run shit smooth, though. And I'm still getting Gucci, still getting pussy. I'm good," Gucci said.

"I like Soldier," Kareem said. "He's smart. He got us doing things more intelligent. Less run-ins with the police. Getting more money. I'm good with that."

Saquon turned to Demarius. "Things change bruh, and you gotta learn to change with it."

70

"We have a problem," Saquon said as he and several members of the crew approached Moses. Caron, a seventeen-year-old member, had been chased through the streets and shot at by three members of a rival gang. He survived by jumping over a chainlink fence and darting through an alley. "You said to bring any beefs to you. We're bringing it to you," Saquon said. Demarius stood behind him. He looked both giddy and angry.

"You know who they are?" Moses asked.

"Yeah," Saquon answered.

"You know where they are?"

"Yeah."

"Good," Moses said.

"Now let's go light them up," Demarius chimed in.

"No. Everybody else stay put. Me and Quon will handle it."

"Nah. I'm coming too," Demarius demanded.

"No," Moses said assertively. "We're good. Saquon and I will handle it." Moses and Saquon walked off and left Demarius stewing.

Everything was purple and orange: the room purple, the television orange, the coffee table purple, the sofa purple, the men on the sofa orange, the pipes in the walls purple, with purple water running through them. There were four orange men in the trap house playing video games with orange controllers. An orange phone rang and one of the orange men picked up.

"Who this?" he answered.

"Bitch, you know who this is. You came at my people today," Saquon said.

The orange man laughed. "Yeah. Almost got that bitch too. But he fast though."

"Lucky for you he is. That's the only reason why we talking right now," Saquon said.

"Ain't nuthin to talk about. You CMK niggas is puss. We coming for you. We gon' take your corners, your block, your building, we taking everything."

"You know, you play too much video games."

A high caliber bullet came through the window into the orange television causing a minor orange explosion. Shocked the orange men dropped to the purple floor and grabbed their guns. Orange man one instructed the other three to check the windows. They took cover behind the purple walls and peeked out but saw no one and shook their heads.

"You looking for me, bro?" Saquon said laughing. "You can't see me, bitch. I ain't even anywhere near you. But I can see you though. I see yo' bitch ass hiding under that table." Another round landed with an orange streak into the purple carpet inches away from the orange man's head. He jumped up, knocking the purple coffee table and all its orange contents over. He attempted to leave the room, but another orange bullet struck a foot away from the direction he was running and stopped him.

"Did I tell you could leave?" Saquon asked.

"Yo, trust me on this one, you are dead, ma nigga." the orange man said.

"No, you're dead." Another bullet came just six inches over the orange man's head, dropping him back down to the sofa he was sitting on. "That coulda been your ass right there," Saquon said. "And believe me, I'm missing on purpose. Let me tell you something. You not on my level, you heard. You ain't know, but

CMK, we carteled up. I told them what you did. And you know the cartel, they wanted to come in there and kill everybody. But I'm just not trying to kill another black man unless I have to. So this, is a warning shot. Take the warning. Cause you ever come at me or any of my people again—" Everything lit up in orange. There was an explosion.

Moses had placed a pipe bomb under one of the gang members cars parked outside the trap house. He just detonated it by phone. Moses and Saquon saw everything through the infrared scopes of their sniper rifle and spotter scopes respectively. It was after midnight and they were two blocks away on the flat roof of an empty two-story house that gave them a view through the front window of the trap house.

"Oh shit," Saquon laughed. "That is beautiful," he said as he watched the orange men scampering around. "Yo, you gotta teach me how to do this."

"I will," Moses said. "I'll teach all of you, when I think you're ready. Now let's hope they take the warning."

They did—all of the gangs did. Word got around that CMK was connected to a Mexican Cartel. Everyone knew to tread lightly. CMK had gained their respect and Moses had gained the full respect of the gang.

71

They met at the barbershop, the one Moses had been go-ing to, Mac's barbershop. All the heads of the major gangs in the Ville, and their Lieutenants, were there. Moses and Saquon were there. It was a big shop but that many people took up a lot of space. They met after nine. The shop was closed. There were no more customers. Everyone there was there for business. They came because Mac, short for MacArthur, had called them. He had one of the most popular barbershops in the neighborhood. He had cut every one of them at one time or another in their lives. They knew him. They trusted him. This meeting was Moses's brainchild but all Mac's doing. No one else could have gotten them to come out.

Mac began, "Five people got shot last week, none of them in the game. One of them was a six-year-old girl. She died. Somebody in here knows who did it." There was grumbling in the room. "I'm not calling anybody or any crew out. This meeting ain't about retribution, this is about change. She was six-years-old, man, and she was beautiful, and she was sweet. She ain't begin to live and she's gone, and for what—for what? Ain't no violation you think another man did to you is worth the life of an innocent six-year-old child."

"You right," one of the gang leaders said.

"I know I'm right, and everyone in here know I'm right. Even the one who did it, even if he ain't here, someone in here knows him." Strangely, like so many of those weekend killings, none of them knew who did it, and none of them knew none of them knew who did, and the killers were never found. "We're here now to make sure that it doesn't happen again. So we're starting up a neighborhood patrol, me and few other brothers and sisters who are fed up. It will be a couple teams of us, we gonna walk the neighborhood, every day, night and day make sure kids can play safe, people can walk about safe. Keep an eye on shit." There was more grumbling in the room. "This is for your benefit as well. All of you got mothers. Some of you got sisters, baby mothers, babies, cousins. A lot of you got brothers, blood and otherwise, who already died. This place is only about one square mile. It's too tight to have people from Brownsville can't walk through Tilden, and Van Dyke and Seth Low."

"So, niggas violate, and you want me to let that shit slide. That shit ain't happening. We came here on the strength of you, Mac. Now you basically saying you gon' be watching us, turning snitch and shit."

"No. The Patrol ain't about snitching and sending more black men into the system. Sell your drugs. We don't care about that. In fact, we'll watch out for you and let you know when the cops are around. And we'll walk with a legal adviser to make sure you always have representation if you're ever being harassed. What we are about is ending the violence and the killing. No robbing. No banging. We wanna make sure that mothers and grandmothers can walk the street safe. Kids can play, and you yourself can walk to the bodega and get a sandwich and not worry about catching a bullet. This benefits you. You can make your money, and not worry about all the other bullshit. All beefs end now."

"What you talking about a truce? Them shits never last."

"That's why I'm talking about forming a coalition. Each gang remains separate, but if any member of the coalition is attacked all members join in. You have a real interest in keeping the truce. You're gonna come together and say you know what, past sins are in the past."

"I hear what you saying, but some beefs can't be forgiven, yuh heard," Kevon one of the gang leaders said, and many others seemed to agree with him.

"It's funny you said that. You especially. Because we have a special bond," Mac said to him.

"What you talking about?"

"Kevon, I know you killed my son," Mac revealed and there was an audible reaction from the other men in the room.

"What? Fuck outta here. I ain't killed nobody."

"Markelle Jones." The name took Kevon aback. He didn't say a word, but the bell rung in his eyes. "I found out it was you while I was away. Now, you ain't know he was my son. Otherwise you wouldn't have come in my shop. I knew from the first time I cut your hair. I had the blade in my hand, and I could have cut your throat. I ain't gon' lie and say the thought didn't cross my mind. But I let it go. I let it go. He was my son. But how am I gonna condemn another man for doing the same thing I did. I tried to take another man's son from him. He lived, thank God, and that's the only reason I did twenty years and not life. When you're young you don't think about that. But you get a lot of time to think in your cell. Your life is filled with moments. Most are bullshit but some can change your life forever. I've spent years sitting in my cell regretting that moment. That one moment cost me twenty years. You feel this rage in you. You don't know why you're so angry. You think you gotta do something. You got a hatred in you for another black man that you can't even understand. You wasn't any different than the man I was. You just caught up like we all are. They don't teach us how to be men. Back in the day, back in Africa, when you got to a certain age, they used to have rites of passage. Men used to teach the boys how to be men. We need to get back to that. That's what I'm trying to do right here. Shit gotta change. And it can. We can make it change."

Saquon raised his hand. CMK was the first gang to join the coalition. Five others followed suit. Only a third of the gangs who went to that meeting joined up. It wasn't everything they wanted but it was a start.

72

Moses drove Saquon back to the Claude McKay Houses after the meeting. "It's crazy how Mac let Kevon slide for killing his son," Saquon said.

"It's not that crazy," Moses said. "He sees the bigger picture."

"You think the coalition is gonna work?"

"Don't know, but we have to try. Either that or we kill each other off, or they kill us off."

Saquon looked around the car. Moses was driving the old Honda he had bought when he was planning to kill Saquon. "Ma dude, what's up with your ride?" Saquon asked.

"What's wrong with it?"

"It's a piece of shit."

"It's not a piece of shit."

"Soldier, it's a piece of shit."

"This piece of shit does everything I need it to."

"But c'mon, Soldier you making money, you can do better than this. We can't have the head of CMK rolling out like this." Moses smiled. "I mean what are you even spending your money on?"

"Guns," Moses said straightly.

"For real? How much guns you talking?"

"A lot of guns. Those are my toys right there," Moses said.

"Where you getting all them guns from?"

Caleb connected Moses to a gun seller in Texas that the Cartel used. The Cartel had bought over two hundred guns from him, AKs and ARs and .50-caliber rifles, over the last few months. The seller got the guns from sporting goods stores and gun shows. He also modified them to make them fully automatic. He sold ammunition and pipe bombs he had made as well. "They think I'm buying these guns to sell to all the gangs so you can kill each other," Moses said.

"Then why are you buying them?"

"Because I see what's coming. I'm gonna start putting some of them in building three as well."

"In case the coalition doesn't work out?"

"Yeah . . . that . . . and anything else. These white boys, they got so much guns. I'm talking hundreds. Some of them have thousands. They're preparing for something. We need to prepare ourselves too."

Moses pulled over beside a street vendor, got out, bought a bouquet of flowers, and re-entered the car. "Oh shit, you bought some flowers for your bitch?" Saquon asked and Moses gave him a stern look. "For your, Girl," Saquon corrected himself.

"Something like that," Moses said and drove off.

Three minutes later Moses pulled over again at a familiar place on Mother Gaston Boulevard. Saquon knew this place well. "Why are you stopping here?" Saquon asked, belying the fact he felt incredibly uneasy being here.

"Come, I'll show you," Moses said. He got out the car. Saquon tentatively followed.

The shrine was in shabby condition. Saquon hadn't come for months now. There was just a filthy teddy bear chained to a tree, two broken glass candles and three deflated balloons. Moses knelt and placed the fresh flowers beside the teddy bear. "My mother died here a year ago," Moses said, and Saquon's heart fell and his pupils shrunk. "She was killed in a drive-by shooting." Saquon's heart rate quickened and it was like a drum beating in his belly. He could see the handle of Moses's pistol, in the back of his pants, poking his shirt. Saquon's mind was racing. Did Soldier know Saquon was the killer? Had he known all along? Had he brought Saquon here to kill him? Saquon had his gun in the back of his pants as well. He should reach for it just to be safe, but his heart couldn't find the energy to do it. Whatever Soldier was going to do, he was going to do. "It was some gang shit," Moses continued. "Some drive-by shooting gone bad. It's the reason why I left the marines. It's the reason why it means so much to me to change what's going on out here." Moses put two fingers to his lips, kissed them, then put them to the teddy bear. He stood up and faced Saquon, who was doing his best to keep all his emotions in.

"Did you ever find out who killed your Mom?" Saquon's subconscious asked, while his conscious mind was kicking him for doing it.

Moses looked at him directly and said, "No."

And Saquon could tell that he lied, and it broke his heart like an ulcer in his stomach. Saquon fought hard to keep it all in. He looked down then looked up at Moses. "I'm so sorry for what happened to your mother," he said.

Moses put his hand firmly on his shoulder and said, "I know." Then he got back in the car and Saquon did as well and they drove off together.

73

There were a dozen or so homeless people who from time to time squatted in building three. The gang used to harass and run them off in the past. Moses stopped that and allowed them to come and go as they pleased. They entered through a different entrance than the gang and kept to themselves on the other side of the building. When your options were sleeping on the trains or the streets, mold and lead paint poisoning didn't seem so bad. Some of the apartments, the ones they were able to pry open, had abandoned mattresses in them. Word got around Brooklyn that there was an abandoned building, still most of the homeless stayed away, for the same reason they stayed away from shelters—because it was unsafe.

One of the homeless was an Iraq war veteran of the first Iraq war. He wore a Desert Storm baseball cap. Over half of the homeless people in the city were black, and a quarter of them were veterans. Moses attempted to speak to him on a few occasions, but he hardly spoke. The extreme shame of being homeless can drive you into a depressive state that's hard to come out of.

There was a homeless woman, Moses often saw. She was in her late fifties or sixties—it was hard to tell. She was worn-down and drug addicted. She was like a brown candle melting. She was a fixture in the community. She would go around begging, "Excuse me, I'm homeless, I'm hungry, I'm trying to get four dollars to get something to eat. If everybody could just give me one dollar, it can add up to four dollars, and I can get something to eat." The first time Moses saw her, he gave her four dollars. She said thank you, then proceeded to the next person and repeated her pitch, "Excuse me, I'm homeless, I'm hungry, I'm trying to get four dollars to get something to eat. If everybody could just give me one dollar, it can add up to four dollars and I can get something to eat." Moses laughed, but then as he watched her, going around, collecting one dollar here and there, an idea came to him.

74

"Now we've all heard the saying that black people don't support each other. It's a myth. It's not true," Yalitza Noel said. There was another community meeting in the basement of the local church. They had been having them the first Wednesday of every month, and it had been steadily growing. There was a little over fifty people there this time. "Well it is factually true, but it is a misunderstanding of what's truly taking place," Yalitza continued. "It's not that black people don't support black business over white business, it's that we're supporting big business over small business. And big business nine out of ten times kicks small business's ass. If you open a restaurant on one side of the street that is white owned and another on the other side that is black owned, both of equal size and prices, black people will predominantly support the black owned business. But now if you were to open a McDonald's down the block, it would kick both businesses' ass. That's what desegregation did. They let us into the Major Leagues, and we foolishly abandoned our own Negro League.

"I want you to imagine something. I want you to imagine a Jamaican restaurant in Chinatown." People began chuckling. "It sounds absurd doesn't it. It's so absurd that it actually hurts your brain, like that can't happen, like it's against the laws of physics. But if that's so absurd, ask yourself why are there so many Chinese restaurants in the hood?" There was a collective hmmm, among the audience. "You see, Asian people understand the value of their dollar. Of the over one trillion dollars we generate annually we spend less than three percent of it with ourselves. If we were to spend just ten percent of our earnings with black owned businesses, we would create a million jobs. The path to our empowerment is in our own hands.

"I propose we create a Trust. I call it AACT, African American Community Trust. There are so many things that our community needs. We need affordable daycare, quality affordable housing, after school tutoring for our young people, and jobs—most importantly we need jobs. If we pull our resources together, we can accomplish all of it."

The audience applauded her, but when it came time to invest in the Trust at the end of the night, most people didn't give and what they gave was paltry. A few spoke with her after the program about getting funding through grants and endowments and contacting some of the wealthier black people for help. Yalitza listened to their ideas but stressed that she wanted to build the Trust organically through the community, so that the community had ownership of it and not a select few.

Like before, Moses waited until everyone who wanted to speak with Yalitza had done so before he approached. "You came back," she greeted, though she had seen him there regularly every month. Her lectures along with the books he and Marcus were reading had fed him. But this was only the second time he felt comfortable enough to speak to her.

"Here," he said and awkwardly took out a dollar and presented it to her.

"What's this?" she asked.

"I'm donating to the Trust."

"One dollar?" She looked a bit offended.

"Yeah and I'll give it once a week, every week. That's four dollars a month," Moses said.

"That's very nice of you, but we're going to need a lot more than that."

"You have a lot more," Moses said.

She was intrigued. "Explain," she said.

"How many people are in Brownsville?"

"Roughly 80,000," she began and they finished saying together.

"That's a lot of dollars," Moses said. "That's a lot of four dollars. That's a lot of fifty-two dollars for the year." Yalitza was beginning to see where Moses was going. "The way I see it, you try to do a fundraiser with folks around here and they'll cry broke and give you all kinds of shit about why they can't donate, while they'll waste it on lotto, and wait in line to buy Jordans. You try asking for twenty dollars, you might get some, but most people will walk right by you. Ten dollars, same thing. They'll even give you shit for five. But one dollar. Don't ask for more don't ask for less—and let them know you're legit using it to build up the community, building that daycare center like you said, you'll get a dollar, and you'll get it every week."

"And with enough dedicated dollars, imagine what we can do," she said, her mind wide open.

75

It had been roughly two years since his mother died. Moses sat in the courtyard of the Claude McKay Houses. It was a nice night and people were out enjoying it. There was Michael Jackson and Prince music playing. There were children running about. There were young girls playing double-dutch. There were young men rehearsing a step dance routine. There were senior citizens sitting outside, fanning themselves and laughing. There were older men playing chess and dominoes, and some younger folk waiting to join in. The gang was there but they were not threatening anyone, and no one felt threatened by them. They existed as a part of the community. There were deals happening in the open. They had eyes out giving warning if any police were nearby. They knew all the anti-crime officers and they knew the cars they drove. No one objected to the drug dealing. If they did, they didn't make their objections known. Everyone seemed to be in an agreeable mood—then the gunshots rang out.

They cut through the revelry. People's ears perked up and mothers went for their children. All the gang members in the courtyard gave each other a knowing look. Moses moved in the direction of the shots fired. It was relatively close roughly three blocks away. He wondered if this may have been a gang hit. He hadn't heard any of the boys mention any escalation with any of the rival gangs. Then again all it took was two boys having words with each other for things to escalate. Not every gang joined the coalition, but the coalition was strong enough that no outside gang would take on a coalition member because they would be at war with six gangs instead of one. There hadn't been any shootings in this neck of Brownsville in months.

As Moses approached, he heard someone say in passing, "The cops just shot him." There were people running away and people running towards the scene. When Moses arrived, there were roughly thirty people there watching and recording with their phones. Moses watched, with his own eyes, a plain clothes police officer pull a bleeding teenage boy out of a shot-up BMW. As he looked around, he saw Saquon and other members of the gang watching. Gucci shouted, "Where the gun at? Where the gun at?"

They watched a flood of police officers arrive—but no EMS for ten minutes. When EMS did arrive, they put him on a stretcher and took him away, but Moses knew it was already too late. He watched the life leave the boy's eyes. Seeing that boy die on the street filled Moses with deep anger and profound sadness. You read about police brutality, you see videos of it on television and the internet. There was something so much more devastating seeing it in person. As people around him became more enraged and vocal, Moses was calm and calculating, and his eyes were on the white officer who had done the shooting.

76

It was night again. The streetlights and the moon coming through the small window provided the only light in the room. They had been going at it for hours. They were hungry, they were angry, they were tired. "You keep bringing up all this shit about the violence going on, like that got anything to do with why you killed my son. Why do I have to answer for every piece of shit that goes out there and kills some kid or robs somebody, like they have anything to do with me? Do you answer for all the pieces of shit who get a bunch of guns and start shooting up a school or a concert? And when you do your shit, you do it big—ten, twenty, fifty people at a time. Do you answer for them?"McNally shook his head with a look of exhaustion. "Can't stand to smell your own shit can you?"

"This is pointless. This is . . . what do you want? What do you want from me? He's not coming back. I'm sorry but he's not coming back. We can go at this forever but nothing we say to each other here will bring him back. Fine, I killed him because he was black. I followed him, I pulled him over, I shot him seven times and I watched him die. That's what you wanted to hear. There it is. Now kill me or let me go. But please leave my family out of this."

"Oh, shut up with that shit. How dare you sit there and try to act like you're a victim," Bishop said.

"No, I'm not a victim. I'm not," McNally said. "But let me ask you this. If you were white, what kind of person would you be?"

"I never wanted to be white. I love being black. I love who I am," Bishop said.

"That's not what I'm asking you? I'm asking you, if you

were born white, what kind of person would you be?" Bishop still looked confused by the question. "Now, you made the point about the dinner table, and all the different kinds of white people at it, old kids, middle kids, young kids—black sheep. So, I'm asking you, you being you, but now you're white, who are you? Are you the one to turn the table over . . . or do you eat?" He watched as Bishop's expression changed from confusion to comprehension to confusion again, and McNally had his answer. "Yeah, you would eat. You would eat."

When Bishop came to an answer, he had to admit, "I don't know."

McNally took some satisfaction in that. "The history of the world is a history of human beings doing horrible things to each other. But we have to find a way to move past it or we'll never move on," McNally said.

"Move past it," Bishop repeated and smiled to himself. "You know, I read somewhere that after the civil war up until 1950 something like 4,000 black men were lynched. And that's only the numbers they were able to count. It was probably way more. It happened so often, they used to put out signs saying another man was lynched yesterday. Shit was crazy. Lynchings were like events. Like a big whole picnic, people came from all over to watch a black man burn. They used to advertise that shit in the newspaper. People used to take souvenirs, cut off ears and noses, fingers, and especially balls. Black balls that was the main prize. And I think about that. And I think about 1950. My father was born in forty-eight. My grandmother on my mother's side was born in twenty-seven. She's still alive, thank God. And so, it hit me that there are still people alive today who went to a lynching. There are still people who were the lynchers themselves who are alive today—who still got their souvenirs. They probably keep them in a back room, like how people have their rooms where they keep their old Nazi shit. You talk like that shit was a thousand years ago. And you keep talking like why do we keep bringing it up, why don't we move on? It just happened. My grandmother lived that—my grandmother. And it keeps happening. It don't stop. Emmett Till happened in like the fifties. But I remember Yusuf Hawkins, that happened in 1989. They shot that boy up just for being in their neighborhood. And that boy that who went into the church and killed all those people, that wasn't four girls in like 1960, that just happened. And you, you shot my son seven times, pulled his bleeding body out of the car, handcuffed him to the pavement and watched him die. You did that. Not your father, or your granddaddy or your great gran-pappy. You did that. You murdered my son, and you have the fucking audacity to talk about moving on."

77

Moses appeared in the doorway wearing his baseball cap and surgical mask. He gave a look to Bishop and then walked away. Bishop knew to follow him. Bishop left McNally in the room and met Moses down the hall. "How's it going?" Moses asked, pulling his mask down.

"It's going," Bishop answered.

"He hasn't given you what you wanted yet?" Moses asked.

"No. Not quite," Bishop said sounding exhausted by the entire ordeal.

"It's been a long day."

"Yes, it has," Bishop concurred.

"You may have to acknowledge he may never give you what you want," Moses said.

"Yeah," Bishop said flatly.

"You did the best you could for your son."

"I don't know about that," Bishop said.

"I think he would be proud," Moses said. Bishop shook his head with an exhausted smile. "Either way we have to bring this to a conclusion." Moses looked at Bishop directly—and Bishop looked at him. "Do you understand?"

"Yeah, I do," Bishop answered soberly.

"You should go home. Let him sleep on it again."

"Yeah," Bishop said.

"I'll walk you out."

78

Moses and Bishop came out of building three of the Claude McKay Houses, walked through the opening in the wire fence and onto the courtyard. They looked at buildings one and two in front of them. Moses looked at all the lights on in each building and all the people living inside. It seemed peaceful. Whatever this was that he was doing, he believed was having an effect.

"Do you have a family?" Bishop felt compelled to ask Moses, recognizing he knew very little about this man he had committed a grave felony with.

"My father died years ago. My mother died two years ago, and I have two sisters."

"I'm sorry about your mother—and father," Bishop said.

"Such is life," Moses said.

"No wife? No children?"

"No wife. No children," Moses answered.

"Girlfriend?" Bishop asked.

Moses smiled at how prying the questions were becoming. Bishop asked because he wanted to know how Moses was able to keep his woman and do what he was doing, as Bishop was finding it increasingly difficult to keep this all from Diane. "No girlfriend," Moses said. "I have a complicated relationship with women."

That sounded odd. "What's the complication?"

"I can't talk to them," Moses revealed. Bishop looked at him quizzically. "I mean, I can talk to them about regular things. But I can't *talk* to them." Moses stressed. "I've been this way since I was young. I think I have a weird phobia. I think I'm traumatized. Shit terrifies me." Moses had never revealed this to anyone before. Before when Caleb would bring women up, Moses would lie, and whether Caleb believed him or not, was uncertain, as Caleb never questioned him.

"C'mon, talking to women is not terrifying," Bishop said.

"For me it is. I've been to war and nothing scares me more."

Bishop had to laugh at that, and Moses laughed as well. "I get it. When you were a kid, talking to girls can be hard, not knowing what to say, trying to be cool. But it gets easier as you get older. And you're built like a brick, bro. That's like three-fourths of the battle."

"You would think, right. But no. I still never know what to say and how to approach them."

"So, what do you do?" Bishop asked.

Moses understood the implied question. "I mostly make do . . . and when I can't I pay for it, which I don't like doing, because it makes me feel dirty."

Bishop couldn't understand this phobia, but he could see the strained look on Moses's face and the toll it took on him. "When this is done. Let's go get a drink again. I'll introduce you to some women."

"I'd like that," Moses said.

"There are so many women out here searching for a good man. And believe me, they love talk. You don't have to say a word. They'll do all the talking for you." They both laughed at that. "Hopefully, God sees us through this," Bishop said, bringing the subject back to the most pressing matter.

"God has nothing to do with it. We're gonna see ourselves through it," Moses said.

Bishop turned and looked at Moses directly. "You don't believe in God?"

"Oh, I believe in God. I just don't believe God gives a shit. I've seen too much shit in this world to believe otherwise."

"I believe in God. I believe God has a purpose for all of us, that God guides us. And that we might not always see it but there is a greater good at work."

"What was the greater good for slavery? What was the greater good for lynchings? What was the greater good for your son dying?" Bishop wanted to answer, but he was honestly too angry with God over the death of Desmond to say anything. He wanted to believe there was a greater good at work. He needed to believe it. Otherwise, what was the point of all this? "Frederick Douglas said," Moses continued. "'I prayed for freedom for twenty years but received no answer until I prayed with my legs.'"

"God helps those who help themselves," Bishop said.

"And that's what we're doing."

A young member of the gang walked over to Moses. "Soldier," he greeted him.

"What's up?" Moses said.

"I need more of that white girl."

"You moved your package already?"

"You know how I do."

"Good. There's more inside," Moses said.

The gang member nodded to Bishop and went through the fence and into building three. Moses could tell that Bishop was disturbed by the exchange. "Say what you're thinking," he said.

"You're selling drugs?" Bishop asked.

"Yes, I am," Moses answered straightly.

"You're selling drugs to our people."

"I'm selling drugs to every people. You'd be surprised how many white and Asian buyers, and dealers, come through here," Moses said.

"And you don't see anything wrong with that?" Bishop asked.

Moses pointed down the block. "Two blocks down there's a CVS, do you see anything wrong with that?"

"C'mon man, don't give me that we're street pharmacists shit. It's different and you know it," Bishop argued.

"Actually, no I don't. They sell adderall in there. It's pretty much the same as meth. And they give that shit to kids. They sell oxycontin as well. It's just as bad as heroin. What's the difference?" Bishop was stymied not having an immediate answer. "The difference is they tell you one is legal, and one isn't."

"Legal or not it doesn't make it right," Bishop said.

"I agree. It's about rights. And people have the right to harm themselves if they want."

"You want people to turn into junkies. We completely disagree there, bredren."

"I'm not encouraging people to turn into junkies. I'd prefer if they didn't. But I don't think it should be illegal. These drug laws are only a hundred years old. We think they've been around forever, but they haven't. And they were made to criminalize black and brown people. America forced the whole world to make them illegal, and because they are, they created all these gangs and cartels and all of the violence and killing and the mass incarceration that comes with it."

"I hear you. I hear you. But we can't fix the problem by perpetuating it," Bishop said.

"The real problem in the hood is not drugs but the violence and the killing. And we're fighting that, and it's working. We got a lot of the gangs to come together. The violent crime rate is the lowest it's been since anyone can remember. The police are taking credit for it, but we did that. We did it. For the first time in years people are feeling safer walking around, coming home late from the subway. Kids are playing in the parks more. Our elderly leave their house without fear of being robbed. People around here see the drug dealing and they don't care. They just don't want the killing."

There was a twisted logic in what Moses said. But in his heart of hearts Bishop couldn't bring himself to Moses's position. He'd seen up close how much drugs can destroy a person and a family. He had uncles and cousins who had been devastated by it. His uncle Dave suffered with heroin addiction for years and it cost him his family and caused early onset Alzheimer's.

At fifty-five he was a fit man, but his mind was gone, and he was institutionalized, and spent his days walking up and down a single hall. "I think you're going to trade in one monster for another," Bishop said

"Listen, when I took over the gang, I thought about stopping the drug dealing, but I realized quickly that shit was impossible. Look around they're just about no jobs here. You think I could tell them to stop selling drugs and have shit else for them to do to earn a living and take care of their families."

"But by selling drugs you're creating more junkies, which is destroying the community."

"I don't think so. I haven't seen it."

"You haven't seen it yet."

"You think these boys selling on the corner is bad. They don't compare to the pharmaceutical companies and the shit they do. I've seen their evil upfront. My mother was dying of cancer and a drug that could prolong her life they were charging 3,000 a month for. It was a tiny little pill and each one cost one hundred dollars. That should be a crime. Those people should be put in prison for that. America, Europe these people built their wealth on crime. I'm alright with us doing the same."

"If we do that, then how are we any better?" Bishop asked.

"The only time you're better than your enemy, is when you've beaten your enemy," Moses replied.

Bishop's phone rang. It was Diane. *Shit.* He recognized he had been out all day. "It's my wife. I gotta go," Bishop said.

"Okay. Go home. We end this tomorrow."

79

It had been over twenty-four hours and a dozen calls— and every call went straight to voicemail. Throughout the day she went from perturbed to perplexed to panicked and had settled somewhere around pissed, as she considered possibly Brian was not at Indian Lake, but somewhere closer.

"Hello," the woman answered.

"Is Brian with you?" Meagan asked, straightforward.

"Excuse me?"

"Is my husband with you?" Meagan clarified.

Shannon was silent.

"Listen. I know. I know, alright." Meagan had known three days before Desmond Bishop was killed. She had packed a bag that night—for him. She was tired of being a cop's wife and this was her out. She was almost relieved and grateful. Then Brian walked through the door blood stained and emotionally broken, and she forgot herself. "But I'm not calling about that," she said. "Brian isn't home. And I just want to know if he's with you."

It took a moment for Shannon to work up the nerve to speak. "He's not here," she said.

"Okay," Meagan said, relieved—and not relieved.

"But he was. He came yesterday in the afternoon."

"That bastard," she blurted from her belly.

"He came to break it off. He was only here for like ten minutes and then he left," Shannon explained.

"What time was that?" Meagan asked.

"Around two in the afternoon."

"Hmmm. Alright," Meagan said.

"Are you saying you don't know where he is?" Shannon asked, sounding concerned.

"He told me he was going to a cabin in Indian Lake. Did he tell you that he was going to a cabin?"

"No. He never mentioned anything," Shannon said.

"Okay. Thank you." Meagan was about to hang up.

"Wait. I just want you to know, I didn't know. I didn't know he was married," Shannon said, apologetic.

Meagan answered flatly, "I don't care," and hung up.

80

Bishop returned home and found Diane in their bathroom. "What is it?" he asked. There was an urgency to her call that had worried him.

"Tell me what's going on," she said. By her calm yet pointed tone, he knew this wasn't an emergency, but was nevertheless imperative.

"What's going on?" He played coy.

"You've been doing something these last two days and I want to know what it is."

"Doing what? Diane, I don't—"

"John," she cut him off. "Don't lie to me."

He didn't want to lie to her, but he also feared her knowing. Beyond her reaction, there's a thing called plausible deniability, and if he told her she would lose that in the case this all went to hell, which it very likely could.

"You don't want to know," he said.

"Yes, I do."

"I don't want you to know."

"I am your wife. We've been together for twenty years and two children. Tell me," she said pointedly. Diane recognized that she had been right. There was something he was hiding and by the grave look on his face it was grave. He knew there was no getting beyond this. She could smell the blood in the water, and she would not relent until she had bled it all out.

Bishop felt a great burden lifted, no longer having to keep this from her. That lasted until the first hit came, as she began pounding his chest and shoulder with the bottom of her closed fist. "What's wrong with you?" she said. "What's wrong with you. What were you thinking? Why did you do that?"

Bishop gave the only answer and defense he had, "I'm a man," he said, baring his teeth, the veins in his brow visible. "I'm a man," he repeated as a sharp whisper. "He killed my son. I had to do something."

"You're a man and I'm a mother. Do you think you loved him more? I'm the one who carried him. I'm the one who chose to have him. Do you remember? It was my choice. Even though with my sickle cell it was an at-risk pregnancy. And I went through damn near two days of labor and the most pain I ever experienced in my life to bring him here."

"I never said I loved him more. I said I had to do something."

"And I'm not doing something? I'm fighting to get justice for him, and I'm doing it by myself."

"Justice? Diane there won't be any justice."

"Don't say that."

"Don't fool yourself. They're playing the same game with us they play with everyone else. They'll tell us to wait for an investigation, then they'll get a grand jury and then they'll get him off just like they always do. Then they'll give us a little money for our trouble. That's what our lawyer is waiting for. And that white man will walk away and have his life and his family, and I couldn't stand that."

"You couldn't stand that, so you decided to make this all about you and not Desmond."

"What?" Bishop was baffled by her question.

"From the moment you spoke at Sharpton's you made this all about you. It's all about your feelings, and what you want, and what you can't handle, and what's best for Desmond has taken a back seat. And you've taken all of the focus away from Desmond and put it on yourself."

"What?" Bishop said, utterly nonplussed. He couldn't believe what she was saying.

"Are you doing it to make up for the fact that you feel guilty for what happened?"

"Guilty? For what?"

"You lent our seventeen-year-old son your car for the night. Why?" she yelled. "You don't even like me driving the car. Did you do it, so that he could pull up in front of his girlfriend and be a big man? While Cece brings home a boy for the first time and you damn near terrify him."

"Is that what you've been thinking?"

"You've been making this all about you. It's always about you. Ever since Desmond was three and he put that basketball through that baby hoop, you've been trying to live through him, wanting him to live the life you feel you had to give up, because you became a bus driver. You let your seventeen-year-old black son drive your BMW knowing damn well what the world thinks when they see him. And you wanna make up for it by kidnapping this man and tearing our family apart even more."

"Stop . . . stop," he said, holding his hand out for mercy as if he was being lashed by a whip. The tears came uncontrollably. "How could you say that? How could you say that?" The ferocity of it all tore Bishop down, and he sat on the covered toilet, with his head in his hands.

Some things you think, some things you feel, sometimes you say things you think but don't feel. Diane felt angry, and the anger was a respite from the unremittent sadness. Her son was dead, her first born, her beautiful boy, not quite a man, but what a man he could have become. She was heartbroken and racked with headaches. She felt tired of giving interviews alone, and having the questions divert from getting justice for her murdered son to what her husband had said. He was the man, and he got to check out and deal with his pain, while she had to deal with her pain, and work, and the lawyer, and the police and the press—and now he had kidnapped this man—and she had to contend with what might befall their already beleaguered family. Men get to deal with their pain. Women must suffer it, as they must consider consequences.

"I just had to do something," Bishop said, teeth clenched weeping. "I had to do something." Diane began crying as well. Seeing him so broken she regretted what she had said. He did not fully know what she was going through, and she did not know what it was like to be a man and to feel the burden of vengeance more acutely. There was nothing served adding to his pain. He was not at fault. The white man who murdered their son was.

She walked over to him standing in front of him, to hold him and hold herself up as well. Bishop held her by the waist and planted his head in her stomach, she held his shoulder and rubbed his head and they wept together. "I'm sorry," he said. She bent over and kissed his forehead, not amorously, just as an involuntary impulse. And they both realized they hadn't kissed each other in so very long, not since the morning before Desmond died. They hadn't held each other intimately either. They missed touching each other. Bishop looked up at his wife and without telling them to, his hands began to undo her pants, and she let him, she helped him, she stepped out of them, and he pulled his pants down as well, to his ankles, and his bare bottom, sat on the bare toilet cover, and it was chilled at first, but warmed quickly, and she sat over him, and they both guided his way inside, and it had been so long, and felt so warm and welcoming and fulfilling and pleasurable and painful.

81

A half hour later they sat in the same place. He was soft but still inside her. They couldn't bear to separate, out of love and exhaustion. They just held each other and had intermittent fits of kissing. In a quiet moment Diane felt her intestines pull on her vocal cords, and the words, "You can't let him go," escaped her mouth. Bishop looked at her to make sure he heard what she said, and she looked at him, and said nothing and said everything.

Bishop never gave much thought to how this would end, but it was obvious this was the only way. If he let McNally go, McNally would go to the police and Bishop would go to jail, which worried him less than the fact that Diane would lose her husband and Cece her father, and after losing Desmond that was something he couldn't bear for them to suffer. He saw now that he had been making this too much about himself and losing sight of his wife and daughter in the process. He had to put them first now. He had started this and he had to finish it.

82

McNally had never felt more tired in his life. A day and two nights he had spent in this humid, musty hell; neck sore, back sore, ass sore; listening to the recurring train, listening to the rats, to the black and Spanish voices passing above him, and the mad people in the halls. Sleep came in half-hour fits between hours of regret and contemplation.

He missed his bed, he missed his children, he missed his

wife. It had been well over a day since they spoke. Meagan must have called a dozen times. She must be going mad with worry. *Jesus*. Would he ever see his family again? He didn't know. He didn't know what was in Bishop's mind. In his heart he felt Bishop was a good man. McNally had absorbed a great deal of what Bishop had said to him. He had nothing to do last night but mediate. Admittedly he missed Bishop. He was his captor, but McNally preferred his company to the solitude of the night and the dread of what else might come into the room.

He heard footsteps in the hall. He was happy and greatly relieved when he saw Bishop walk in. As he did yesterday, Bishop brought water and food.

"Good morning," McNally said.

Bishop said nothing. He gave McNally a bag with another turkey sandwich. After the long night it smelled otherworldly good. McNally didn't know to be grateful or afraid. Was this his last rites? Was this his last meal? He bit in and his teeth tore through the roll, the vegetables, the cheese and the meat, and it was so good. It excited every taste bud; electric currents went off in the back of his tongue. It evoked memories of childhood.

He was four and his brother Joseph was six. Their twelve-year-old cousin Shauna was babysitting. She didn't know how to cook and the only things in the house to eat you had to cook, and they were all very hungry. She took the boys to the market and bought corned beef, fresh bread and a packet of orange Tang. When they returned, she made Tang and corned beef sandwiches. At the time it was the best meal McNally had ever had. This sandwich was now a close second. He chewed it slowly and made certain each bite was paste before he swallowed.

While he ate, he looked at Bishop who sat in his chair silently; always the gun visible in the front of his waist. Bishop hadn't said a word. He just sat and looked at the eroding wall. Though he looked as if he was looking beyond the wall into something else entirely.

McNally finished and said, "Thank you," and Bishop said nothing. He just kept looking through the wall to the side of Mc-

Nally's head. He looked heavy. That look told McNally today would be different than yesterday. Yesterday was a marathon. Today would be a sprint. "I understand, you know," McNally found himself saying. You think something, you don't plan to say it, but then it starts coming out of your mouth like puke catching you off guard. "I understand why you did it." That took Bishop out of his torpor and he turned and looked at McNally. "If I were you, and it had been my son, my daughter, my wife, I would have done the same." Bishop smiled slyly, not fully trusting what McNally was saying.

"I've been on the job eight years, and every day she still says make sure you come home. Make sure, Brian. And every day I promise her I will. She never liked that I became a cop. At first, I didn't want to either. I wanted to be a ballplayer, but I wasn't good enough. I wanted to be a lawyer, but I wasn't smart enough, or maybe I just wouldn't dedicate myself enough. I goofed around a little bit, then I met her, I fell in love, she got pregnant, and I needed the security. Law enforcement was there for me. It always was. It saved me. But it worries her, every day. So, I made her a promise to always come home . . . and that's what I was doing that night. I was keeping my promise."

"I made a promise too . . . when I threw dirt on my son's coffin," Bishop said.

"And have you kept your promise?" McNally asked.

Bishop shook his head. "Not yet." Bishop leaned in and began pointing the gun at McNally, not threateningly, more conversationally. "But you see, McNally, if I do, I make you the victim. But if I don't, I stay being the victim. And I gotta tell you, I'm real tired of being the victim."

"I'm tired too," McNally began. "I haven't slept. Not just since I've been here. I haven't slept, not since . . . I keep seeing his face." You are how you were born. Your views evolve over time but in the most pressing times you go back to basics. McNally was born Catholic—and he let it out. "I was sick that day—that night. I usually work the four to twelve. But I left early because my ulcer started messing with me. I'm heading home, I leave the precinct, I'm in a department unmarked car. I notice this BMW drive by; the color catches my eye. Baby blue. You don't see that shade of blue every day, so I look at it . . . I see the driver. It's a black guy. He's grown but he's a kid, and this is Brownsville. Kids don't drive BMWs around here unless they're in the game. But I'm off, my ulcer is killing me. If he is a dealer he'll keep for another day. He turns on Mother Gaston, and I turn as well. I usually take Rockaway home, but I can take Mother Gaston. So, I follow him and I'm behind him for about six blocks. Then I see him pull over by this church behind this Nissan. A white guy wearing a backpack, looks like he's in his late twenties maybe thirties, looked like one of those guys who always got a slight green smell to them, because they're vegan and don't like wearing deodorant. Looked real out of place around here. I see 'em in Bedstuy, sometimes, Bushwick, Williamsburg, definitely, but not the Ville. I get the feeling something is going down, so I lay back at the stoplight and I watch. Five minutes later white guy gets out the car, gets back into his Nissan and both cars pull off.

"I'm off, I should just go home. My heart is telling me just go home. But something in my gut says I know something went down. There's a high likelihood they have drugs on them. High likelihood of a gun as well. Lieutenant had just chewed us out about not getting any guns in the last two months. My head is telling me this is an easy score. And they haven't been easy to come by lately. They're at an intersection, the Nissan is going straight, and the BMW is turning. I can't follow them both. I gotta choose but at the time I didn't think it was a choice. I follow the BMW. I follow your son. I put on my lights, I put on my siren, after I've made the turn. The car drives about a block and a half. I'm guessing he's not sure if the siren is for him. The car I'm driving doesn't have a loudspeaker so I can't tell him to pull over. So, I ring the siren again. He gets the message this time and he pulls over on the next block. He pulls over at the bottom of the block. I wanted him to pull over in the middle to give me room to pull up behind him. But again, I don't have a loudspeaker, so I can't give him orders. If I pull over on the block I'm on, the light's about to change, if traffic starts going, he can easily take off and I lose him. So, I go through the intersection, I go past him and pull over a few yards ahead.

"It's nine at night, but it's Brooklyn, it's summer, it's live. There's a playground across the street. People are out. They're playing ball, they're watching people play ball. Subway is nearby. People are getting off. A lot of talking, a lot of noise and . . . I'm alone. And it hits me how alone I am. My unit isn't with me. No one to watch my side or my six. It's just me. People are walking by, they look at me, they can tell I'm a cop. I don't know, but I feel like they hate me just from looking at me. I'm on edge and . . . I'm afraid. I hear someone say pig, or maybe I just imagine it. A car drives by, music is playing loud, some rap song I've heard on the radio, but I don't know the song or who sings it. I'm regretting doing this already. I wanna just get back in my car and drive off. But I'm already in it, so I gotta follow through. I just saw a deal go down. I know that for certain. This kid definitely has some drugs on him, I'm telling myself, and I'm thinking he's a dealer, so he probably has quantity on him. And he likely has a gun. And as I'm walking towards him, I put my hand on the grip of mine. We're directly under the train tracks and the train is going by and it feels like it's literally shaking everything. There's a man and woman down the block cursing at each other, looks like they're about to have a fight—or maybe they're just playing. My mind is a mess. I realize I'm looking at them too long. I look back at the car and I see hands out the window. I see hands and I swear I see a gun. I swear I see it. It's right in his hand. Every time I dream, I see it. Even now I'm still seeing it. My heart rate spikes. I feel it in the back of my throat. I say drop the weapon—in my head—and I'm firing at the same time. They say I fired off seven shots—but It felt like three. To this day I swear it was one, two, then three, but it was seven. Now shit goes crazy. People run; they scatter. But not everyone. I can hear their voices. It's like a foreign language. You don't understand most of it but every once in a while, you pick out a word, "he shot him, he shot him." I approach the car. The car is shot all up. The alarm is going off like an old rotary phone. I see him and he's alive, but he isn't moving. I train my gun on him. I'm telling him don't move, don't move, but he can't. He just looks at me and his eyes, his eyes are big, and they're wide open. It's like he can't blink. And he's so scared. He's so scared. And so am I. I'm the most afraid I've ever been in my life. He's probably dying and I'm not seeing a gun. There's no gun on the ground, anywhere. For a second there I wonder if someone had taken it up before I got to him. That's what I was thinking at the time. But maybe the gun was in the car. I ask the kid, your son, Desmond, I ask him where's the gun, and he says nothing. I say get out the car, but he can't move. He's bleeding and all he can do is look at me. I undo his seat belt with one hand and with the same hand I pull him from the car. I lay him belly flat on the ground. He's in pain but he doesn't have the energy to scream. I see he's bleeding badly but he's still alive. Procedure say you always secure the suspect because you just never know. So, I pull his arms behind him and I handcuff him. I look in the car. I'm looking, I'm looking but there's no gun. And he's agonizing on the ground, and I'm still looking. I call my sergeant. I tell him there's a shooting. I tell him where I'm at. He tells me to secure the gun, but there's no gun, and I'm scared—and he's bleeding. I call in EMS. I'm thinking don't die, don't die, but I'm also thinking, fuck me there's no gun. I see he's scared. I tell him you're going to be alright, EMS is coming, but it wasn't soon enough. I watched him die. I watched the life leave his eyes right in front of me. I see it now. I see what I did. I see everything I did. I see what I took from you. I killed your son . . . I killed your son . . . and I'm sorry," McNally said and looked up.

The gun was six inches from McNally's head. Bishop had listened to all of it. He took it all in. He didn't interrupt. He tried not to breathe for fear that an exhale might throw McNally off. McNally saw Desmond. He saw his skin, he saw his youth, he saw the car, he followed him. He saw a drug deal and decided Desmond and not the white man was the dealer. He pulled him over. He put a gun in his hand that wasn't there. He shot him seven times—not three—seven.

He had vision enough to make every shot land but couldn't see that there was no gun in his hand, because the gun was not what made him a threat. He called his sergeant and searched for a gun that wasn't there before he called for help. He watched Desmond die and him being sorry didn't change any of that. McNally looked up at him with shimmering eyes. He was trembling, surrendering to whatever his fate may be.

Bishop's finger massaged the trigger . . . and pulled.

With a bang and a flash of light McNally's head went back and then slung down.

Bishop saw it.

He saw him dead. McNally breathed and looked at him, but Bishop saw him dead. Bishop couldn't pull the trigger. He wanted to. His entire body was tense, like one muscle. He bit down on his teeth so hard he felt they might shatter. He wanted to kill him, he needed to kill him, but his mind couldn't send the signal to his finger. He dropped his hand, released the tension in his body and dropped back in his chair. Both men looked at each other in silence for another ten minutes, then Bishop got up and left the room.

83

Bishop rented a U-Haul van for the day. He drove it to building three and parked it in the back. He did as he had been doing for the last two days, entered through the back door and walked a flight down into the basement. With a nod, he walked by the four boys congregating in the hall and entered the room McNally had been kept in.

When McNally saw Bishop, he didn't know what to make of him. He seemed different from before, more convicted. Before he seemed like a man searching to figure out what to do.

Now he appeared to have made a decision. Bishop took the keys from off the desk in the room, walked over to McNally, pulled out a black piece of cloth, which was an old t-shirt, Bishop had ripped, wrapped it around McNally's eyes and took his sight away. McNally was more afraid now than he had been this entire time.

Bishop undid McNally's handcuffs from the radiator, leaving his hands handcuffed in front of him. Bishop helped McNally to his feet as he didn't have his sight and minimal use of his hands. Bishop held McNally by the shoulder and began to guide him out.

McNally felt like asking what was going on, but imagined he wouldn't get an answer, and if he did it wouldn't change what was going to happen anyway. He remained silent for now and followed Bishop's guidance. Bishop walked him into the hall by the four boys who he passed before. They seemed surprised to see McNally out, but were unsure what to say, until one of them asked, "Yo what's good?"

"What's good?" Bishop replied.

"You done with him?"

"Yeah, I'm done with him."

"Soldier said we was taking him out?"

Bishop debated for a beat before replying, "Yeah."

The boys looked at him dubiously for a moment before replying, "A'ight," and returning to their dice game.

Bishop lead McNally out of the building. For the first time in days McNally felt the sun on his skin and breathed fresh air. It didn't last long as he was quickly ushered into what appeared to be the back of a van. Bishop sat him down on a milk crate and rechained him to a handlebar in the van. Bishop then got out closed the van doors and got into the driver's seat. After a bit of ambling they got out of wherever they were parked and made it onto a road. Where they were going McNally didn't know but he was certain wherever it was, it would be the end of this.

84

The van stopped and his heart rate quickened. He heard the engine turn off. He heard the car door open. He felt the dip in the van as someone got out the driver's seat. He assumed it was Bishop but couldn't be sure. He heard the footsteps on pavement as they came around, the clank and the clink of the door opening, felt the light sting his periphery, felt the weight of someone stepping into the van, the footsteps approach, the blindfold came off.

He squinted as he regained his sight. Bishop sat across from him. They both sat on opposing milk crates. They just looked at each other. They didn't say a word. Bishop still had his gun. It was visible in his waist. The standstill could have lasted a minute. McNally was going to break the silence when Bishop said, "Give me your hands," McNally raised his hands and Bishop removed his handcuffs.

You wear handcuffs for two days straight and it's amazing how much a part of your body they become. They become not just accessories but appendages. Your body feels almost unnatural without them. He felt so much lighter. Handcuffs weigh roughly one pound, but after two plus days they felt more like twenty; twenty pounds he just lost. His wrists were red and raw. He soothed them with his thumbs.

Bishop had uncuffed him, but McNally remained seated, not exactly sure what to do next. Bishop shook his head. "Go. Go home to your family," he said. McNally still didn't leave right away, as if he was asking Bishop internally, "Are you sure?" Bishop nodded. McNally stood up and began leaving the van. Before stepping out he turned to Bishop and asked, "What are you going to do?"

"I'm going home to my family," Bishop said. They both shared a nod and McNally departed.

Bishop leaned back and let out the deepest breath of his life. Having let McNally go he felt lighter as well. He wasn't sure if he had done the right thing. However, he felt undeniably lighter. Now he just wanted to see his family.

85

Bishop let McNally go somewhere in Flatlands, Brook-lyn. He was roughly three miles from his home in Marine Park. He decided to walk it home. Go two days in a filthy, humid, moldy basement, without showering and you begin to look almost homeless. At least that's how he appeared to himself as he passed his reflection in storefront windows. He smelled ripe as well. People walking by got a passing whiff of how rank he was. He didn't care, he just wanted to get home. Beyond his house keys, he had nothing in his pockets otherwise he would have taken a cab. It took him a little over twenty minutes to get to his house. He had never been so happy to see his front door and he thought he might collapse right there at the door mat. He found the strength to push through. Before he entered, he surveyed the block. He remembered that video Soldier showed him, with the man outside of his house with the gun. There was no such man outside presently and he felt relieved.

His daughter, Sarah, saw him first. As soon as she heard the door open, she knew it was him. Meagan was in the kitchen preparing dinner and calling his phone for the umpteenth time. Meagan was an hour away from calling the precinct and reporting him missing, when she heard Sarah yell out, "Daddy."

Meagan walked briskly into the living room and found him kneeling hugging his daughter. Meagan was so happy to see him, but then she looked at him. He looked dirty and worse for wear and, "You smell Daddy," Sarah commented.

"Yeah, I know. But I was up at Grandpa's cabin, only the water had gotten shut off, so I didn't get to shower while I was there. And then when I was driving home, my car broke down, and I had to walk the rest of the way home."

Meagan heard his story. She didn't believe any of it, but figured it was good enough to tell the kids. She let it stand—and beyond that she was just so happy to see him.

"Hey," she said.

"Hey," he replied.

86

McNally didn't feel up to recounting the events of the past two days, but he knew brushing Meagan off wouldn't do, and he didn't have the energy to lie. So, he told her. He told her everything. He even told her about Shannon and going over there to end it. Meagan told him she knew about Shannon. He was shocked.

His iphone was acting up, and he brought it into the apple store to have it repaired, only he wasn't able to pick it up and asked Meagan to do so for him, and he forgot he had unlocked his phone before giving it in, and when Meagan got it a text message came in from an unstored number, and the message was a bit too familiar. A brief search revealed everything. Meagan was set to confront Brian and leave him the night he shot and killed Desmond Bishop—but that changed everything. Nothing else seemed as important, and Megan did what she had always done for her family, she sacrificed.

McNally was ashamed and speechless. But Meagan told him that didn't matter right now, that they would deal with it at another time. She told him to move on in the story. He did as she requested. He got to his being taken, being chained to a radiator in that room and meeting the father of the boy he killed.

"And what happened?" she asked.

"We spoke."

"About the shooting?"

"About everything. It was so much."

"For two days?" she asked.

"Basically, yes."

"Brian, you have to report him."

"I'm not going to do that. I can't do that," he said.

"Brian, him and these other people kidnapped you. They could have done whatever to you. You have to."

"I'm not going to do that. I killed that man's son. I did it, Meagan. I killed his son. And I did it because he was black . . . I can see that now. And he could have killed me, so many times, but he didn't, and he found the strength to let me go, knowing that I'd probably go to the police. And truthfully if I was in his place, and it had been Aiden, I don't know if I would have had that strength. So, I'm not going to report him. I'm not going to do anything more to that man and his family."

87

Cece was a junior at Brooklyn Technical High School in Fort Greene. It was one of the better high schools in Brooklyn. Living in Canarsie, she was not zoned for that school and had to earn her way in. Cece had always been a bright child, always got top marks. She cried the one time she got a C in middle school. Bishop and Diane had to console her and tell her it was okay.

It was two weeks into the new school year. Bishop pulled up outside of Cece's school in the U-Haul van, got out, stood beside it and waited to see his daughter among the flood of students leaving for the day. After five minutes, Cece and Josh walked out together.

Bishop was still not sold on the idea of the two of them, but he was warming up to it. From what he had heard Josh had been very helpful during this time and Bishop had met his parents at Desmond's funeral, and they seemed like fine people, and were appropriately condoling.

Bishop waved to get Cece's attention and ushered them over. Surprised to see her father, and standing beside a U-Haul van, Cece walked towards him with a bit of trepidation.

"Daddy?"

"Cece."

"Are we moving?" Cece asked while looking over the van.

"No."

"Then why are you driving a U-Haul?"

"I just needed to move something today, so I got it."

"Oooookaaay. So why are you here?"

"You can ask question eeen. Mi can't come pick up mi daughter?" Bishop said in patois.

"No. You never do that."

Bishop laughed. "Well, I'm doing it today." He turned to Josh. "Hello Josh," he greeted.

"Hello Mr. Bishop." They shook hands.

"How have you been? How are your parents?"

"I'm good. They're good. Thank you. How have you been Mr. Bishop?" Josh asked.

"I'm . . . I'm . . ." Bishop struggled to answer. He was finding it even hard to bullshit. "I'm figuring it out," he said. It didn't make much sense but that's what came out of his mouth.

"Okay," Josh replied with an understanding nod.

"Now Josh, if you don't mind, I'm gonna drop Cece home. Just need a little father daughter time," Bishop said knowing they usually took the train home together.

"No," Josh said. "I'll see you tomorrow," he said to Cece.

"I'll text you tonight," Cece replied. They shared a platonic hug and Josh departed.

Cece and Bishop got in the U-Haul and drove off. They weren't two blocks away when Cece asked, "Okay, what's going on? Did something happen? Is Mommy okay?"

"Nothing has happened. Your mother is fine. I just realized

we haven't talked much since . . . and I just wanted to see how you were doing."

"Um, I guess, I'm like all of us, just trying to figure out how not to break down every day."

"I'm right there with you," Bishop said.

"I just try to be helpful as much as I can with you and Mommy, because I know what you're going through."

"And you have been. You've been great. I've meant to tell you that."

"Thank you," she said.

"How has it been at school?" Bishop asked.

"It's been okay. Everybody has been really supportive—students, teachers, a lot of people have really reached out to me," she said.

"That's good to hear."

"And some people have been a little too supportive," she said.

"What do you mean?" Bishop asked.

"Well some people are talking about doing marches and protests, but the way they're talking, it sounds like they might wanna do some crazy stuff, and I don't wanna be a part of it."

"Good. Don't. Stay away from them. Some people have their own agendas and they wanna exploit Desmond's name as a part of it."

"Okay," Cece said. "They love you by the way," she added. "They think the speech you gave was great."

Bishop chuckled. "Let them think that. Let me be the one crazy person in the family." Cece laughed as well. "Look, I know right now, it seems like everything is all about Desmond, and it seems like it sucks up all the oxygen, but I want you to know that I haven't forgotten you. I love you and your mother more than anything, and nothing in the world means more to me."

There were tears in her eyes. "I know Daddy, I know," she said. She then broke down. "I just miss him. I miss him so much."

Bishop fought hard not to break down as well. "I know. I miss him too." Bishop stretched his hand out and touched her head affectionately, his fingers sinking into her curly hair. "But we're all gonna get through this alright. We're gonna get through this together."

88

Diane came outside when she saw the U-Haul pull up. Bishop and Cece came out hugging each other as they walked up the driveway. Diane was happy to see them happy together. For a moment the weight of everything else was lifted, and she imagined this was how they would move forward as a family. Perhaps they could find a way to be happy again.

"Daddy picked me up from school," Cece said.

"I see . . . and in a U-Haul," Diane said.

"I had to move something," Bishop said.

Diane understood what he meant and everything that was dark in the world was brought back into focus. "Okay," she said. "Cece head inside. Give me and your father a moment."

Cece gave Bishop another big hug and then went inside.

Bishop and Diane looked at each other for an extended moment before, "I didn't do it," he said.

Diane let out a very audible sigh of relief "Thank God. Thank you, Jesus." They both laughed uneasily.

"I couldn't do it. I just couldn't do it," Bishop said.

"Thank God, you didn't. I wanted to call you and tell you not to. But then I thought maybe you had already done it, and I might make things worse by calling and telling you that."

"I'm just happy you think I made the right decision."

"You did," she said. "So, you let him go?" she asked.

"Yeah. Whatever comes next, I don't know."

"Whatever it is, we'll deal with it together," she said.

They hugged each other.

"I love you," he said.

"I love you," she said.

"I have to go."

"Where?" she asked.

"I have to go back. I have to talk to Soldier."

"What do you think he'll say?"

"I'm thinking, I'm hoping, he should be fine. He did this for me. And McNally only saw me. I wanna make sure he and the other men know no matter what happens, whatever McNally does, this will only fall on me, and I won't give up him or any of them."

89

McNally slept for the first time in three days. The last forty-eight hours had been a hellish ordeal. He had prayed to make it home to his family and his bed and, after he had showered for a half-hour and steam washed it all away, his bed had never felt so welcoming. It was eighty-nine degrees out. He turned the air conditioning on as high as he could and wrapped up under the covers. His head hit the pillow and sunk.

He slept.

He slept for an hour.

He was jolted awake. Meagan was shaking him. "Brian, wake up, wake up," she said, sounding frantic.

"What?" he said, drunk with sleep.

"Get up. You have to see this."

"See what?"

Meagan used the remote and turned on the bedroom television. She turned it to the news. There was a breaking news banner at the bottom of the screen. An Anchor Woman was making an announcement. "In what police are calling a coordinated terrorist attack, six former NYPD police officers have been shot and killed execution style in their own homes."

Hearing the news, whatever bit of grogginess in McNally's system was shot through with adrenaline. "Holy shit," he said from his intestines.

The news anchor continued, "And it seems these former officers all have something in common. They were all involved in the shooting deaths of unarmed black or Hispanic men." Those last words gripped McNally's heart like a vise. Meagan looked at him and without words they were of the same mind.

"I'll get dressed," he said.

"I'll get the kids ready."

Within twenty minutes the McNallys were in Meagan's sports utility vehicle. Meagan and Brian did a quick pack with three sets of clothing for everyone. All Meagan told the kids was that they were going out. She didn't tell them where. She didn't know where. "Where are we going?" she asked Brian as the children blithely played with their tablets in the back seat.

"My parents?" McNally suggested.

"What if they know where your parents live?" Meagan asked.

McNally hadn't considered that. "Then where?" he thought out loud.

"I think you should go to the precinct. I think you should tell them what happened. I think you have to now."

McNally was reluctant but Meagan was right. Things had changed drastically in the last two hours. "What about the kids? We take them to the precinct too?" he asked.

"Yes. I don't want us separated," she said.

"Okay," he said, "okay."

90

They reached the 65th Precinct in a half hour. Things were a good deal more frenetic than they usually were. Everyone was on high alert. McNally approached the desk sergeant.

"What are you doing here, McNally?" sergeant DeMarco asked.

"I heard," McNally answered.

"You believe this shit?"

"I believe it," McNally said.

The desk sergeant looked over and saw Meagan and the kids. You brought your family. "That's smart. We don't know if this is over."

"Any news?" McNally asked.

"Not much. Said it was done by guys dressed in UPS outfits. That's about it right now."

"I think I might have some information," McNally said. "Let me talk to Bertrand."

91

McNally and Meagan were in the interview room. Detec-tive Monroe, Lieutenant Cashman and Deputy Inspector Bertrand, the precinct commander, were in the room as well. Riley, Daniels and Roberts watched through the one-way mirror in the adjacent room. McNally had just told them about his abduction, omitting Bishop from his narrative.

"And you think the guys who kidnapped you may be responsible for the killings?" Cashman asked.

"I can't be certain, but maybe."

"Did you hear any names?" Detective Monroe asked.

"No," McNally answered quickly more as a reflex to protect Bishop. But then he thought for a bit. "Soldier. There was someone they called Soldier. I think he was the leader."

"Okay. Was it him that let you go?"

"I can't say. I was blindfolded. Whoever it was, put me in a van, drove off, uncuffed me, left me twenty minutes' walk from my house and then drove away."

"Why did he let you go?" Deputy Inspector Bertrand asked.

"I can't say. I'm just relieved he did."

"What happened while you were abducted?" Monroe probed.

"This one guy just badgered me again and again about the shooting. My shooting," McNally said.

"Was it this Soldier?"

"I can't say if it was or wasn't. He didn't give his name. And they were always covered. Baseball caps and surgical masks."

"Could you get a sense of his race?" Cashman asked.

"He was black. He could have been Hispanic. Beyond that I don't know."

"What did you tell him?"

"That the shooting was justified. That I was sorry, and I just wanted to get home to my family."

"That's it?" Monroe asked.

"We really just talked a lot about black and white people and race and racism."

"Did they try to get any information from you? Did he mention doing anything to other officers?" Monroe asked.

"No. Not that I recall."

"Do you think the guy who let you go is the same person who questioned you?" Inspector Bertrand asked.

"I'm not sure. The guy who let me go never spoke to me." McNally said, trying his best to tell as much of the truth as possible, while leaving Bishop out of it.

"Why didn't you report your abduction as soon as you got away?" Bertrand asked.

"I was tired. I was just relieved to get away and I just wanted to see my family."

"Anything you can tell us about where you were?" Cashman asked.

"It was somewhere in Brooklyn," McNally said.

"How do you know?" Monroe asked.

"When I asked the guy, who questioned me where we were, that's what he said."

"Do you believe him?" Cashman asked.

"That's what he said, and I took it for the truth."

"What can you tell us about the room you were in?" Monroe asked.

"It was underground. Dirty, old, rundown, paint chipped. A lot of mold and mildew. Could have been a boiler room, maybe of a building."

"So, it was a building?" Monroe tried to clarify.

"I'm not sure. I can't say definitively," McNally said.

"What else? Was there anything you kept hearing?"

"From time to time, I could hear people outside walking above me. It was the hood. They were mostly black. I heard Spanish here and there."

"Did you smell anything?" Cashman asked.

"Not really. It was kind of musty and damp."

"When you were in the van how long do you think you were driving before he let you go?"

"Hard to say. But roughly twenty minutes," McNally answered.

"Twenty minutes to Flatlands, and then you were a twenty-minute walk from your house in Marine Park," Monroe deduced.

"Yeah, that's about right," McNally said.

"Is there anything else? Anything you heard?" Inspector Bertrand asked.

McNally thought for a minute. "You know there was a train. I kept hearing a train."

"Subway?" Cashman asked.

"Yeah. But it wasn't underground. It was definitely above. It fell like it could have been one block at most two away. It felt real close."

"So, we're looking for an old rundown building in Brooklyn, real close to an elevated subway line," Cashman said.

"Oh shit," Riley blurted from the adjacent room, having a light bulb go off in his head.

92

Bishop walked through the maze-like machinations of the boiler room and came to the old office where a few hours ago McNally had been held. He could hear arguing. The room was filled with people. There was Moses and four of the older boys, and two of the younger ones. The younger two were the ones Bishop walked by when he left with McNally.

"So, you just let him stroll that man outta here?"

"Soldier, you said you was working together. I thought he was doing what you wanted," the younger boy tried to explain. The younger boys had no idea McNally was a police officer. Soldier and Saquon had told them that he was a drug dealer who had stolen money from the crew, and they were holding him to gather information from him. At that age, the boys didn't pay much attention to the news. They had heard of Desmond Bishop but didn't know John Bishop was his father. Soldier told them Bishop was an army buddy of his who was good at torture and interrogation. They took Soldier at his word and thought nothing more of it.

"You thought? Did you hear me say he could take him out?" Soldier railed at them.

"Nah, but he said—"

"Nah, but nothing. You don't listen to him. You listen to me God dammit."

Bishop walked in and intervened.

"Don't blame the boy. It's not his fault. I'm the one who took him out." Holding in his rage like biting his tongue, Moses looked at the two younger boys and told them to go home. One of the boys gave Bishop a sour look as he walked by, mad he had gotten them in trouble. Moses turned his attention to Bishop, "And where is he now?" he asked, though he was fairly certain of the answer.

"I let him go," Bishop said.

"You let him go. Did I tell you, you could let him go?" Moses asked.

"No, you didn't."

"No, I didn't. In fact, I told you specifically, to finish what you were doing because we had to resolve this situation."

"Yes, you did."

"And you knew what I meant?"

"Yes, I did . . . but I couldn't kill him."

"Remember before I picked him up, I asked you if you wanted me to do it, knowing what the consequences would be, I asked you, and you said yes," Moses reminded him.

"I know what I said."

"So, you forgave him," Moses said, shaking his head.

"I didn't forgive him. I just couldn't kill him. I tried. But I couldn't bring myself to do it."

"I never told you to kill him."

"Yes, but even if I left him for you to kill him. I'd still be killing him."

"I told you before that we all must play our part. I am a soldier. My role is to be on the frontlines, to defend us and do the hard things that need to be done. Not every man is a soldier. You are a father and your role is to raise strong black children who know and love themselves. That is important as well."

"I heard you . . . but in the end, it was my decision."

"It was not your decision." Moses took objection.

"He was my son."

"Nigga fuck yo' son," Moses roared. Surprising many of them in the room. They had never seen him display this level of anger before. "You think I did all this just for your son? I did this for him and him, and his son and his daughter and all the sons and daughters to come, and have come and gone. Get your head out of your ass. This shit is bigger than you. And by letting that man go, you put every man in here, brothers who put themselves on the line to help you, in danger."

Bishop was stunned by Moses's ferocity. "You're right. It's bigger than me. And I appreciate what you and everyone in here did for me, I do. But I'm the only one in danger, alright. He ain't seen none of you. And I blindfolded him before I took him. And I ain't take it off until I got him far away. He only knows me. His beef is with me. And if he goes to the police, I'm the only one going down. And I'll never give any of you up. I promise you that. I promise you all that on the soul of my son. I came back here to tell you that."

"So, you're saying we're safe?" Moses asked.

"You're safe. I'm the only one who'll go down for this."

"Let me ask you something, how many senses do you have?"

"What?" Bishop remarked, thrown off by the question.

"Do you only have one sense? Is sight the only sense you have?"

"No."

"Alright then—listen," he said.

"Listen to what?" Bishop asked.

"Just shut the fuck up and listen," Moses retorted bitingly. "Everybody quiet," he said to the others. Everyone did as Moses said. Bishop as well. The regard and respect Moses showed Bishop had eroded mightily, and it had been replaced with contempt. For the first time he looked at Moses and felt unsafe. He had to do what he was told. Like the others he listened.

They didn't know what they were listening for. At first, they heard nothing at all, beyond their beating hearts and the sound of their respiration. Then they heard the ambient noises, the traffic outside, the voices of the people walking above them on the sidewalk, the sound of an airplane flying overhead, the sound of the elevated subway train two blocks away. And then it hit Bishop—the train. He had heard it as well every five or so minutes for the last two days. He never paid it any mind. Why should he? It was just noise. But if he heard it, then McNally heard it, and, "If he knows he was in a building, by the look of it abandoned, next to an overhead subway train," Moses began.

"Oh shit," Saquon blurted.

"Assume he's already been to the police," Moses continued. "Assume they've already questioned him. It won't take them long to figure out where we are. We're compromised. We gotta break everything down and get outta here."

Gucci walked over to Bishop and said, "Yo, you fucked us, homie."

"Look, I know I fucked up. I see that now. I shouldn't have taken him out without telling you. And they'll find this place. But look, he still only knows me. And I swear, I swear, I'm not giving up any of you."

Saquon approached him shaking his head. "This ain't just about your cop."

"What?" Bishop asked looking bemused.

"It's not just your cop. There's six others."

"What are you talking about? You kidnapped six other cops?"

"No, not kidnapped," Kareem said, and then Moses began to explain.

93

Three weeks ago, Moses had a meeting with Kareem, Sa-quon, Demarius and Gucci. It took place at Moses's home, in his mother's house, in her living room. Moses had never invited them into his home before. The fact that he did let them know this meeting was important.

"What's up Soldier?" Kareem asked.

"I only asked you four to this meeting because this ain't for everybody. You guys are the Lieutenants and I trust you above all others. In this last year, you've earned my trust and I hope I've earned yours."

"Okay," Saquon said, curious to know what this was all about.

"Now we all know about Desmond Bishop," Moses said and asked at the same time.

"That's the kid the cop shot," Demarius said.

"Right there on Livonia too, yo. Watched homie die right there in the street," Gucci said.

"Yeah, they shot him up seven times," Saquon added

"Yeah, and I'm gonna hit them back for it," Moses said.

"Hit who? The police?" Saquon asked jokingly.

"Yes," Moses answered with conviction and no emotion. "But not just any cop. I'm going to hit the cop who did it. And not just him alone. Six others as well. One for every bullet he shot. I wanna send a message." They were all taken in, just absorbing the gravity of what Moses was saying. "Now I can do a few myself, but like I said, I want to do seven, all on the same day, all around the same time. Tactical, efficient. I can do about 3 or 4, but I'll need help with the others. I can't be everywhere at once." Moses let that sit for a beat, before asking, "Who else is in?" They were all very sober—and silent. It was the first time he had ever seen them speechless, even Gucci, and that boy never stopped talking. Their trepidation was understandable. "Look I understand what I'm asking of you and I won't knock any man for not doing it."

"I'm in," Saquon said. Saquon felt a special bond with Moses, especially after learning he had killed Moses's mother. He owed him a great deal and Moses's forgiveness was something he felt he could never repay. Beyond that he had seen the difference Moses's leadership had on the gang and all the gangs in Brownsville in fact. He trusted him, possibly more than he trusted his own brother. He would have followed Moses anywhere. If Moses believed doing this was worth it and would make a difference, then Saquon believed it as well.

Kareem joined in next. With Moses he didn't feel like a gangbanger, he felt like a soldier, like he was fighting for something greater than himself. Hitting back at the police for all the killing and abuse they had committed and gotten away with felt noble to him.

Gucci was in once Saquon was in. They had known each other the longest and had been getting into scraps together since grade school. He wouldn't let his brother go into a fight alone. And over the last year he had come to see Moses and trust his judgment. He had the utmost respect for him and liked the world he was trying to build.

Demarius was the most reluctant. Though he had come around to respect Moses like the others, he wasn't sure if he could follow his lead here. What turned him around was the fact that if they had asked him to go do a hit on a rival gang, he would have been the most gung-ho. "But before I say anything, I need to know how you plan to do this? How we gonna get away with it? I'm not trying to go to jail for this. I love getting pussy out here too much." They all chuckled at that, though they took what he said very seriously.

"I respect that," Moses said. "I'm not trying to go to jail either. I don't wanna be a martyr. I don't want any of you to be martyrs. I wouldn't trade your life for the life of any of these people. I wouldn't ask you to do this if I wasn't sure of us being successful." Moses then broke down the plan.

Moses took out his laptop. He had Intel on hundreds of police officers. When they asked him how he got this, he informed them he got it by hacking into the NYPD database through the computers at the 65th Precinct. "How the hell did you do that?" Kareem asked. Moses held up a thumb drive.

Three days prior, Moses went into the 65th precinct and filed a missing person's report for his mother. This was of course a ruse, given Moses's mother was already dead. He told them she had dementia and had wondered off. An officer took Moses into the back by their computers to fill out the report. While the officer was working on the report, Moses asked for something to drink and the officer seeing how distraught Moses appeared, kindly went to get him some water. Moses took the opportunity to kneel and pretend to tie his shoelaces but in fact placed a malware infected thumb-drive in one of the computers USB ports. He bought it from a seller based in China off the dark web using bitcoins a few days prior. As soon as the thumb-drive was inserted it began downloading the malware. It was done in less than thirty seconds. Moses removed the thumb-drive and was back to sitting upright before the officer returned. They then completed the report and Moses left.

He returned two hours later and said his mother had been found by a relative in Bedford Stuyvesant. Apparently, she had traveled to an old apartment she used to live, and a neighbor recognized her and called the family. Moses thanked the officer again for their help. Moses went back to his house and opened his computer and he was in the NYPD database. He had information on police officers, past and present, their addresses and mobile numbers. He even had a layout of all the surveillance cameras in the city—and he knew which ones were working and which ones weren't.

There were seven targets on their list. McNally and six others. On the day of the hits McNally had already been gotten and was chained up in the office next to the boiler room of building three of the Claude McKay Houses. For the other six, they broke into three teams; Kareem and Gucci, Saquon and Demarius, and Moses who was a team onto himself. Moses would do the lion's share. He assigned himself four targets.

Saquon asked why he was taking on so many. He explained that they were all within a twenty-minute drive of each other. He could do them all in just under two hours. Also, three of the targets had families, wives and children. Dealing with these variables would be tricky and he only trusted himself to do it. He stressed repeatedly that they were only meant to take out the targets and no one else. If they were forced to take someone else's life they were to abort rather than proceed. If they killed anyone but the targets the message they were trying to send would be lost.

They needed cars for the job. Moses already had the old used Honda he had bought when he intended to kill Saquon. They got McNally's Buick after they abducted him. Moses bought another car, a Chevrolet Impala from an independent seller for again a little over two thousand. Moses brought all three cars home, removed their hoods and removed their vin numbers, and then put their hoods back on.

Moses then took a trip to Newark, New Jersey and bought three pairs of old license plates from a junkyard. They placed each set of plates on each car. They got three prepaid burner smart phones and installed a cell phone tracking app on each. Their own personal phones they left on and at home. Moses created dummy accounts and bought five UPS uniforms from three different costume sellers on eBay. Moses then bought three refurbished laptops for cheap on Amazon. He didn't want the laptops; he just wanted the official Amazon boxes fashioned in a way to make someone believe a valuable piece of electronics was inside. He then had sticker print outs made with the name and address of each target. They finally bought three police radios, so each car could keep track of any police activity in their vicinity. They were set. Each team knew their targets and the exact routes they were supposed to drive.

Target one:

Moses arrived at his home in Nassau County at exactly ten am driving McNally's Buick. He placed the packaging sticker on the box with the laptop. He put on a UPS baseball cap and tied a surgical mask around his neck and left it hanging below his chin. He put on a pair of nitrile latex dip work gloves. He placed his gun with the silencer already attached in the front of his pants, and let the shirt hang over it. He placed a small roll of duct tape in one of the shirts front pockets and several police grade flexicuffs in the other front pocket.

He left the vehicle with the package and went to the house and rang the bell. The Target's wife answered. He told her he had a package for the Target which required a signature. Not expecting a package, she seemed confused and called to her husband in the other room if he was expecting something from Amazon. When the husband entered the room, he found the UPS delivery man, now wearing a surgical mask, standing behind his wife with one hand firmly over her mouth and another with a gun pointed at her head. He was stunned and before he could say a word Moses put the gun to his lips in a gesture to be quiet. Moses then led both the Target and his wife to the sofa. "Take anything you want, man. We don't have much but just take it," the Target said.

"I don't want your money," Moses replied. He threw the Target two flexicuffs and instructed him to bind his wife. The Target was reluctant. "I'm not here to harm your wife. Don't make me have to." The Target understood and given how in control of himself this man was, he knew he meant what he said. The Target bound his wife, who was now crying, by her hands and her feet. Moses then threw the Target the duct tape and instructed him to cover his wife's mouth. The Target again reluctantly did as he was told. He then asked, "If this isn't about money, what is this about?" "You know," Moses said, and promptly put a bullet dead center in his chest and then walked over and put one in his head. The wife screamed but it was muffled by the duct tape.

Moses looked around the house for the door leading to the

basement. He found it opposite the kitchen. He returned to the living room and grabbed the wife by the hand and pulled her, as she pleaded for her life, downstairs. There was a large metal pole in the middle of the basement. Moses carried her over to the pole and attached another flexicuff around the pole and around the cuffs on the wife's hand. She was attached to the pole and would not be able to move. Moses left her crying in the basement and then left the house with the Target dead on the living room floor.

It was a fifteen-minute drive to Target Two and then a twelve-minute drive after that to Target Three. The hits proceeded in a similar fashion. Target Two opened the door when Moses rang, and so he led him inside and shot him in the foyer. Moses found the wife unaware cooking in the kitchen. He promptly gagged and flexicuffed her hands and feet behind her and left her struggling on the kitchen floor.

Target Three was the most difficult because he had children, a fourteen-year-old girl and an eleven-year-old boy, who were both unexpectedly off from school, and Moses had four people he had to contend with. He had to repeatedly stress to the Target that his family would be fine, and he had no intentions to harm them. "If I meant to harm your family, I wouldn't need you to bind them." After Moses had the Target bind and gag his family, Moses took him into the basement and shot him there. He then attached each family member to a different immovable object in the house and left.

Target Four was divorced and lived alone. When Moses rang the bell, he didn't come to the door. Moses heard him watering his lawn in the backyard and met him there.

"What are you doing back here?" the Target asked.

"You have a package. I rang but no one came to the door," Moses said, while studying the backyard and looking to see if anyone was around. There wasn't anyone.

"So, you just walk onto someone's property?" the Target angrily asked.

"Yeah," Moses flatly replied, then took his gun out from his pants and put one in the Target's chest and walked over to him and put another in his head. He then grabbed the body by the armpits and pulled him into the house out of view.

Moses had gotten the Target's blood on his UPS shirt, but it didn't matter, he didn't need the uniform anymore, his jobs were done. However, he couldn't drive around like this. He went in the Target's closet and took one of his t-shirts. He then took off the UPS shirt and put it in a plastic grocery bag, put on the Target's t-shirt and left the house, got in the car and drove off.

Target Five lived in a shitty apartment building in the Bronx. His life had spiraled downward since his shooting. No formal charges were brought against him, but the Department found him guilty of misconduct and he was released from the force. He had a series of affairs and his wife eventually left him and took the children.

He was high on crack when he opened the door for Kareem and Gucci. He didn't recall ordering a package but then again, he didn't recall not ordering a package. The apartment was squalid with beer cans and old pizza boxes piled up in the corner as if they were modern art. It smelled like week's old body order and sweat. Kareem and Gucci looked at him and how pitiful he was. He looked at them wondering why they weren't leaving. Then they took out their guns with the silencers attached and the Target knew what this was. "What took you so long?" he asked. "I've been waiting for you. I've been waiting a real long time. But you don't have to kill me, man. I'm dying already, I'm dying already. I'm killing myself slowly. I'm dying already. You don't have to kill me."

Kareem and Gucci looked at him as if they were momentarily sympathetic but then raised their guns together and unloaded on him. The bullets riveted his body and knocked him into his love seat. Gucci then walked over to him in disgust and spat on him. Kareem went nearly apoplectic. "You spit on him?"

"Hell yeah, piece a shit. You remember what this bitch did?"

"So, what. You don't watch TV?" Gucci looked confused.

"DNA, bitch, DNA. Wipe that shit up," Kareem said. It then hit Gucci what a dumb thing he had done. He got two pieces of paper towel from the kitchen and wiped the spit off, and a good deal of the Target's blood as well. Kareem though knowing DNA can be found in weird places in very small amounts, found bleach in the kitchen and doused the body for good measure.

Target Six lived in Astoria, Queens. He came to the door while talking on the phone and gestured with his hand for Demarius and Saquon to wait while he finished his conversation. This annoyed them and they considered shooting him right there at the door, but Moses had told them it was better to do the hit inside. After hanging up the Target looked at the package and simply said, "I didn't order anything," and began closing the door.

Demarius stopped the door from closing, and said "It has your name on it, and it needs to be signed." The Target became suspicious as he had never known UPS delivery people to come in pairs. He also recognized that there was no UPS truck outside. However, most importantly he asked Demarius, "How do you know it has my name on it? I never told you my name." At this point it was time to give up the ruse.

Demarius took out his gun and rushed the Target, pushing him inside. The Target grabbed both of Demarius's hands and held the gun away. Saquon hurried inside and closed the door. In the time Saquon took to close the door the Target, who was a man in his early forties and in very good shape, had gotten the upper hand on Demarius and thrown him to the floor when Demarius went for his gun, the Target fell on top of him and wrestled it out of his hands. Saquon shot him through the side of his head from temple to temple. The body fell and Saquon helped Demarius to his feet. "You good?" he asked Demarius.

"Yeah," he replied. "It's a good thing we came in twos. The man was strong, he woulda had me."

"Don't worry about it. You did good. Let's go. They picked up the Amazon package, put on their surgical masks, left the house got back in the Chevy and drove off.

94

Bishop was utterly horrified at what he had heard. "What have you done?" he asked. "You killed six cops. I didn't agree to this. I want no parts of this. You were only supposed to go after one cop. My cop. That's it."

"You keep thinking this is all about you," Saquon said.

"Yeah, you selfish, homie," Gucci said. "This shit is bigger than you."

"Your son was the spark, but he wasn't the cause," Moses said to Bishop. "The cause has been building for a long time now."

"That maybe. But killing cops—that don't work. That won't accomplish shit. Dudes done that before. Went crazy, killed some random cops. It didn't do anything but cause riots and get themselves and other people killed," Bishop argued.

"See that word you used—random. That was the problem. They went out and killed random cops. Cops who weren't directly involved in any killing. That was wrong. You have to kill the ones who did the deed. Having another pay the bill on someone else's debt won't stop that man from cheating you. You gotta collect from that man directly. Then things will change," Moses said.

"What do you think is gonna change?"

"Everything. Power concedes nothing without a demand. Once a cop knows if he kills someone in our community unjustly that his life is forfeit, you best believe he's gonna talk to you first like a human being, and make sure it's really a gun and not a cell phone, or a toy, or a lead pipe or nothing at all. Wasn't that what your son had? Nothing—just black skin. You have to hit back. I learned that a long time ago when you're dealing with bullies. Even if you get your ass kicked, even if you get killed, you have to hit back."

The gravity of everything that had happened and was about to happen hit Bishop like a massive headache. "What have you gotten me into? You should have told me you were going to do all this. I would have told you no, that I wanted no parts of it," Bishop said.

"Maybe I should have. But it's too late now."

"I gotta get outta here. I gotta get to my family," Bishop said sounding frantic and turned to leave. Moses gave a look to Demarius and Kareem who were behind him. They understood instinctively and blocked Bishop's path. They didn't reveal their guns but by their posture, standing with their hands in front of them at the ready, Bishop knew they were armed.

"You're stopping me from leaving?" he asked Moses.

"I can't let you go. Not right now."

Moses started walking towards Bishop and Bishop in that moment feared for his life. Bishop pulled his gun and aimed it at Moses. The other boys pulled their guns as well. With a silent gesture Moses stayed their hands.

"You pull a gun on me?" Moses asked.

"You're not giving me a choice. Let me go."

"You pull the gun I gave you on me?"

"I don't want to. But you're not letting me go."

"You pull a gun on the man who helped you after your son got killed, while you let go the man who killed your son."

"Because you killed six other people, and I'm connected to it, and you're going to get more people killed."

"Well go ahead then. Shoot me. Put me down," Moses said calmly and continued walking towards Bishop.

"Don't do this. Don't force me. Just let me go."

"I can't let you go. Not now." Moses stood right in front of him. The gun trembled in Bishop's hand. "You can't do it can you?" He asked. "Because you're not a killer. And that's alright. There's no shame in that. Moses easily took the gun from Bishop's hand. I bet you never really held a gun before." Moses handed the gun to Demarius

"Yo, this shit is light. What is it empty?"

"Yeah, it's empty," Moses answered Demarius and looked at Bishop. Bishop was stunned to find out the gun had been unloaded the entire time. "And you never knew," Moses said to him. Moses unloaded it because he knew Bishop was in an emotional state, and he feared he might get too close to the cop and the cop might take the gun from him.

He held Bishop with forceful affection by the back of the neck, and brought him close to him, heads tilted down, forehead to forehead. "See, I never expected you to kill the cop. That was for us to do. I just gave you the gun to give you leverage while you talked to him. But from your speech, from what you said, about pain and suffering, I expected you to understand and support what we were doing. But I was wrong about you, and now I can't let you leave because I can't trust you."

"I'm sorry alright. You made your point, but now—" before Bishop could finish his sentence Moses cocked his head back and butted Bishop right on the bridge of his nose, breaking it instantly and flooding his nose and mouth with blood. Moses released his neck and Bishop immediately fell to his ass.

"Cuff him to the radiator, same as we did the cop." Bishop felt like he was drowning and falling asleep at the same time as Saquon and Demarius dragged him to the radiator and hand-cuffed his left hand to it. Moses walked over to him and handed him a rag for his nose. "I'm sorry. When I asked you for a drink this is not how I intended things to end."

95

"When are they coming?" Kareem asked.

"It's hard to say," Moses said. "It could be in an hour. It could be hours. It could be tomorrow. But it won't take them long to figure out. Let's operate on the basis that they already know."

"We gotta get outta here," Saquon said.

"Yes, we do. We need to get a van," Moses said. We need to get all our product, equipment and anything that can link us to anything out of here."

"Where are we getting a van from?" Demarius asked.

"I have a van," Bishop said, through his broken bloody nose, using the rag to keep himself from swallowing his own blood. They all turned to him. "I got one to take the cop away. It's outside."

Kareem went to the basement window and looked out. "He's right. There's a U-Haul van outside."

"Good. Maybe the universe is on our side with this. Start packing it up," Moses said to the boys.

Moses walked over to Bishop, went into his pockets, and got the keys and Bishop's phone. "Just let me go, man. I'm sorry for what I did. I didn't understand but I do now. I won't tell anything about anything. Just let me go to my family."

"I appreciate you giving us the van. But I told you, I can't trust you anymore. I wish I could. When we've moved out and everyone is safe from anything you can say, then I'll let you go." Bishop sighed disappointedly, trying to keep the blood from going in his mouth. "Have faith," Moses said. "Pray. It works sometimes. Maybe it will see you through. Maybe it will see all of us through this."

96

"And why has NYCHA abandoned this building?" Dolan, the Commanding Officer of the Emergency Service Unit, asked as they were in the conference room of the 65th precinct going over the details of the raid. The ESU was a component of the Special Operations Bureau. ESU provided specialized support and advanced equipment to other NYPD units. They were the cops, cops called. They were stationed in ten squads around the city for deployment whenever needed. They were all focused on the current task at hand. Commander Dolan had over twenty years on the job. He had been a member of the ESU for the last ten years and had been leading it for the last five. He took this task especially personal as he had been good friends with two of the Targets that had been killed. He had been on vacation but came out of it when he heard the news to lead this effort.

"It's my understanding that the building was no longer liv-able," Deputy Inspector Bertrand explained.

"So, we abandoned it to gangs and derelicts?" Dolan asked.

"It was NYCHA's plan to relocate all the residents of the complex and then bring down all three buildings together but finding housing for that many people has been difficult, and plans have stalled." Bertrand said.

"So why not sit a patrol unit by the building at all times?"

"We have from time to time, but we just don't have the man-power to dedicate to one abandoned building on a consistent basis," Lieutenant Cashman said.

"So how many people do we think are in there?" Dolan asked.

"Those projects are run by CMK. They're one of the smaller gangs, unaffiliated with anyone else. We estimate them to have anywhere from fifteen to twenty members," Riley answered.

"So, we could have upwards of twenty armed suspects inside," Dolan said.

"I'm having a hard time believing CMK is involved in this. They're stupid kids who get into Instagram fights with rival gangs. They don't have the balls or the tactical expertise to pull off a coordinated attack like this. Those hits were done by professionals. I think we should go in soft with two units at first and get a sense of what's going on inside that building." Cashman said.

"Well officer McNally's description of where he was held matches this building. And if they had the balls to kidnap an NYPD police officer off the street, detain and interrogate him for two days, I don't think we should presume what they can or can't do. And I'm not about to risk the lives of any officers doing a soft entry when they are possibly twenty armed men inside," Dolan said.

"I agree. We'll go in hard. I'd rather go in there hard and come out with nothing, than risk any officer being injured because we weren't fully prepared," Bertrand said.

Dolan turned to Riley. "You guys are familiar with the layout of the building?" he asked Riley.

"Haven't been in building three in years. But we're familiar with buildings one and two. Building three shouldn't be much different," Riley said.

"Alright good. Gear up."

Riley and all the officers taking part in the raid began putting on their protective vests. McNally entered the room and approached Riley. "Hey Riley, me and Meagan and the kids are heading out. They're putting us up in a safe house until this all blows over."

"That's good. That's good."

"Just wanna say good luck out there."

"Thanks. And you did real good today. You were sharp and kept your wits about you during this whole thing and you lead us right to them. And we're gonna get them for you, and for all the cops they killed."

"Thanks," McNally said. They shook hands and hugged, and then Riley continued gearing up. As McNally was walking away, he looked at a picture of the Claude McKay Houses they had projected on the big board. Building three was circled. This was where he had been held prisoner for the last two days. It occurred to McNally that it was only four blocks away from where he shot and killed Desmond Bishop. Seeing the force that was being deployed, McNally thought about John Bishop, and he hoped to God he had went home to his family, as he said he would, and was nowhere near what was about to go down.

97

It had been almost twenty minutes Bishop had been chained to this radiator. Bishop's left wrist was already sore from being handcuffed and he was going stir-crazy. It was eighty-five-degrees now, but he could feel the cold from the floor seeping into his ass. The entire room made you want to itch every part of you. This was what McNally was going through. Bishop huffed with a smile.

Continuously trying to stop his bleeding nose, Bishop considered all his actions that brought him here. He regretted many things. He regretted telling Moses to get McNally. Whatever satisfaction he gained from his and McNally's talks, it wasn't worth any of this. The saying, when you go looking for revenge dig two graves came to mind. Bishop had let McNally out of the grave, only to fall in it himself.

He could hear Moses and the boys rushing to pack the van. He wished they would let him help. The faster they were packed and out of there, the faster Bishop could be set free. All he could do now was sit back wait . . . and . . . what was that? It was a whirring vibrating sound, coming closer and closer. It was a helicopter. "Damn it," Bishop said out loud. *They're here.*

98

Buildings one and two of the Claude McKay Houses were fourteen stories tall. Building three was sixteen stories tall. At its height when all three buildings were fully occupied, there was an estimated 700 to 1000 people living in the entire complex. The estimate could vary this wildly as many apartments held more occupants than they were slated to have. After building three was closed, buildings one and two held an estimated 600 people.

Moses looked out the third story window with his assault rifle at his side. He saw two ESS armored trucks pulling up on Riverdale and another two on Powell Street. They were here sooner than he would have liked but it was expected. "Alright, they're here, and it looks like they're coming in heavy," he said to the boys. There was no way they would be able to finish packing the U-Haul and drive off now. There was no escape. Now it was about survival. Fortunately, they had packed the latest shipment of drugs in the van first. They had assault rifles and thousands of rounds of ammunition in the building still. They would have to make a stand here. Saquon and the others soberly took in what they were about to get into.

"Alright let's do this then," Gucci said.

"No, Moses said. "We can't win this fight."

That deflated the crew who were trying to psyche themselves up for something they were wholly unprepared for.

"You want us to just give up and turn ourselves in?" Demarius asked.

"That's a choice each man has to make. I won't begrudge any man for his decision. No one should. They all thought on that for a second. "But that's not what I'm suggesting."

"What are you thinking, Soldier?" Kareem asked.

"Right now, they're getting ready to come into the courtyard and cut us off. We need to keep them from getting in here. Because once they're in, we're done. So, we need to lay down a shitload of suppressive fire. We're not trying to kill anyone, we're just trying to back them up get them out of the courtyard, get them back on the street. Then we make a run for building two. It's less than fifty yards away. We can make it. Once we get to building two, we'll blend in with everyone else. There will be no way for them to know who's who. They'll come in and arrest some of us for just being part of the crew, but we had already worked out our alibis for today. We hold tight to our stories and we're good."

"I like it," Saquon said. "I like it."

"Yeah shit's Gucci," Gucci said. This was the first time he had ever said Gucci with a twinge of fear. His heart rate kicked up a few notches.

"So how do we keep them from getting in?" Saquon asked.

99

Moses had six pipe bombs in the building, which he purchased through the buyer in Texas. He and Saquon set a bomb at the doorway of each of the three entrances; one for the two ground entrances and one on the roof. He didn't conceal their presence. He placed the wire very visibly at the front and he placed other wires throughout the hall to give the impression it was all rigged. The bombs had enough explosive power to be a deterrent. If you were close enough it would kill or cause great bodily harm but not bring the structure of the building down. He wanted to keep the police away but in case a bomb went off he didn't want the explosion to be bad enough where they might be trapped inside. "That will delay them from coming in. For now," Moses said.

"But what about when we need to get out?" Saquon asked.

"Don't worry, I know how to dismantle them. But if something were to happen to me just step over the wire and you're fine. The whole hall isn't rigged. I just want them to think that."

"Good," Saquon said.

"Now we have to take out the snipers," Moses said.

"They have snipers? You've seen them?" Saquon asked.

"No. But I know they're there."

Moses was right. There were two snipers. One on the roof of building one and the other on the roof of building two. Presently, they were surveilling building three, and relaying any movements back to command. Moses had to take them out. There was no way they'd be able to get to building two with them there.

Moses and Saquon were on the fifteenth floor. They were in one of the apartments that had a view of both snipers. Moses saw them through the scope of his M40 sniper rifle, its bi-pods braced on an old chest of drawers Moses laid on its side. Saquon saw them through his spotter scope. Moses took two minutes calculating each shot then practicing the movement he would make as his target moved from the first to the second sniper. He had to take down one then quickly swivel and take out the other in seconds. Moses nodded to Saquon.

Saquon sent a group text message to Demarius, Kareem and Gucci, who were on floors three, seven and ten, respectively, each on a different side of the building. NOW, the text read. Saquon then took the butt of his gun and shattered the glass window in front of Moses, giving him an opening to shoot. Simultaneously, Demarius, Kareem and Gucci did the same. They broke the windows then immediately took cover.

"We have some activity here," Sniper One relayed. "We have windows being broken on floors three, seven, ten and fifteen."

"Do you see any suspects?" the voice over the radio asked.

"Not yeahh—shit," Sniper One said, just as a bullet struck the barrel of his rifle, shattering it. The sniper shuddered and snapped back and began to radio what had happened.

The second sniper had just gotten the radio message. He also heard the shot. He had an idea of where the shot came from. He twirled to the side and found Moses, but not before Moses had him. The bullet shot the gun from under the sniper as well as two of his fingers.

Using his spotter scope, Saquon saw both snipers slink away. "You only shot the guns. Did you miss?" he asked.

"No. That's what I was aiming for." Saquon looked confused. "They're just men doing their jobs. They got families like we do. Some of them may have served. We're not trying to kill anyone unless we have to. We just want to get them to back off to give us room to get out of here."

"I got you," Saquon said.

Gucci ran into the apartment out of breath after just running up from the tenth floor. "Yo. They're coming in from the front and Riverdale side," he alerted them.

"Alright let's get back downstairs," Moses said.

100

Riley and Daniels were with ESU alpha team as they ap-proached the building coming through the courtyard in tight formation. Two men led the way carry active shooter ballistic shields and they were ten men deep. Riley was the middleman behind shield one and Daniels was the middleman of shield two. They came to the door. Immediately the Sergeant in front saw the wire and the pipe bomb.

"Hold," he said and held up a closed fist. "Bomb."

"We got a bomb here as well," Bravo team radioed from the Riverdale entrance, where Roberts was.

Moses saw their confusion from the third floor. "Let's back them up," he said. "Don't aim for anyone. Shoot the ground."

The boys did as Moses said, and unloaded a fusillade of gun

fire from their modified AR-15s. The automatic weapon fire sounded like popcorn popping at the highest decibel.

"We're taking fire, we're taking fire," the officers shouted. It seemed like it was coming from everywhere. "Pull back. Pull back." The ESU officers began pulling back through the courtyard and the street, while returning fire at wherever they saw the muzzle flashes coming from. Within a minute they had regrouped and taken cover behind their armored vehicles.

Inside of the building, Moses shouted to the others, "Get to the stairs." Without question they followed his commands and ran to the nearest stairwell. Moses knew they needed to be where they would have the most cover. Within seconds of them making it to the stairwell it began.

After the ESU officers had all taken cover, they unloaded on the building from their Colt M4 Commando Carbine automatic rifles. Tearing into the facade and windows in and around the third floor apartments. From the stairwell, Moses and the others could see the dust and debris kicking up, as sustained gun fire eat into the walls. It sounded like a hurricane, like the lashing of torrential winds and rain.

101

"How about entry from the roof," ESU Commander Dolan asked from inside the Mobile Command Center, a fully armored RV. It was a tactical office on wheels. It was parked outside the Claude McKay Houses, surrounded by other ESS vehicles.

"No go. Our helicopter eyed it. The roof is wired as well," a member of the aviation unit said.

"Any idea how powerful the bombs are? Can we send the robot in, to detonate it?" Dolan asked.

"That's an option but they'd likely see it before it gets there and shoot it down. And they have snipers at least two."

"I thought these guys were supposed to be a street gang," Deputy Inspector Bertrand said.

"I'm not buying that. This ain't CMK. Especially after what we've just seen. These people are organized and coordinated," Lieutenant Cashman said.

"Whoever they are, I think it's safe to say they are the ones responsible for the assassinations earlier. And we must resolve this situation as quickly as possible," Dolan said.

"How do we do that?" Bertrand asked.

"Well I'm not risking any of my people going in there. We don't know what they could be walking into. The best bet would be to force them out." Dolan said.

"I agree. What do you suggest?" Bertrand asked.

"We fire bomb them."

102

"You want to drop a bomb in a highly populated residen-tial area in Brooklyn?" The Mayor asked as he sat in his office in Gracie Mansion doing a video conference with the Commissioner, the Chief of Department and Dolan.

"We believe the most expedient way to end this is to drop a tactical incendiary device on the building, yes, Mr. Mayor," The Commissioner remarked.

"It's my understanding that during the fire fight that they shot at the ground and not at any officers. And that their sniper shot the rifles of our snipers and not the officers themselves."

"There's no way to know if that was done on purpose Mr. Mayor or if we were just fortunate. They have already killed six police officers today, and they killed them in front of their families. So we know they do not have an aversion to killing. They are terrorists," the ESU Commander said.

"There's no way we can take the building and ensure no further police casualties," the Chief of Department said.

"Mr. Mayor," the Commissioner began, "you don't want it to come out that you could have ended this crisis without any further loss of police life, and you opted not to."

"Hmmm," the Mayor said, not liking the veiled threat. But he had no choice. They were all of one mind—and if you lose the police, you lose the city. "Are we sure that they're only terrorists in the building? Could they possibly have hostages?" he asked.

"To our best confirmed knowledge only the terrorists are in the building." The ESU Commander said, knowing he had heard that there may be homeless people inside. "And if there were hostages, they would have made demands."

"And this bomb, can we make certain that it hits just this building and the fire is contained to that building alone?" the Mayor asked.

"Yes, Mr. Mayor," the Chief of Department said.

"Because we cannot under any circumstances have this spread," the Mayor stressed.

"I agree," the Commissioner said. "It won't. We'll have FDNY there to control the fire after we've gotten the terrorists out."

"Then gentlemen, you have my go."

103

Diane was worried. Bishop should have been home by now. He said he had to go back and explain things to Soldier. She imagined it wouldn't be too bad given Soldier only did this on John's behalf. It should be John's decision to let McNally go, and McNally had only seen John. Then she saw the news of the six former police officers who had been killed; men who had killed unarmed black men and not been prosecuted. She wondered if this Soldier was somehow involved with that as well, and by extension was John caught up in it too. She had been calling him and his phone kept ringing out. Her heart was racing as if she was doing a brisk walk. She wanted nothing more than to see her husband walk through the door, or at the very least have him answer the phone and say he was okay and on his way in. The phone was ringing. "C'mon John, pick up, pick up."

Cece rushed into the bedroom. "Mommy have you seen the news? Have you seen what's going on?"

"What? What's going on?" Diane didn't want to hear any news. *Please no more bad news.*

Cece turned on the television.

"We're here at the corner of Riverdale avenue and Powell street outside of the Claude McKay Houses, where police are in an intense stand-off with the people they believe are responsible for the terrorist attacks earlier today, taking the lives of six former New York City Police Department Officers."

"Oh Jesus Christ," Diane blurted from her soul.

The look of absolute terror on her mother's face terrified Cece as well. "What Mommy, what?"

"Your father," Diane struggled to say. "Your father."

"What about Daddy?"

"I think your father is in there," she said.

"What? Why you think that Mommy? Why is Daddy there?"

"I have to go." Diane grabbed her bag and started heading out.

"Mommy where you going?"

"I have to go there. Stay here," she said to Cece. "Stay here."

"No. I'm coming with you."

"No, Cece, you stay here."

"No, Mommy, I'm not staying. I'm coming with you."

Diane didn't have the strength to argue with her. "Alright, come, come," she said. "And they left."

104

Bishop heard the phone ringing. It had been ringing just about every fifteen to twenty minutes for the last two hours. He knew who was calling. He knew she was worried, and he was worried sick for her. The phone was on the table across the room, completely out of reach. Moses leaving his phone in the room was a bit sadistic of him. If Bishop could at least get to the phone, talk to her, if only just to hear her voice, if only just to comfort her, tell her everything would be alright, even if it would be a lie.

He couldn't see what was going on, but he heard. He heard when the officers were approaching the building. He heard their footsteps. He heard their voices, their radio chatter. He heard when they said there's a bomb. *There's a bomb,* he thought. He heard when they said they have a sniper and he heard when the gun fire started. It was loud, near deafeningly loud. It was like being right next to the fireworks as they went off during the Fourth of July. He felt like he was trapped in the middle of a war zone that was steadily contracting in diameter.

He tried pulling and kicking and yanking that old radiator, but though it would creak and shake it wouldn't give. The handcuffs wouldn't give as well, and he had nothing to pry them loose. He kept trying to make his hands smaller, trying to squeeze them through. His hands were too large. The skin on his wrists were raw and peeling and bloody, and still he couldn't get his hand through.

He had to get out. He couldn't stay here. His only thought now was breaking his hand, maybe by breaking enough bones he could make it small enough to squeeze through. He slammed his hand against the ground and slammed it again as hard as he could. And though it hurt like hell, the ground wasn't hard enough to break the bones. There was only one thing in reach hard enough to do that. He looked at the radiator. He couldn't believe he was going to do this, but he had to. He gritted his teeth and flung his hand as hard as he could against the old rusted iron.

105

Day had turned to evening. The sky was orange. The po-lice had pulled back to the perimeter behind the cover of their armored vehicles, and they had stopped shooting, but there were officers blocking the nearest entrance to building two. If the crew attempted to make a run for it, the police would see them and pick them off. Moses knew this and was trying to a formulate a way to get out without unnecessary bloodshed.

Moses heard the helicopter. There had been a helicopter earlier but then it left. This helicopter, however, was different. It had a familiar whirl—very heavy. Moses had heard it hundreds of times. This helicopter was military grade. It was much louder than commercial helicopters and the ones the NYPD usually employed. This one had about seven blades, five more than the normal two. This increased its uplift force and weight capacity. And it needed this to be able to carry the extra weight. It was no doubt carrying ESU officers who were trained to rappel down onto their target.

He knew they had seen that the roof had been tripwired. It was quite possible they were prepared to detonate it and breach through the roof anyway. If they were going that route that meant they were willing to take the building by any means. Things were going to get very ugly. People would die.

These young men had grown to trust him over the last year and a half. They had trusted him enough to take part in the assassinations. He had led them into this, and like his brothers in the corps, he wanted to lead them out safely. His life didn't matter to him as much. If he needed to be the diversion so that everyone else could get out, so be it.

Then they heard it—and felt it—one big explosion. It was actually two, but one caused the other, and they came so close to each other they felt like one. The foundations of the building shook. For about ten seconds it felt like the epicenter of an earthquake. "What the fuck," Demarius blurted.

Moses smirked. *Touché,* he thought. He knew exactly what had happened. "It's a firebomb," he told them. "It's on the roof now, but it's going to spread. They're trying to burn us out."

"So, what do we do? Do we try to put out the fire?" Saquon asked.

"No. We don't have the means. And it's gonna spread fast."

"Then we gon' burn up if we stay in here," Kareem said

"We'll die of smoke inhalation first," Moses said.

"Then fuck it. Let's shoot our way out," Gucci said.

Moses nodded. "Push comes to shove. That's what we'll do. But for now, let's hold tight."

106

The occupants of buildings one and two of the Claude McKay Houses had been watching the events unfold. They saw when the police arrived in armored trucks that looked like mini tanks. They saw when they disembarked in all black in full military gear. They saw when they attempted to enter building three with their riot shields. They saw and heard when the gunfire broke out and the police were forced to retreat, and then returned fire ferociously for fifteen minutes.

They watched their televisions and were living and watching the news simultaneously. The streets outside were filled with news personnel from all the major networks, and many people who were watching and live streaming on social media. This was their home that was being shot up and it was being broadcast for the world to see.

A few of them knew the people currently in building three. They were sons and brothers, fathers, baby-fathers and cousins, nephews and uncles. And for some who weren't related to them, they were friends. For many others they were just a gang, and many had previously wanted to see them all locked up— many still did. However, in the last year the gang changed the way they behaved, and many of the residents had begun to view them differently.

The news were calling them terrorists. They said they were responsible for killing six police officers. That seemed incredible. They were a small gang not ISIS. Most of the residents didn't believe CMK could have anything to do with what was going on. And if it was true, there were those who believed that it was justified for the litany of killings and abuse the police had committed over the decades and gotten away with.

Things had gone quiet for the last hour. The longer this stand-off went on the worst it would get for the people inside, for their family, for their friends, for their fellow tenants. Then they saw it. They saw the helicopter fly overhead in the evening sky, hover for thirty seconds, then drop its payload.

It landed on the roof and felt like a minor earthquake and sounded like standing next to thunder. The sky turned a brighter shade of orange for about a minute then settled into rust. A chorus of "Oh my Gods," went through the two buildings; disbelief, fear and outrage bubbled over. "Was that a bomb?" "That was a bomb." "They dropped a bomb on them, yo." "They dropped a bomb on us."

107

The ESU Commander watched as fire began to slowly en-gulf the top floors of building three. It had been ten minutes. FDNY was on standby. They were waiting for the call to go in and stop the fire. They had been prepped and were at the ready. When given the go, they would need to act quickly before the fire got out of hand. If it did, it could spread to the grass and trees of the compound, and to the other two buildings, and that would be a disaster of monumental proportions.

Dolan was staid. He was a patient man. He had his men ready at every exit for when the terrorists attempted to make their escape. And they would attempt to escape or choose to die by fire. And he didn't believe these terrorists had the spiritual conviction for that.

There was another tremor as the roof of the building collapsed onto the top floor. Things would proceed this way until the entire building came down.

108

There were a dozen or so homeless people who had made building three their refuge. They kept to the upper floors, stayed to themselves and out of the crew's way. Now they were caught in the middle of this warzone. They had no idea what the cause of all this was but smoke had begun consuming the upper floors and was seeping through the entire building. The homeless had no parts of this and they wanted out.

A homeless man in his twenties coughing profusely from the smoke made his way to the front lobby. He never received the memo about the entrances being trip-wired. Moses heard the explosion go off and knew immediately it was one of the pipe bombs. He peaked out the window down at the main entrance. There was smoke and debris caused by the bomb going off. He wondered for a moment if the ESU was attempting a breach again but there were no officers around.

There was another homeless man who had been a few yards behind the man who triggered the bomb. He was blown back but not terribly injured. However, the bomb had temporarily deafened him, his ears bled, and he was incredibly disoriented. Despite the wreckage of the bomb, which had blown through the front doors, and dug holes into the side of the walls of the lobby, he could still see outside, and he still wanted nothing more than to get out. He continued forward and stepped over the wreckage and the mangled body. With a single-minded focus of getting out, he walked through what remained of the entrance, walked through the opening in the fence and stepped out in the open. He was only out for five seconds when a bullet struck him in his upper torso and spun him around before he fell.

109

The other homeless people saw it. Moses and the crew saw it. Many of the people in buildings one and two saw it. The news crews heard the shot fired but were not at a vantage point to see it. "Target down," the shooter radioed. The officers had given a verbal command to get on the ground. They gave one command. Four seconds later the shot was taken.

The Commander had given the order to take down anyone coming out of the building. He knew as well that getting to building two was the best path of escape. He had officers guarding the entrances of buildings one and two and had guns trained on the exits of building three to prevent that from happening.

The fire at building three was eating it away floor by floor and tree by tree. One of the adjacent trees caught fire and it spread to another. The FDNY official made the ESU Commander aware of this.

"Can you still put it out and contain it?" Dolan asked.

"Yes," the FDNY official answered cautiously but stressed that the longer it went on the less likely that would be, and that every minute counted.

"Then let it burn . . . just a little bit more," Dolan said.

The Commander wanted to buy a few more minutes. That's all it would take. The fire was already beginning to force them out. If he sent the FDNY in to contain the fire now he would lose control of the scene. The terrorists could escape the building and he wouldn't be able to stop them.

110

It had been an hour since the bomb went off. Night had come but the fire made it look like sunset. Moses and the crew wore their surgical masks to protect themselves from the smoke that had reached the bottom floors. It wasn't stifling yet, but it would be in minutes. They were all on the first floor, meters away from the front entrance, which was the closest exit to building two.

They had all seen the homeless man who tried to leave get shot down. Obviously, the cops were not accepting surrender and they would die if they stayed in the building. They all rifled up and placed extra magazines in their back pockets. Their only option now was to shoot their way out. Moses had wanted to keep unnecessary deaths down but now there was no choice.

He looked at his squad, these gang members, who he once contemplated killing, who he had come to look at as little brothers, and who looked at him as their leader. Some of them wouldn't survive getting out of this building, if any. But if that was the case Moses was ready to give his life to get as many of them out.

The homeless stood behind them coughing. Moses was responsible for them as well. The Desert Storm veteran came forward. "Lance Corporal Jones, reporting for duty sir," he said to Moses. This was the first time Moses had heard him speak; the first time he appeared to be in his right mind. "I'm ready to go in sir." Moses looked at him intently for a moment then he looked at Saquon. "Give him a gun." Saquon did as Moses said and gave him the handgun he held in his back. Their numbers had just increased by one, but they were still woefully outnumbered.

To get everyone out, Moses would take out the two officers guarding the entrance to building two then provide cover so the crew could make a dash for it. There was a great deal of smoke from the fire, it should help conceal them. Moses told them the plan and they all nodded they understood.

There were eight terrified homeless people who wanted to get out of the building as well. The best he could tell them was to run when they saw everyone else running. He felt sorry he had gotten these people caught up in this and just hoped that as many of them as possible would be able to make it out. Moses was getting ready to lead them out when they saw a flood of people rush out of building two into the courtyard.

The fire had spread from tree to grass to tree to the westward facade of building two and was beginning to climb the building. Tenants had been held back and kept from entering or exiting buildings one and two during the siege. However, as the fire spread panic grew, and tenants began pushing their way out. There were too many for the officers to hold back.

Seeing the blaze now spread to building two the FDNY stepped in and instructed their firemen to put out the fires without even asking the ESU Commander. Firemen began mixing in with the tenants. It was chaos and it was just what Moses needed.

"Take off your masks, drop the guns and just run," he said. "Blend in, they won't be able to make you out from everyone else," he instructed them. Seeing their opening and their weird fortune, the crew did exactly as Moses said and began running.

Officers saw them running from the building but didn't dare take a shot, and after a few yards they lost them in the crowd. Moses and Saquon were ushering everyone out, the homeless included. It was time for them to go. They were about to run out together when Moses remembered something. "Go," he said to Saquon, "Go. I'll catch up."

"Where you going?" Saquon yelled.

"I left something behind," he said and Saquon watched Moses run back into the smoke and fire.

111

"Our Father who art in heaven, hallowed be thy name. Thy kingdom come. Thy will be done, on earth as it is in heaven. Give us this day our daily bread; and forgive us our trespasses, as we forgive those who trespass against us; and lead us not into temptation but deliver us from evil. For thine is the kingdom, the power and the glory forever and ever . . ." he hesitated then said it ". . . amen," then he looked up.

There was this thing called Devotion. Every Wednesday morning before classes began all the students and all the faculty gathered in the front of the school. There was no auditorium but there was a dais, four steps elevated from the ground, where the faculty stood separately, while the students, grades one through five, in their khaki uniforms, stood in the oppressive heat, as the principal played pastor and held a church service. Giving devotion to our Lord and Savior, Jesus Christ. Dunrobin Primary School was not a religious school *per se*, but Jamaica was overwhelmingly a Christian country, and this was a practice held in all public schools.

Seven-year-old John Jacob Bishop hated every minute of it. If you were born Jamaican, you more than likely grew up Christian. Your parents were Christian as were your grandparents and just about everyone you knew. Bishop was a casual Christian. He went to church only on special occasions and weddings and funerals. He had just been to a church four weeks ago. On that day he hated God for taking his son from him. Not just McNally but God had taken Desmond.

Was God testing him, like he tested Job? Bishop had always found Job to be a sadistic book, where God and his Adversary played a horrible game on God's most devoted servant simply because they could. If this was Bishop's test, then he had failed. He couldn't understand why God had taken his son. He couldn't accept it. He had held McNally hostage to get an answer, not just from McNally but from God. He had received McNally's confession, but God was silent. Even as he held the gun to McNally's head, God said nothing. Bishop couldn't pull the trigger. Knowing that there were no bullets in the gun now made that moment comically tragic. He couldn't have killed McNally even if he wanted to. He freed McNally and as a sick twist of fate he had taken his place. Were God and his Adversary up above having a good laugh? The Adversary was winning this bet.

Nevertheless, here in his darkest moment Bishop found himself saying the Lord's prayer and pleading to God to forgive him his sins and, "Please bring me back to my wife and daughter." He prayed with only his right hand. He made it a fist and held it under his chin. His left hand was inoperable. It had become a mangled, bloody, swollen mess. He had slammed it repeatedly against the radiator. He was quite certain he had broken several bones and had lost the ability to move his fingers. His brain would send a signal and the fingers would at best shiver. He had done all this and was still unable to get the handcuffs off.

He yanked and he tugged. He tried massaging it slowly and tried yanking it violently, almost tearing his shoulder out, each way hurt and each failed. The pain came in waves of excruciating and unbearable. His last resort was to cannibalize himself and begin eating through his hand in hopes of getting free. If he had a saw or a knife, he would have cut his hand off already but as much as the thought ran through his mind, he couldn't bring himself to eat through his hand.

He put it to his mouth but couldn't do it. But he had to get out. He had to get back to Diane and Cece. Every now and again the phone would ring. He would cry every time he heard it. They were reaching out to him. "God get me through this."

Down here Bishop couldn't see what was going on but what he heard sounded terrible. He heard when the bomb hit the building and felt the ground tremble. He knew the end was coming. He could see signs of fire through the basement window. He heard when a smaller bomb went off, and he heard when a single high caliber gunshot was fired. He saw as the smoke slowly seeped into the room and watched as it kept seeping and seeping with ominous intent. With his teeth and his right hand, he removed his shirt and tore it into a rag and wrapped it around his mouth and nose. It helped with the coughing, but it would not suffice. He could feel the walls getting hotter. This building was going to hell and he was in the ass of it. Bishop had tried saving himself, now he put his head down and asked God to save him.

He looked up and there was Moses. Bishop's head fell from exhaustion. He was happy to see him but didn't have the energy to smile. Moses rushed over. "You came back," Bishop said.

"We don't leave any soldier behind," Moses said. He saw Bishop's left hand, and he imagined what Bishop had been through down here. Moses simply said, "Sorry."

"It doesn't matter," Bishop said. "Let's just go." Moses however didn't have the key for the handcuffs, but he did have his gun. He pulled his handgun from his back pocket. Both he and Bishop shielded their heads and Moses shot the chain. Bishop was finally free. He couldn't have ever imagined what being free from bondage was until that moment. Moses helped Bishop to his feet.

"Can you walk he asked him?"

"Yeah."

"Can you run?"

"Yeah."

"Alright good, because we gotta hurry."

They ran out the room but then Bishop stopped. "Wait," he said. "I forgot something." He went back into the room and grabbed his phone. He then met Moses in the smoke-filled hall, and they navigated their way out through the boiler room and up the stairs.

They were on the first level, fire was on all sides, the air was thick with smoke, but there was a distant light that showed the outside and it was only roughly twenty yards away. That light shot Bishop with a jolt of hope and energy as both men navigated their way through the flames and debris.

Bishop's phone rang again, and it was in his hand, and he looked down and Desmond's graduation picture was his screen saver and Cece was calling. Seeing his son's face and his daughter's name, tears came to his eyes, then Bishop heard a creak from above, his thumb clicked answer and he looked up.

112

Diane and Cece arrived at the Claude McKay Houses roughly an hour ago. They had parked the only place they could find, four blocks away in front of a fire hydrant. They didn't care if they were ticketed or if the car was towed. They got out and ran the four remaining blocks.

There was a police barrier around the perimeter of every building. No unauthorized personnel were allowed in or out. If you lived in buildings one and two—too bad. You were not entering your home until this had all been resolved. There was a mother who was a Nurse's Aid who was returning from work, who's children were alone in her apartment on the fourth floor of building one and they would not let her in. The scene was manic. There was media, and wannabe media, and spectators.

Diane approached a police officer and implored him that her husband was being held hostage in building three. He radioed someone about what she said but he got back no response but informed her they were doing everything possible to get everyone out safely. Then they saw the helicopter drop the bomb. Cece yelled, "Oh my God," and Diane fell silent, and prayed and prayed. When she saw that the building didn't collapse after the bomb fell, she believed there was hope.

She continued praying and in between praying she called John's phone. The response was the same. It rang out. She took solace in that. If it had started going straight to voice mail that meant something had changed with the status of his phone, which could have meant something terrible. The fact it kept ringing for now was a good thing.

Then they watched the fire grow and they heard another explosion, and with every event all the people around them gasped and they heard a solitary gunshot, and many people ran, but Diane and Cece ran closer to the ESU command center, and she heard over the police radio, someone say target is down. *Target? What target? Who?* She tried telling them that her husband was a hostage inside, but no one would listen. They told her and Cece to get back. There was nothing more Diane could do but as they say, let go and let God.

She began praying again—and her eye began twitching, and it twitched so much she closed it and just prayed. She didn't watch as the fire grew and spread but Cece did. And she along with the crowd screamed at the police to put the fire out. And there was a near riot building in the streets. The situation was becoming unsustainable. There were roughly four police precincts on the scene, and it was insufficient. The situation had gotten to a boiling point. The tenants of buildings one and two pushed their way out of the buildings, and the FDNY finally stepped in to battle the fire. Cece told her mother and Diane watched nervously.

They heard chatter over the police radios that the targets were escaping building three and blending in with the crowd. They heard the word escape and were hopeful. Diane told Cece, call your father because Diane didn't have the energy to do so again. Cece pressed Daddy on her phone and it began ringing, and after three rings it finally picked up, and Cece heard what sounded like the inside of a building on fire. "Dad, Daddy," Cece screamed. Realizing Cece finally got through, Diane came to the phone. "John, John," she called, then they heard a roar and looked up as the center of building three crumbled in onto itself. Diane's heart dropped as she dropped to her bottom and the phone went silent.

113

Saquon and the others were able to blend into the flood of people coming out of buildings one and two. The homeless were not so fortunate. Riley and the ESU officers advanced into the courtyard. There was fire in the trees and the grass, and thick smoke in the air. Like vines, fire climbed the outsides of buildings one and two. Building three was a caved-in inferno. Riley and the other officers had seen people running through the fence leaving building three but then they would lose sight of them. This angered Riley that they might be getting away. Some of the homeless, the ones who had their wits about them, were able to blend in, but many stuck out like a sore thumb.

They approached the Desert Storm veteran. "Get on the ground, now," they shouted. He stopped and looked at them as they came in black through the smoke. "Now you see me," he said. "Now you see me. You ain't seen me all this time. Now you see me." Most of the officers couldn't hear him over the chaos. "Get on the ground," they shouted again. "Fuck ya'll," he replied, flicked them away with his hand and walked forward.

They fired for five seconds. His body was ravaged. He fell to his knees and then his face.

People screamed and ran, trying to get out of the courtyard, while fire fighters ran in trying to put out the blaze. The mad man walked coughing through the smoke, one hand over his mouth, the other holding up his pants. Riley and the ESU officers approached him next. "Get on the ground," they shouted. He saw them and there was madness and fear in his eyes. "Now," they commanded.

He trembled and said the only thing that came to mind, "The world is round but when I walk all is see is flat. Flat, flat, flat. Sunny day, planes fly, strange clouds in the sky." Some of the officers didn't hear him. Those that did couldn't make sense of what he said enough to care. "Clouds not clouds," he shouted trying to get their attention. "Look, look—" His hand went up. Riley fired first—and second—followed by a shower of bullets.

When the shooting stopped two men had fallen. "Officer down," an ESU officer shouted and ran to give assistance. Riley laid on his back, shot through the neck, through his carotid, bleeding badly. They applied pressure, but his blood flowed like running water . . . until it stopped.

114

Within an hour, buildings one and two along with three, which had collapsed, were engulfed in flames. Five engine companies battled what encompassed two city blocks throughout the night and into the morning. All the tenants of buildings one and two evacuated in time but now they were six hundred plus newly homeless people on the streets of Brownsville. Most residents sat in the streets dumbfounded and angry. Mothers were beside themselves holding their crying children. Some people took to the streets in protest—a few broke out into a riot. Every nearby precinct came to the scene and the Governor declared a state of emergency and deployed the National Guard.

Saquon, Demarius, Gucci and Kareem did what Moses had told them last. They blended in with the crowd, sitting among the other tenants. Saquon especially told them and all the other members of CMK to sit with their families and not together so that they wouldn't stand out.

The siege and the bombing were the front page of every newspaper and the headline of every website. Social media was filled with images and stories.

"I lost everything. Everything. They bombed us. And they saw the fire was spreading and they let it burn," A building one tenant vented, wiping her tears away as she spoke.

"This is America, we are Americans. How are they going to drop a bomb on us? This is not Iraq. We are not terrorists," a building two resident said.

"The city has been looking for an excuse to begin tearing down the housing complexes for a very long time now, and they used this so-called terrorist action as their excuse to do it. This is a crime of unimaginable proportions," Yalitza Noel said.

"Excuse me, I'm homeless, I'm hungry, I'm trying to get something to eat. If everybody can give me one dollar, I can get four dollars and get something to eat," the homeless woman said to the sea of cameras.

It took three days for the riots in Brownsville, in Detroit, in Baltimore, in Chicago, in Compton, Toronto, Paris and in London to subside. However, that would not be the end of it. Hundreds of people had been displaced. The city had to house them in hotels, and ships they brought into the Hudson river. Finding permanent housing for all these people would be a monumental challenge. National charities came in to aid as well.

115

Seven people died during the siege on the Claude McKay Houses: Gerald Douglas (26), Ronald Davidson (42), Desert Storm veteran Emmett Jones (49), Malachi Washington (32), Robert Moses (35), John Bishop (40) and NYPD Sergeant Jason Riley (36). The U-Haul van Bishop rented was found at the scene with a cache of drugs inside. It gave the appearance that Bishop was involved with the terrorist attack.

Diane argued desperately that her husband was in fact a hostage and had nothing to do with any form of terrorism, but it was hard for her to explain the U-Haul van and why he was there. Powell, her attorney, advised her not to speak anymore, lest she incriminated herself.

Diane and Cece watched the news with tears in their eyes as Bishop's name was pilloried. Moses and Bishop's pictures were placed on the screen side by side. For Moses they used his Marine portrait. For Bishop they used a still frame taken from his speech at Al Sharpton's.

"Police believe these two men, former Marine, Staff Sergeant Robert F. Moses and John J. Bishop were the main orchestrators of the terrorist attack, taking the lives of six former NYPD police officers and eventually leading to the standoff with police at the Claude McKay Houses in Brownsville, Brooklyn, which lead to the bombing of the complex, all three buildings being brought down, and five other people dying, including NYPD Sergeant Jason Riley."

Though Riley had been shot by friendly fire, his death was attributed to Moses and Bishop. "John Bishop you may remember is the father of Desmond Bishop, an unarmed teenager who was shot and killed by officer Brian McNally earlier in the summer. You will remember the speech he gave at Reverend Al

Sharpton's National Action Network, where he called for officer McNally to feel pain and to bleed and suffer."

"Well we can see that John Bishop acted out those vengeful words," a male political pundit remarked, "not only going after officer McNally, who they kidnapped and held hostage for two days before he was thankfully able to escape, but also going after six former police officers, who were lawfully cleared for any wrongdoing, but who these terrorists saw fit to murder."

"And what about Robert Moses? He is a former marine and fifteen-year veteran, with two bronze stars with valor for his service to his country. How did, what looked to be an American hero, become involved with this?"

"Well we believe that during his many years deployed in Iraq and Afghanistan, that Mr. Moses was radicalized at some point by ISIS. He left the marines without completing his final tour and obviously came home with ideas of taking the knowledge he had learned in the marines and using it to plan attacks on American soil. Police recovered a dozen automatic and semi-automatic assault rilfes in the wreakage of building three, along with hundreds of rounds of amunition. They also found thirty other guns of various kinds and thousands of rounds of amunition in his home, along with pipe bombs and C4. And to execute his attacks, Moses went after the most vulnerable in our society, coopting the homeless and the hungry, into his terrorist plot."

116

Detectives were looking at five monitors at the same time. They were going over footage of the siege on building three and the killings of the six former police officers.

"Freeze it right there," the detective said. They were looking at a wide angle shot of building three taken from a police helicopter. "You can see that gunfire is coming from at least five sources. So, there were at least five of them in there who were involved in this."

"That gels with what we know about the killings. They all took place between ten am and twelve pm on the day of. We think there were three teams. Two teams of two, and Robert Moses who acted alone. We believe he was responsible for Targets one through four. We have surveillance footage of officer McNally's black Buick pulling up to each of the Targets' homes, a man in a UPS delivery uniform getting out with a package, he enters the home and in three instances he's out between five and ten minutes. Except for Target three, where it took him thirteen minutes, because he had four people to deal with. Though he's wise to keep his hat on, and most times he had the surgical mask on as well, the suspect fits the build of Robert Moses and also there is an efficiency and professionalism to how Targets one through four are killed. Always only two shots. One to the chest, one to the head. He kills Target four last. We actually see him here leaving the Target's home not wearing the UPS shirt but a t-shirt instead."

"Why do you think he changed his shirt there?"

"Guessing he probably got blood on it. He moved the Target's body from where he shot him in the backyard to the living room."

"And where does he go after the last hit?"

"So, he's in Queens and we've tracked him up until he's gotten to this block here, and that's where we lose him."

"How did we lose him?"

"It's a dead zone. No surveillance footage from any angle."

"Interesting. How did he know to park there?"

"He hacked into our system."

"No shit?"

"Yeah. When we recovered his laptop we found that he had access to the NYPD database. Looked into it. Found a malware in the network at the sixty-fifth precinct."

"How did he do that?"

"Don't know that yet. So, he parks and that's it. No sign of him or the car leaving that block. Officers went there looking for the car—no car. I had a hunch maybe it was towed. I called up all the private tow companies in the area and one of them had towed a Buick from that block."

"Good."

"It was towed to a lot five miles away. The plates are bullshit and the vin is gone, but we knew this car was McNally's car."

"Alright. Let's move onto the others."

"Okay. Target five was in the Bronx. We see the two men in UPS uniforms enter the building and leave sixteen minutes later. And this one is a complete mess. They put eleven bullets in him, and then threw bleach on the body."

"They probably thought they made a mistake and were trying to cover themselves. Did we find any DNA?"

"No, we did not. Target six now was done by another team in Astoria. He was shot once through the side of the head. This one is a lot cleaner than the Bronx but there are signs of a struggle. He put up a fight before they put him down."

"So, they drive off, where do they go?"

"They're all the same as Moses. They drive to these blocks with no surveillance and then they essentially disappear. Again, the same as Moses, the cars were towed to a nearby lot. The plates are shit, the vins are gone. We don't know their history."

"Okay, instead of going forward let's go backward. Let's

track them from Claude McKay, see if any of these cars come by there."

"We can't. There's no CCTV in Claude McKay."

"What do you mean?"

"Two thirds of NYCHA buildings have cameras. Claude McKay was part the one third that didn't."

"I've seen cameras in buildings one and two."

"Apparently they're dummies. They haven't worked in years. NYCHA didn't think it made good sense to upgrade the cameras in buildings that were gonna be torn down."

"So, what the hell do we have?"

"Well we know there was definitely five people directly involved. Moses and the other veteran Emmet Jones. After he was shot down, they found the gun that was used to kill Target Six on him."

"Good. And then we have Bishop and two others."

"I'm not so sure about Bishop. The wife says he had nothing to do with any of it and that he was a hostage."

"I'm not buying that. Why does he have a U-Haul rented under his name filled with drugs."

"The wife said Soldier—Moses—she calls him Soldier, kidnapped McNally on his own, and then contacted Bishop about it. When Bishop found out about it, he was horrified, he wanted no part of it, and he rents the U-Haul the next day and he's the one who sneaks McNally away. This jives with what officer McNally told us."

"So after he sneaks McNally away, why does he go back? Why doesn't he go to the police if he's so horrified?"

"I can't really speculate on his motivation there, but there is evidence to support he was a hostage. When we found Bishop's body, he still had a handcuff on his left hand. The other half had been shot off and was still attached to the radiator in the boiler room. Also, his nose was broken as well as several bones in his left hand. The coroner said, these were injuries consistent with someone who was desperately trying to escape his handcuffs."

"Hmmm—I'm still not buying Bishop as an innocent. I just

can't. He and Moses died together. Obviously, Moses went back to the boiler room to get him when he could have just escaped like the rest of them. Why would he do that if he and Bishop didn't have some kind of connection?"

"That I don't know. And in that case, we have at least two maybe three more people involved. Officers on the scene, said there were well over a dozen people who ran out of building three. There was too much smoke to make any of them out."

"Most of them were homeless and out of their minds."

"Not all of them. Unfortunately, we lost a lot of them in the crowd."

"I don't know. I'm just not feeling this whole homeless revolution angle."

"Well if that's not the case, we'll have to explain why we killed three homeless people for no reason."

"Well we can let the media run with the homeless for now. But I like the gang better for this."

"Alright. Well then, let's bring them in."

117

"I was home," Saquon said, as he was being questioned in the interview room in the 65th precinct by Detective Monroe with his attorney present. "I was playing video games until things started popping off. Then I went to the window to see what was going on. Until ya'll dropped a bomb and started a fire and burned down my whole building, and me and everyone else had to run up out there. Now we all homeless and got nowhere to go."

"Records show that he was home," Saquon's lawyer said.

"Records show his phone was in the house. It doesn't mean he was."

"I was playing and live streaming like we always do."

"Have you verified that?" the attorney asked.

"Yeah. And it's convenient," Monroe said.

"It's not convenient. It's proof that he was home."

"You run CMK," Monroe said to Saquon. "Your brother founded it. Moses and Bishop were operating inside building three and you want me to believe you had nothing to do with it and knew nothing about it. We know they didn't do this alone."

"We don't really mess with building three, since it got boarded up. A lot of homeless people took it over."

"And what about the drugs we found in the U-Haul van?"

"That's something you'd have to ask Mr. Moses and Mr. Bishop about," the attorney said. "I've heard stories that Mr. Moses may have been connected with a Mexican cartel. Perhaps he was trafficking guns and drugs to help finance his acts of terrorism."

"And he was doing all this, in building three, and you and your gang were fifty yards away and you had no idea," Monroe said to Saquon.

"Yeah we seen homeless people move in and outta there. We don't pay attention to them."

"You have no idea who else was working with Moses and Bishop. You're trying to attach my client to them simply because he lived in the complex," the attorney said.

"Because he ran the gang that lived in the complex. And I find it impossible to believe that he wasn't involved or at the very least knew what was going on."

"I didn't know nothing about nothing. And CMK is not a gang."

"Claude McKay Killers. And you're not a gang? Cut the shit," Monroe said.

"When my brother Marcus was running things, yeah we used to be a gang. But once they got arrested, we weren't in that gang life. We were just friends, hanging together and keeping each other safe so we wouldn't get attacked by other gangs."

Monroe laughed incredulously.

"I'm sure you've checked their social media. There is nothing gang related in any of it. They are just regular young black men who happen to be growing up in the projects. Do you have anything to connect my client to this? DNA, video—anything?" Monroe was silent. "Then you have nothing to hold my client on Detective. He came in here for this interview on his own free will. And now he's leaving."

Saquon and his attorney got up to leave.

"Alright. You can go," Monroe said. "But this ain't over. We're watching you. All of you."

"What's new? You been watching me all my life."

118

The night before the hits Moses went over the plans me-ticulously with Saquon, Demarius, Gucci and Kareem. He had his laptop out and it showed the blocks where there was no surveillance. "Kareem, Gucci, after you've taken out your Target, you'll drive back to the block where you got the car. You park the car. Park in front of someone's driveway. Change out of the UPS outfits inside the car. It's better to wear them over your clothes, so you just slip them off."

"Got it," Gucci and Kareem said.

"Good. Now after you change, you put the UPS outfits in a garbage bag and back in your back packs. You'll wait twenty minutes in the car, then you'll leave like how you came—separate. There is a high school two blocks away. There are subway stations four blocks away in either direction. Seniors will be leaving out of school around this time, and they'll be headed to the trains. You'll go in different directions. Wear your hats, wear your book bags. Take off your gloves, put them in your book bags, leave the block and blend in with the high school kids. Get on the subway. Head back to Brooklyn. Get off two stops from where you normally would. Find one of those large garbage bins. Make sure it has a good amount of garbage in it, then drop the garbage bag with the UPS outfits and your gloves inside in the bottom. The next day is garbage pick-up day. After that get a two-dollar cab and take it back to Claude McKay, like you did when you left in the morning, and go home."

Gucci and Kareem nodded that they understood. Saquon and Demarius would be leaving from Astoria after taking out their Target, but the details of their egress were fairly the same. "We'll all meet in building three at three-thirty. We'll take out McNally. Then we'll dig a grave right there in that room. I already checked. Under the tile the ground is soft. It shouldn't be too hard for us to dig. We drop the body in and fill the hole."

"Sounds good," Saquon said.

"And let the other members know to stay away for the day. Let's just have four guys watching the building and that's it. The fewer people know about what we're doing the better."

"Got it," Saquon said.

"Now, about your alibis?" Moses asked.

"We're all set," Kareem said. "For the last three weeks we've been playing video games online, and we've been live streaming while we do it. On different days we each recorded ourselves playing and live streaming. And like you said, we did it for different times, between four and half and five and a half hours. Tomorrow we'll all head out at our set times, we'll start streaming our prerecorded sessions just before we leave. "

"And when you recorded your sessions you all made sure that there was a TV visible in the background and that it was playing the tapes, right?"

"Yeah," they all said.

Moses imagined the cops might argue that the live stream could have been prerecorded. So, Moses looked at the schedules for cable networks that showed syndicated television shows. He bought copies of the episodes that would be airing on the networks during the hours of the hits. He recorded commercial breaks from the specific networks and he edited them into the copies he had bought. Fortunately cable networks run the same few daytime commercials repeatedly. The boys played the edited shows on thier TVs in the background as they live streamed.

It gave the impression the shows were broadcasting on television at the times they were scheduled to.

"We're ready," Moses said as he looked at these boys and what they were about to embark on. "I'm proud of you guys."

"You think this is gonna change things?" Saquon asked.

"I think it's going to be the beginning of a change."

119

"Are you pleading guilty voluntarily?"

"Yes, Your Honor."

"Do you understand that by pleading guilty that you are admitting to facts that make up a criminal offence?"

"Yes, Your Honor."

"Do you understand the consequences of a guilty plea, including that you are giving up your right to have a trial by pleading guilty?"

"Yes, Your Honor."

"It is my understanding that you turned down any plea arrangement between your attorneys and the state."

"Yes, Your Honor."

"Why did you do so?"

"I acknowledge that my actions in question on the night of were unlawful, and I am prepared to face the proper judgment for those actions."

Pre-trial, the Police Union argued McNally was being charged solely because of the political climate as a result of the destruction of the Claude McKay Houses. He was being scapegoated they said. In private the District Attorney in not so many words expressed a similar sentiment to the head of the Union.

When McNally decided to plead guilty, and not even seek a plea agreement he did not inform the Union beforehand. He however did inform his attorney, and as his attorney was brought on by the Union, the attorney told the Union. Pacheco, his union representative argued vehemently against McNally doing so. "If not for yourself and your family, think about the precedent you're setting. Think about how this might impact fellow officers in the future."

"I am," McNally told him. His mind was set. He would not be moved from this position. He had thought long and hard on it. Pacheco urged him to at the very least not plead guilty outright and work out a plea agreement, which the District Attorney was very open to—but again McNally said no. He didn't want to plea bargain his way out of this. He knew in his heart of hearts that he had done something wrong and needed to take responsibility for it. He needed to atone. His soul would not be at peace until he did.

McNally and Meagan had spoken about this exhaustively before he made his plea, and though she understood and respected his decision, she didn't want him to do it. No wife wants to see her husband and the father of her children sent to prison. Also, at great issue was the financial burden his decision would place on her to have to provide for the kids alone while he would be away. However, that turned out to be not so much of an issue. A GoFundMe account had been set up on behalf of McNally and his family. It had raised upwards of four hundred thousand dollars. That at least set McNally's mind at ease that financially his family would be okay for how many years he would be gone.

McNally's sentencing took place a week after he had entered his guilty plea. Brooklyn Supreme Court Justice David Hart began by saying, "After reviewing the facts of the case and giving it great consideration, I am reducing the sentence from second degree manslaughter to criminally negligent homicide." There was a shudder in the courtroom for which the judge quickly called things to order. He continued, "And though Officer McNally has plead guilty for the tragic death of the victim Desmond Bishop, Officer McNally, was also the victim of a very heinous crime, perpetrated by terrorists who would go on to commit even greater acts of terror. And I find that given the defendant's background and given how truly remorseful he is that it would not be necessary to incarcerate the defendant to have a just sentence in this case. The sentence is for three years' probation and community service." That was the sentence. Mc-Nally would not see a day in jail. There was muted applause from the police side of the courtroom and cries of outrage from activists and community members who had attended.

McNally had been prepared to hear a sentence of three years, which was the minimum mandatory sentence for second degree manslaughter. Though he also knew that the judge could throw the book at him and he receive the maximum sentence of fifteen years. A reduced charge and three years' probation had not been in his calculation.

McNally plead guilty with the full estimation he would serve a significant amount of time for killing Desmond Bishop. Yet seeing the joy on his wife's face and knowing he was going home to his children made him feel relieved—hollow but relieved.

He looked behind him in the courtroom. His family was there: his father, mother, Jessie and his brother Joseph who had traveled from California to be at the trial. Joseph and his parents were overjoyed. Jessie gave McNally a supportive yet plaintive smile.

Daniels and Roberts were there, and they smiled and applauded, Daniels less so than Roberts. Daniels had been promoted to sergeant and was now the head of their anti-crime unit. There was no Riley. All three of them attended his funeral months ago. Riley, like the six other officers who died the day of the siege, got the equivalent of a state funeral.

McNally kept looking behind him, through the happy supporters and the angry community members, believing possibly that Bishop's wife and daughter might be there—especially today of all days. However, they were not in attendance. They hadn't shown up the entire trial.

120

McNally wore a suit and Meagan wore a formal dress, much the way they dressed when McNally went to court. He held her hand tightly as he rang the doorbell. As a police officer he had given six death notices to family members through the years. It was always difficult to do. You're anxious, your stomach is in knots. You search for the right words and tone. And you can say everything perfectly and it still goes terribly wrong. This wasn't a death notice, but he had come to speak to the family of John and Desmond Bishop. Cece opened the door for them and let them in. He could feel the pit in his stomach tightening.

The afternoon sun shone through the window. They sat in the living room opposing each other. McNally and Meagan sat on the sofa, a coffee table with water and an assortment of fresh fruit was between them. Diane sat on the loveseat her husband preferred to sit in. Cece sat on the edge of the seat by her side. After the pleasantries and the compliments about the house, it was time for McNally to say what he came to say.

"I just wanted to say, me and Mr. Bishop, me and your husband spoke a great deal in those two days I was, we were, together. He was a good man. He was a very good man. He wasn't a terrorist like they're making him out to be. I don't know how he got caught up with the other people involved, but I believe he wasn't a part of anything else they were doing. He let me go . . . he let me go, and in doing so, it probably cost him his life. I think about that. I think about Desmond. I think about that night. There are so many things I wish to God I had done differently. There so many things I wish I had known before. I learned a lot in the many talks I had with your husband, conversations that I will take with me for the rest of my life. He was a good man.

I am profoundly sorry for what I have done, for the hurt I have caused you and everything your family is going through." He finished. Meagan held his hand lovingly. They both had tears in their eyes.

Diane and Cece appeared sober and unmoved. They had listened, they had been receptive but were inured. They had cried too much in these last few months. Sometimes they wondered if they could ever cry anymore or have feelings the way they used to. "I believe you," Diane said. "I believe you are sorry. And I do respect you owning up to what you did to my son and pleading guilty for it. I can see that your time spent with John has changed you. You're right, he was a good man. He was a damn good man. He loved his son, his loved his children, he loved his family, more than anything, more than himself, and he just wanted some accountability for what happened, because you're never, ever, held to account. Never. Even now, even with you, as you came out and said I was wrong, I did it, I'm guilty. They said it doesn't matter, you're free to go. You said you're sorry, and like I said I believe you, but if you're here for forgiveness, I don't have any to give. The decisions you made that night took away my son and her brother and ultimately my husband and her father, no matter how you feel about that now you're going to walk out of here, and you'll have your wife and you'll have your children, and you'll go on and live your life in whatever capacity you see fit. And I don't care. I don't care about what lessons you've learned. I don't care that you've changed. I don't care about you, or about what or how you think, or how you see me or us anymore. I am tired. I am so tired. I am tired of the pain. I am strong." She held Cece's hand. "We are strong. But we're tired of being strong. Our men aren't coming back. Our men aren't coming back and that we have to live with."

121

McNally and Meagan left the Bishop home and walked
to their car. They were quiet. All four had shaken hands and
respectfully said goodbye before leaving. McNally didn't know
what to expect from meeting with them. Something in his soul
said he owed it to them to face them and say he was sorry. He
felt relieved he had done it but still felt empty. Had he wanted
forgiveness? He didn't believe he went there with that in mind,
but he did want to embrace them, and in some strange way have
them embrace him. He felt connected to this family and felt he
owed them a great deal. He felt he had an eternal debt he had to
repay. But they wanted nothing from him, and he understood it
and he accepted it. He and Meagan got in their car.

"Thank you for coming with me," he said to her.

"Of course," she replied. "They're in a lot of pain. And my
heart breaks for them, and I hate that we are the cause of it. But
you're a good man as well, Brian."

"I don't feel like a good man."

"You can be a good man and make a mistake even a horrible
mistake. It's what you do afterwards that matters."

"Yeah," he said sounding unconvinced.

"So, what do you want to do now?" Meagan asked. They had
the day and their lives ahead of them.

"I don't know . . . I feel like turning over some tables," he
said, then looked at her and smiled, brimming with new energy.
"You feel like turning some tables over with?" he asked.

She didn't know what he meant but she liked the look on his
face as he said it. "Yeah," she replied, trusting him—again.

He took her hand and kissed it. "I love you," he said to her.

"I love you too," she replied.

They drove off.

122

Cece watched the McNallys drive off through the window as a cry rang out from above. Both her and Diane looked up, and proceeded up the stairs to Diane's bedroom. A cry came again and it was the most joyous cry. There in the room close to the bed, in the baby's crib, laid two month old John Desmond Bishop. He was born premature, just over seven months just six pounds one ounce, but he was a fighter and in the NICU he grew stronger everyday. They brought him home a week ago and he brought life to their house. He had his father and his brother in him, not just their names but, in the face and the eyes. He was beautiful. He was living light and every time they looked at him they couldn't help but smile and laugh. Diane picked him up and held him, and Cece held them both, and Diane cooed his cries and said, "I love you Desmond. I love you John."

123

On the night of the siege, the fire had spread to buildings one and two. Dozens of people were running into the courtyard. Saquon and the others ran with them. And as he was doing his best to blend in, Saquon looked back at building three. Fifty yards away through the fence, the smoke and the flames, he saw into the lobby. He saw Moses. He was running out and Bishop was behind him.

"C'mon, c'mon," Saquon kept repeating under his breath. He was almost out. Moses looked ahead and he saw Saquon as well . . . then he looked up . . . then he looked back at Saquon, nodded his head and gave him a knowing smile . . . then the ceiling caved in.

It was a year after the seige and Saquon still remembered that last look Moses gave him. He remembered what Moses said to him when he took him to his mother's shrine, and why he forgave Saquon and why he did everything he did.

Saquon stood in the barbershop speaking to all the heads of the gangs and their lieutenants. "We are an endangered species. We're going to kill each other off, or they are gonna kill us off. Either way we're dead. Unless we change. I seen what's coming. Nothing else matters, nothing else matters," he said, and there in that barbershop somewhere in Detroit, they heard him, and Demarius spoke in a church basement somewhere in Baltimore, and they heard him, and they heard Leandro, Gucci, somewhere in Chicago, and Kareem somewhere in Compton . . . and somewhere in Philly, and somewhere in Memphis, and somewhere in Dallas, and somewhere in Rio, and somewhere Paris, and somewhere in Soweto, and somewhere . . . and somewhere . . . somewhere . . .

ABOUT THE AUTHOR

Heru Ptah is a novelist, poet, playwright and filmmaker. As a poet he has appeared on HBO's Def Poetry Jam and CNN with Anderson Cooper. His first novel a Hip Hop Story was published by MTV Books and given a feature story in the New York Times. Heru was also the book writer for the Broadway Musical Hot Feet based on the music of Earth Wind and Fire and the choreography of Maurice Hines. Somewhere in Brooklyn is Heru's sixth novel and seventh book.

ACKNOWLEDGEMENTS

To my love, my heart, my backbone and bride to be, my beautiful Monifa Powell, thanks again for coming into my life. Since I have met you, you have been my greatest inspiration, and without you and what you have taught me I could not have written this book or any other. Thank you for being my best friend and most trusted confidant and reader.

To my mother, Venice, the first and most profound relationship in my life. The same love, same respect, and infinite gratitude applies like always. I'm still working on the house with the island in the kitchen. It's been a long time coming but it's coming soon.

To my brother, Tehut-nine, thank you again for your loyalty, your love and your nobility. We are Tehut-nine and Heru forever. Special shout-out to Marcia, Masai and Zaniah.

Special acknowledgement to my inner family: Michelle, Jay and Shanice. I love you all. To my father, Anthony Richards—Tony Brutus—Rest In Power. Live forever.

To Sharon Gordon, thank you for your support, your energy and your passion. To Amir thank you for your service and your military expertise. To my awesome legal advisor I can't thank you enough. I would have been lost without you. And to all of the people who bought and read Show Me a Beautiful Woman, on the street, in the salons and especially on the trains, I thank you so much. You have no idea how much your support has meant to me. You saved me.

To the Creator, Ausar Auset Heru. Thank you for my life and my light. I am striving to live up to the name you gave me. The next book is for you.